The Company Plan

John D. Whipps

Bloomington, IN   Milton Keynes, UK

authorHOUSE®

AuthorHouse™
1663 Liberty Drive, Suite 200
Bloomington, IN 47403
www.authorhouse.com
Phone: 1-800-839-8640

AuthorHouse™ UK Ltd.
500 Avebury Boulevard
Central Milton Keynes, MK9 2BE
www.authorhouse.co.uk
Phone: 08001974150

First published by AuthorHouse 12/4/2006

ISBN: 978-1-4259-6712-3 (sc)
ISBN: 978-1-4259-6713-0 (hc)

Library of Congress Control Number: 2006908652

Printed in the United States of America
Bloomington, Indiana

This book is printed on acid-free paper.

Acknowledgements:

I could not have completed this book without giving credit to a few of the people that made this possible. First I would like to thank my family who gave me the encouragement to complete this work. Thanks to Ruby Jean who steadfastly helped me put words to paper and Amy for helping me through the tough times. My special friend and mentor, Mel, gets special recognition for his unwavering friendship, technical expertise and suggestions. Lee, a good friend, gave his insights into the literary world and suggestions to make the story ring true. I would also like to especially thank the men and women of the United States Armed Forces who valiantly put their lives on the line daily to protect our way of life in the hopes that there is a better future for our children and our country. God Bless you all.

John D. Whipps

Chapter One

FLYING OVER THE BALKANS

"Secure channel, Fruit Tree, Fruit Tree, Apple One. SITREP request as we approach LZ."

The speaker's voice oscillated slightly, shaking in a rhythm that matched the whir of the helicopter's rotors.

The pilot of the chopper, full of elite Army Green Berets, was asking his tactical headquarters for a situation report before setting his chopper down in a landing zone. He was about to deliver or "insert" a special operations "A Team." They would be landing in a hostile enemy fire zone.

In the All Source Intelligence Center or ASIC, the commanding General asked his deputy for the latest report.

"Sir, satellites and high altitude surveillance aircraft monitored people just twenty minutes ago, walking from the village to the small clearing where the chopper will be landing."

The General nodded to the lieutenant at his side, in front of the communications console. The lieutenant made the call, "Apple One, Apple One. Fruit Tree. ASIC reports path from LZ to town clear. No hostile 'rec' of your aircraft."

1

Headquarters was reporting that the path leading from the landing zone through the forest to the target village was clear of mines and booby traps.

ASIC, a clearing house of "all sources" of satellite, electronic jamming and surveillance aircraft, sensor and human intelligence information combined, provides the clearest and latest operational situation analysis. ASIC also observed that no enemy electronic warfare equipment had noticed the helicopter flying deep into its territory.

Air Force electronic jamming aircraft flying in the area were disabling enemy radar sites. The helicopter was hugging the terrain, "nap of the earth", as it flew, clearing hills and trees by just a few feet, defeating enemy radar units looking up into the sky for intruders.

The helicopter was completely black with no lights inside or out. The chopper set down in the LZ amid the dim glow of the waning dusk. The pilots monitored their instruments on a "Heads Up Display" shown on the inside of their helmet visors. The laser generated, computer graphics were displayed directly into the pilot's retina. The aircrew and soldiers behind them wore night vision goggles or "NVG's."

"Apple One. Fruit Tree. ASIC thermal sat has two, at your two-seven-five degrees, forty-five yards."

The pilot and the commandos looked in that direction. They saw two orange, glowing figures starting to take notice of their landing. The images started to un-shoulder their rifles to fire at the helicopter, figuring out that they were not "friendlies."

"Splat, splat."

"Splat, splat."

From inside the chopper a Green Beret sniper shot a silenced rifle. The two orange images fell to the ground. The pilot did not have to wait to see them fall before saying,

"Roger, Fruit Tree. We got 'em."

He trusted that the sniper behind him had instantly picked them off.

Major Nick Dentworth was the team leader. He pointed to each of his four other men and then out the door, mouthing, "Go," to each of them. Just before he leaped out of the helicopter, Nick reached over from behind and firmly patted the pilot's right shoulder twice indicating that the guys were successfully out and it was okay to take off. Nick was the last one out of the chopper.

The pilot radioed headquarters as he lifted off and rose into the growing darkness.

"Fruit Tree. Fruit Tree. Apple One. The seeds are planted. The seeds are planted."

Nick hit the ground running. He followed his men, who were hustling for the cover of the thick forest surrounding the open clearing. Once they were safely inside the treeline, they all clustered in a circle facing outward to protect all sides. Nick took a few moments to survey the area around them. The sound of the chopper was fading. Nick watched and listened for any signs of a threat or any trace that someone had noticed their arrival. After a few minutes, waiting in silence, Nick silently signaled each of his men to follow him.

NVG's demand a lot of practice because they have a deceptive depth perception. After so many years of training, all the men were expert in their use. Nick and the other four commandos began running at full speed down the forest path leading to the village. They knew that time was of the essence. Every second could determine success or failure of the mission.

The five man team wore bullet proof vests and a TA-50 equipment harness, with attached pouches of ammunition, first-aid, minimal food, water and other such necessities. They wore heavy coats because it was winter. There was no snow. Yet, it was very cold. They were camouflaged from head to toe in green, brown and black colors referred to as forest green. Even their faces were painted in colors to blend in with their forest surroundings. They each had side arms, an assault machine-gun, grenades and knives. One of the men carried a crossbow.

They had to run as fast as they could for about a mile. As they ran, they took special care not to make noise. One could only hear the slightest of heavy breathing from their exertion. They were in top physical condition. Their clothing and equipment was made so as to not rub or clank together making a sound that could give away their position. Even their jump boot laces were tucked into their anklets so they would not snag any bushes or items that might make sound or trip up the commandos. As they passed by, they moved like swift, smoke rings in the dark.

About twenty yards from the edge of the trees and the beginning of the village, they noticed another glowing, orange figure fifteen feet off to the left of the path. It was a soldier, his rifle leaning against a neighboring tree. He was squatting down, preparing to relieve himself. He was a perimeter guard assigned to the path's entrance to the town. The five U.S. commandos never broke stride.

"Thump."

The crossbow arrow went right through the man's heart. The number two man, the team's Serbo-Croatian speaker behind Nick, dispatched the guard while on the run. They could not afford any chances of immediate discovery. It would imperil the success of their mission. Nick recalled the

4

General's briefing as to what their mission actually was.

"Major Dentworth, you will be taking a hand-picked team of four other men to bring out an agent of ours from that village. Since the President has cut back so much on our human intelligence and special operations capabilities over the last seven years, this man is one of the few assets we have in place among the population there. We sent him in under cover. He has been providing a huge volume of very high quality intelligence reports on enemy intentions, build-up and actions in the area.

We have been warning the President and his staff for years that the enemy would be launching another 'ethnic cleansing' campaign in that region. When they did, our man was considered by the enemy, as just another of those to be cleansed. Our last, secret communication from him was that it had begun with a horrific ferocity. He requested immediate extraction in fear of his life. If they kill him, we will lose a very valuable man. If they capture and interrogate him, we will lose a valuable man and a lot of precious secrets as well.

Your job, Major, is to go and get him out before they get to him. My deputy will provide you with all the necessary background information and intelligence you need. You have thirty-six, no, now thirty-five hours to get this done. Any questions? Good. That is all. Dismissed."

About ten yards before the trees ended, Nick quietly held his right arm up with a fist, indicating that the men were to immediately stop and take cover together. They caught their breath before venturing into the town to try and find their man.

Once Nick was satisfied that no one knew they were there, he signaled to his men to follow him. Communication was done with slight movements of the wrist and the pointing of fingers. Nick indicated what was happening and where they would go first, by pointing to the building nearest to them. He had studied detailed satellite imagery that showed incredible detail of the village. The last photo he saw of the route he and his men would take was downloaded from the satellite just minutes before they took off in the helicopter.

They did not have to speak to one another to understand what each person was to do. They were all highly skilled in the art of clandestine movement through dangerous areas. They all knew in precisely which farmhouse in the village they would find their man. Or, at least they hoped to find him there. Under the cover of night, they leap-frogged one another from one building or large object to another. Their NVG's made it look like it was daytime, giving them total vision of their surroundings.

They moved down only one side of the street to minimize the chance that someone might see them crossing the open road. The area was still "hot" with enemy soldiers around and in the village. The team had to penetrate the village about one mile, to the house where their man had been clandestinely operating.

As they moved from building to building, they saw dozens and dozens of dead bodies. Many were women and children. They passed by two or three piles of five to ten men laying in front of a wall. The team could tell by the numerous bullet holes in the wall behind the bodies that they had simply been lined up against the wall and machine gunned to death.

Suddenly, the team heard the sound of a racing, truck engine approaching from their rear. It was speeding up the road. A handful of soldiers in the back of the truck were raising their Kalashnikov rifles in the air and loudly whooping and laughing as if they were a bunch of teenagers riding around after a high school, football team win. They wore regular Army uniforms. A couple of the bandits in the truck fired their weapons into the air in celebration of their great victory that day, the slaughter of hundreds, if not thousands, of defenseless men, women and children.

Nick and his men hid themselves behind the nearest object they could find. One of his men was in the process of dashing between buildings when the truck approached and had nothing to hide behind. He simply dropped to the ground. Hiding his weapon, pretending to be dead. Although it would have been simple to kill all of the men in the truck and blow it up, the U.S. servicemen did nothing. They were not there to engage enemy units and unnecessarily kill soldiers. They were there only to retrieve one valuable life, one man.

The truck turned to the left a few blocks up the road and raced away. Without a moment's hesitation the soldier playing dead hopped up and continued running, just as if nothing had interrupted the team's progress as they made their way through the town. As Nick passed by the doorway of one house, an enemy soldier came walking out. He was casually stepping over the dead body of a man he had killed an hour before. The enemy soldier was surprised to see Nick come within two feet of him. The soldier was picking his teeth with a small knife after having eaten a meal from his victim's kitchen. He hurriedly tried to un-holster his pistol on his right hip.

"Splat, splat."

He was too late for Nick's quick reflexes. Nick took a moment to drag the soldier's body behind some fifty gallon barrels lined up a few feet away, to limit any other soldier's curiosity as to who might have killed him. The A team moved on.

After twenty minutes, Nick recognized the street on which their man resided. They turned right.

"Third house on the left," he remembered.

The team quickly and quietly assembled on either side of the front door. They stood motionless, catching their breath and listening for any sounds from inside the house. Like so many other houses and structures they saw on their sprint into town, this one too had been shot up and set on fire. The wooden doorframe was still smoldering when the team made their tactical entry into the small three room house.

The men had done many similar entries in the past, hunting terrorists and other enemies. The men knew what they had to do. Each of them had a specific task and they performed it like clockwork. The first man in, Nick, opened what remained of the door, jumped inside, stepped to the right and immediately swept the room with his eyes and weapon as the second man charged in and took up the same position on the left side. The third man went to the second room, the fourth man to the third room. The fifth man stayed at the doorway providing rear security towards the outside of the building. Within a few seconds they had established and gestured to one another that "all was clear," there were no hostiles in the place.

The interior had been trashed. All furniture and belongings had been strewn about and broken. Then one of the men noticed a boot sticking out from under a jumble of wood, clothes and buckets.

Nick signaled his men with his hands. "Watch for booby traps."

They looked for any signs of wires or explosive devices that might be covered by the debris. They quietly and carefully removed the items from on top of the person lying beneath them. They found nothing as they uncovered the man underneath. The place had been simply ransacked with a hateful rage.

They found a man, lying face down on the floor. But was he the right man they had come after? The face resembled the photograph the team had been shown during their mission brief. Nick had to make sure.

Nick pulled out a small device from one of the utility pouches on his web belt. He turned it on and extended a small, retractable tab. He took a black colored cotton swab and soaked it with blood from the man's bleeding head wound. Then, Nick smeared the blood-soaked swab on the tab. He pushed the tab back into the device which immediately began to chemically compare the DNA signature from the smeared blood, with that of a blood sample taken from the undercover spy before being sent on assignment to this village over two years ago. The digital readout indicated a perfect match. Nick nodded.

"He's our man."

Nick replaced the DNA tester and the cotton swab into his pouch. The medic on the team quickly established that although he had been shot in the back of the head, execution style, the man was still breathing. The medic whispered to Nick.

"He's still barely alive, but with a very weak pulse."

"Can you stabilize him, Doc?"

"I don't know. He's lost a lot of blood. But, here, I'll need your help."

"Anything."

As the other three men in the team provided perimeter security around the building, Nick and the medic furiously worked trying to stop the head wound from bleeding. They used several bandages, some gauze and tape to hold the field dressings in place. After doing so, the medic tried to normalize the injured man's vital signs and breathing. He patched the man up as best as he could. He looked at Nick.

"That's all I can do."

"Can we move him?"

9

"Very risky. But it's the only chance he's got. If he stays, he'll die for sure. It's your call."

Nick as the senior officer and team commander had to make the decision. He only had to think for two seconds.

"If he's going to die, he's going to die with us and go home. I will not leave one of our guys to rot in this God forsaken place. Do it. Let's get him the hell out of here!"

Nick gathered up the packaging from the bandages and put them in a utility pouch so there were no any traces that they were there. If the enemy found such evidence, they might figure out that someone had come to get someone important enough to save. They might deduce that the saved man was a spy and wonder what he might have told his agent controllers. It was best to keep all knowledge or conjecture of the spy's activities as secret as possible.

The medic reached behind him and pulled out a light weight, camouflage colored, foldout, aluminum and nylon stretcher. He had it strapped to his back. They carefully placed the injured man on the stretcher and belted him to it so he could not fall off. Nick gathered his men and whispered his instructions.

"Okay. Out the door and to the left. It's straight down the street about one-half mile, then into the forest. About fifty yards to the left is another path that will take us another half mile to the pick-up point."

Nick pointed to the Serbo-Croatian speaker, then to the other men.

"You follow me. You two carry him. You are rear security. Let's move out. Every second counts, guys."

Off they went leap-frogging again but this time, the man in front of and behind the stretcher bearers covered for them since their hands were full. About a quarter mile down the road Nick raised his fist halting the column in its tracks. Everyone stopped and crouched down to lower their physical profile against the background.

Nick heard a rustling sound coming from a destroyed and burned out house. After a few moments, a figure started to appear from the rubble. The person was carrying a small lit candle in one hand. The NVG's automatically adjusted to the intensity of the firelight to keep the men from being blinded. Nick could hardly believe his eyes.

A little five-year-old girl came crawling out over the shattered bricks. She was shabbily clad in torn and dirty clothes. Her light brown hair was tangled and matted. In her other hand was a two-foot-long stick with a soiled, white shirt attached to it. She was nervously showing him a big, toothy smile obviously trying to please the giant, green men with guns that were before her. Instinct made her hope that her forced smile might help to convince them not to hurt her. She waved the little flag back and forth. Her small, exposed legs stumbled toward him trembling with fear and feeling the winter cold. She kept repeating a phrase over and over again as she walked toward the scary silhouette in front of her.

Nick's heart broke in two as he saw this small child coming toward him "surrendering" herself.

Several thoughts flashed though his mind.

"How is it that she knew to do this? How sad it is that someone probably her parents, had to teach her to do this in the hope of surviving this terribly brutal war. And where are her parents? Probably dead or they wouldn't have let her expose herself in such a way. She probably hid in the root cellar when the bad soldiers came to her house. She was obviously desperate and starving."

Nick signaled the linguist behind him to come to his side.

The little girl was now about twenty feet from them.

"What's she saying?"

"She's saying, 'Please don't kill me. Please don't kill me. Please don't kill me'."

Nick's eyes filled with tears at the thought that this beautiful, innocent child was afraid that because they were soldiers, they were there to kill her. Yet, this precious child still offered herself, relying upon their mercy. He cringed inside at the thought of what this little one must have seen to make her say this to him. He could see the terrified expression in her cute face. Nick got down on his knees and put his weapon down. He extended his open arms to her as she reached him. She kept repeating her plea over and over. He choked back his tears and tight throat and told his linguist, "Tell her we're not going to hurt her. Tell her she's safe now. Tell her to be very quiet and to come with us."

The linguist did as he was told as Nick blew out the candle and took her in his arms. He held her tight, feeling her shivering, shaking body. Her teeth were chattering. A tear rolled down his cheek. Her heart was pounding with fear.

"Tell her again."

The linguist complied as Nick took his coat off and put it around this angel caught in the fires of hell. Nick held her close trying to warm her up as quickly as he could by briskly rubbing her body. He softly whispered in her ear.

"Shhhh. Shhhh."

He looked over his shoulder at his linguist.

"Strap her to your front. She's coming with us. Those sons of bitches are not going to get a second chance to get her. Tape her mouth and explain why. Tell her it won't be for long."

The linguist explained about the duct tape and had the girl wrap her legs around his waist, her arms around his neck. He repositioned his TA-50 web belt and connecting straps to hold her against him inside his coat. Nick signaled to his men that they were late and that they had to hurry, for fear of missing their recovery. The team moved out. Once again, they started down the road. They had exactly ten minutes to get to the LZ for "Extraction."

Special operations are planned and executed when possible, right down to the second. Being an instant too early or late could mean a compromised mission or worse, dead soldiers, your soldiers. This was especially true in a hostile fire zone. So even the unplanned, momentary delay of the five-year-old girl threw off the mission's timetable. Nick just didn't have the heart to leave her behind. It was a calculated delay he thought was worth the risk. The team was naturally aware of that and anxiously cognizant of the time lost. Murphy's Law always seemed to occur. When something can go wrong, it does.

Some minutes later after much exertion, they reached the pick-up point. They were twelve minutes late due to finding the girl. Adding to their delay was the fact that carrying the man on the stretcher was difficult and took longer than expected.

There they found their helicopter right on time, waiting for them in the exact place they were supposed to be. Although they did not show it, the whole team was relieved to see their ride out. The pilot's rule book said that if your operators were more than ten minutes late you leave and let them try to go to their secondary rendezvous point and time for retrieval.

In the minds of these two pilots and crew, they were not going to leave without their men on the ground. They didn't want to leave those guys in peril any longer than absolutely necessary. Every second the chopper sat there hovering just off the ground waiting for the team, they risked discovery and death. Finally, Nick's team appeared in the clearing and started to make their way to the aircraft's open door.

ASIC belatedly radioed the pilots that thermal, highly magnified imagery from two-hundred miles up in space indicated a threat. "Enemy troops approaching your position!"

As Nick's men were crossing the field, a squad of enemy soldiers arrived in a jeep of some sort. They were now at the edge of the clearing. They started shooting at the commandos and the helicopter. They had heard the chopper blades whirring for over ten minutes. They knew that there were no helicopters from their army scheduled to be in the area, so they came to the clearing suspecting trouble. They found it.

Just as the chopper's door gunner was swinging the swivelled gun around to begin firing at the enemy squad, he was shot in the face and instantly killed. The copilot saw what happened and hurriedly unbuckled his five-point, aviation seatbelt. He jumped out of his seat and leaped over to the mounted machine gun. He opened up on the squad with the high-powered machine gun that sprayed fifty bullets a second, for as long as you pulled the trigger.

He was trying to kill the enemy soldiers and provide a fierce distraction to give Nick and his team enough time to reach the chopper. Nick and the other two men not carrying the stretcher also fired at the squad. There were no tracer rounds from any of the Americans, eliminating a path of light that an enemy could follow to their target.

This was another reason NVG's were so useful. You could see where your bullets were going without visually identifying one's self as the source of a stream of bullets. The enemy soldiers were totally cut to pieces with the tremendous firepower of the helicopter's machine gun and that of Nick's men.

During the ferocious firefight, the linguist with the five-year-old girl, the men with the stretcher and Nick, all clambered into the chopper. Nick was the last one to get aboard. As soon as the pilot saw Nick stepping in off of the skid, he lifted off and disappeared into the night.

He shouted into the radio, "Skids Up!"

They left the area as fast as possible. The pilot radioed his flight operations center, which was monitoring the mission.

"Fruit Tree. Fruit Tree. Apple One. The crops are harvested. The crops have been harvested, but in very hot weather. One farmer down. We are in route to the barn."

The pilot had told them that he had recovered the team under fire, that one man on the mission had been killed, and that they were on their way back to base.

Once they were safely airborne, the linguist removed the tape from the little girl's mouth. Nick had a flack vest and coat put around her. The gun battle surely alerted the troops and radar units to be on the lookout for them. Even with the U.S. planes jamming their radar, enemy ground troops could still get lucky and shoot at them flying by. The skill of the pilot and the electronic jamming kept them out of danger until they were over friendly territory.

Later, just after sunrise, they landed at their base. As soon as they hit the ground Nick and his linguist searched for and found a United Nations worker busy handling the hundreds of refugees that flooded out of the war-torn country every hour. The atmosphere was chaotic, noisy and tense. People were yelling, wailing and crying. Nick approached what appeared to be the harried supervisor of the refugee effort at the nearby border crossing.

"Excuse me, Sir. I have a child for you here that needs attention."

The American aid worker did not look around to see who was talking to him.

"Pal, I got fourteen thousand men, women and children here who 'need attention'. Take it to the first aid tent. I got too many already."

Nick spun the man around and looked him square in the face. The UN refugee supervisor's eyes widened with surprise. He saw two completely camouflaged soldiers with green berets, in full battle gear. One was holding the girl, wrapped in a military coat. Nick took his index finger and pushed it repeatedly into the man's chest. The Green Beret Major spoke with a very menacing and serious tone of voice.

"This kid better be on the first plane to the United States or I'm going to kill you as you stand right here, right now, Sir!"

The UN man gulped hard believing every word Nick had said to him.

"There's a diplomatic mission plane that's leaving in five hours. I'll, I'll get her on it."

"She'd better be on it. I'll know. If she's not, I will find you."

A small wet spot started to appear in the groin area of the UN man's pants. "I guarantee she'll be on that flight, Sir."

Nick and his linguist handed the five-year-old to the man. Nick looked directly into the man's eyes then nodded once, reaffirming his threat to him. As they walked away, Nick looked at his team member and gave him a wink and a little grin.

The next day Nick found himself in his dress green uniform, in front of the General.

"Major, I've read your report. The man you retrieved was immediately sent to Ramstein Air Base Hospital, in Germany. The doctors worked on him throughout the night and into this morning. They had to work on him a lot. They tell me they think he'll pull through all right. They said that if you had gotten him an hour later he wouldn't have made it. Good work, son. I'm recommending that you, your team, the pilots and the door gunner get the Silver Star."

Nick audibly let out a sigh of relief and smiled at the General.

"Thank you. With all due respect, Sir, the door gunner killed and the pilots are the ones who really deserve it. We were just doing our job. I'm very glad to hear that our guy will be okay. That's what it's all about, Sir. That's what it's all about."

TRIPOLI, LIBYA

The university had well watered and manicured lawns and gardens. The buildings were constructed by some of the finest masons and craftsmen in the Arab world. The scene was quiet except for the chirping of some birds in the surrounding trees and bushes. There was a soft and cool breeze. It was just enough to gently tumble a few fallen leaves across the walkway. Suddenly, the pastoral serenity was shattered by a tremendous sound. "Crash!"

Maryam Sabbah leapt through the second-story window accompanied by a thousand razor-sharp shards of glass. The splintered pieces showered down like a lethal waterfall of diamonds. With her face covered she could only hear the tinkling of the deadly daggers as they fell down around her and onto the grassy lawn. They shimmered and sparkled with color.

"Ugh."

Her right forearm broke upon impact with the ground. A cut opened up on her forehead and she sustained a few more lacerations on both hands. Her eyes were wide open with fright. She was amazed that she had survived the jump at all. There was no time to think.

Maryam screamed in her head. "Get up. Get up!"

She quickly but groggily picked herself up and fled across the university grounds.

It was a school day. Several startled students and a teacher walking to his next class all stared with disbelief at what had just happened before them. They looked at each other as if saying, "Did you see that?"

Although no students came forth, a faint recognition of their professor was reflected in their eyes. Only one student tentatively spoke. "Professor? Is that you Professor Sabbah?"

Maryam felt a trickle of warmth down her neck. Fortunately, there were no major arteries cut. But her right cheek was bleeding profusely. The heavy object she hurled through the window just before her leap had loosened much of the brittle window glass. It lessened the resistance of the ragged edges when they met her exposed flesh.

A guard dressed in a boxy, poorly tailored suit appeared in the shattered office window and pointed a gun at her.

"She's an easy target at this distance."

"No, idiot! We want the traitor alive," said the Major, now behind him.

He was also looking out of the window. He instantly growled a command. "Well get going!"

The secret policemen ran down the stairs and out of the building after Maryam, the professor, the spy.

The Major extended his bare hand then wiped a smear of blood onto his forefinger from one of the dangling, remaining broken panes of glass. He slowly rubbed his fingers together feeling the smooth consistency of the blood, her blood. He slowly stuck out his pointed tongue and tasted the blood. He never took his eyes off the escapee now fleeing into the distance.

The Major was now alone in the office. In a cold voice, he said aloud to the absent professor. "The further you run my dear, the closer you get to me."

He then angrily punched the broken remains of the window outward. He sent them clattering down to the carpet of winter grass and glass below. He snarled a mean sound from his slit like mouth. He looked around one last time then left the professor's office.

Maryam clumsily climbed on top of a barrel and rolled over a six-foot wall blocking the alley between two buildings. She mistakenly put her broken right arm down to break the fall. The pain shot through her entire body like a bolt of lightening.

"Argh!"

There was nothing quite like the truly guttural sound of deeply felt pain. She nearly passed out. The arm was just now stiffening and starting to dramatically swell. Soon, it would be completely unmovable. A knee cut was being rubbed raw by the fabric of her wool pants.

The secret policemen urged themselves on. "Go, go, go!"

Maryam felt like a small, furry animal being pursued by a pack of voracious, wild and starving wolves. Swooning in pain, she got up and dashed down familiar paths and around building walls. The throbbing of the forearm seemed to echo the pounding of her heart and feet across the well-worn footpaths. The intense pain now stretched throughout the entire right arm and shoulder.

She desperately asked herself a question. "Which way? Which way? This way!"

Around a corner she briefly stopped, breathing hard and scared. A tear of fright welled up in her eyes. She gulped in the cool air. It made her cough, causing even more pain. The university had been a home to her for so long. Now, it was becoming a maze of death. Glancing quickly from right to left, she decided to bolt toward the river. Her heart was beating faster and faster as she ran and became increasingly terrified. Her pursuers' footsteps could be heard not far behind.

She spoke aloud to herself. "Keep going. Keep running! Don't stop!"

Maryam pushed on in desperation towards the nearest river bridge. The jarring motion of her run made the pain unbearable. Part of her was already exhausted and just wanted to lie down and sleep.

Instead, she ordered herself out loud. "Keep going, Maryam. They'll catch you! Must keep running!"

She was strengthened by the knowledge that even this sickening agony was preferable to what the Major would inflict if they caught her. She stumbled onto the bridge, her stamina and legs starting to fail her. The pain half-blinded her.

As she was about midway across the bridge, the thundering herd of footsteps behind her stopped. She glanced over her shoulder, only to see that the men had stopped running. They had slowed to a trot. She then whipped her head back around and tried to focus on the other end of the bridge. Her eyes were blurring from the blood dripping from her brow. She reached up with her good arm and wiped the blood from her eye with her hand. Cars blocked the traffic and men with radios were coming from that direction.

They were closing in.

"I'm trapped!"

The secret policemen got closer. She began to panic and looked over the side of the bridge. The current was swirling and swift. She felt a strange calmness come over her. The professor in her started to resurface.

"Even if I survived the initial plunge, the cold and fatigue would surely make me drown."

The men got closer. They started to run again when they realized that their soon-to-be captive might jump. With impending death so near, Maryam's senses were on heightened alert. She searched for any option of self-preservation. It was do or die, fight or flight. She certainly could not fight them.

A tug boat chugged ahead underneath hidden from Maryam's view by the bridge beneath her.

The men drew nearer. She strained to listen for the tug boat fifty long feet below.

Then she looked at the pursuers.

The men screamed at her, pointing their guns.

"Don't do it. Don't do it!"

Fifteen seconds.

Ten seconds.

Five seconds more.

Just as the policemen reached her position, she quietly resigned herself to her decision. "Oh, God."

She rolled over the railing. Grasping hands just missed her. Passing the point of no return Maryam prayed the tug boat would get there in time. She also hoped that she would not be killed if and when she landed on the tug.

Without a sound, she floated down through the air. It was as if she were in ultra-slow motion. The academic's life rapidly passed before her eyes. As she fell she instantly recalled the morning's meeting that led up to her precarious flight.

Chapter Two

REVOLUTIONARY COMMAND COUNCIL HEADQUARTERS, LIBYA, THAT MORNING

Outside the headquarters a few remaining leaves wafted their way down through the crisp morning air. The gray sky boded more severe weather on the horizon. A blustery wind blew the clouds about, allowing an occasional sliver of sunlight to peak through. Although threatening at the moment, the weather was expected to improve as the day progressed.

Inside the building, the expansive opulence of the office fit the high ranking of the Libyan official pensively gazing out of the window onto the courtyard below. His forehead was deeply wrinkled as he thought of the difficult situation he faced.

General Ahmed Al Kafar was the Minister of Political Affairs for The Socialist People's Libyan Arab Jamahariya, commonly known as the country of Libya. Many years of hard work, risk, military service and political maneuvering had led him to rise to the top echelon of his government's leadership. Even so he had to be very vigilant.

So many wanted to unseat or discredit him so that they could take his important position. The room was silent. Lost in thought, the man's eyes rapidly blinked at the sharp knock at the door.

"Come in."

Maryam entered.

"I came as soon as I got your message."

Her face was still flushed from the cold, outside air.

"Thank you."

Once she was inside and had closed the door Ahmed handed her an envelope.

He then talked to her in a hushed tone. "You must get this to the Bull. We don't have much time. The conference will be upon us soon."

Ahmed's position was among a small circle of the powerful elite. He did not have to fear hidden microphones in his office. Nonetheless his instinct told him to quietly talk.

He explained his tone of voice to Maryam. "It seems there is always someone listening at the doors of this headquarters building."

Maryam nodded, acknowledging the instructions, then cautioned him. "For me to deliver this message would be dangerous. You know I am under suspicion. It could fall into the wrong hands."

In a low and earnest voice, Ahmed replied. "You're the only one I can trust."

She wearily sighed.

"Very well. But I'm on borrowed time. I fear that this is the last time I will see you".

With that their eyes met and great sadness descended over them. Their secret, conspiratorial relationship went back a long time. They had grown personally close over the years. Their double lives depended on the other's silence. Their very existence was interwoven with a sacred trust. They fondly embraced. The two Libyans looked at each other for the last time, knowing that surely one or both of them would be dead within two weeks.

TWO HOURS LATER AT QUADAFFI UNIVERSITY, TRIPOLI

Maryam took a circuitous route to the university to throw anyone following her off track. On the office door was her name and the inscription, "Professor Emeritus, Arabic Literature."

After a jingle of keys and twist of the knob, the spring hinged door opened, then closed behind the academic. She removed her gloves and jacket which she had hung on the coat rack countless times before.

In the spacious office a dusty beam of sun light was transformed by refraction into a spectrum of colors that pierced the room. The large, old window opposite the door was six feet high by four feet wide.

The wavy texture of the imperfect sections were like prisms brilliantly projecting every color of the rainbow. The magical illumination throughout the office seemed almost surreal in the midst of such somber circumstances. It washed the deceptive life away if only for a few seconds, leaving the devoted teacher. She smiled, enjoying her brief moment with beauty. Sure enough, a cloud passed to block out the sunlight making the rainbow vanish before her eyes.

"What a pity,"

Sometimes she wished that the heavy burden of silent service be lifted from her shoulders and mind. It was so exhausting to live two lives. It was like having two full-time jobs, one during the day, the other at night. But, you had to keep your daytime colleagues from knowing that you even had a night job, let alone what it entailed. Maryam had been looking over her shoulder for a long time. She was getting tired of the necessary lies.

She moved around the room in silence touching everything. Her fingertips caressed the books on the wall shelf with gentleness as if she were lost in the fond memory of an old friend that had since passed on.

Twenty-five years earlier she had graduated from the elite University of Tripoli with the highest honors. She was spotted by and subsequently recruited into the Libyan Secret Intelligence Service, or LIS. She served several years as a spy in Europe and America. She was recalled to Tripoli when LIS headquarters became suspicious of her loyalty.

"You are becoming too close to the American way of life, straying from the pure path of Islam."

In fact, she was secretly very sympathetic towards the U.S.A. Once she was exposed to the real West she realized that the devilish image portrayed in her training just was not true.

Back in Libya she was forced to pursue Arabic Literature Studies, as dictated by the LIS. She became the youngest professor of Arabic Studies at the university. However, her inward enthusiasm for America remained undimmed.

The man she met just hours ago, Ahmed Al Kafar, was also code named "Daphne," and was already a spy for the American Central Intelligence Agency or CIA. Kafar was on staff with the university when Maryam arrived to follow her "chosen" field of study.

Ahmed saw that internal passion for Western life in her. Over time he cautiously convinced her to more actively help America. For many years she had risked everything working for him.

Suddenly awakening from her memory, Maryam looked around her office again. She felt that this mission would be her boldest. It may also be her last.

Her shoulders sank with a heavy sigh. The melancholy soon returned at the realization that never again would the Arabic Studies expert sit at the old desk grading graduate research papers. She was taking a terrible chance to even be at the office. Maryam owed it to herself to take in the familiar, musty smell of the aged leather bound books just once more before... .

LIS Major Farid Bashak kicked open the office door.

"At last we meet face to face."

The Major strode in and plopped himself down in the wing chair across from the professor's desk. Removing one glove he twirled it with his finger.

Major Bashak was a fanatically dedicated spy catcher and interrogator of the most ruthless kind. He was completely devoid of a sense of humor. Music irritated his ears. As a workaholic he lived and breathed only for his job. To him there was nothing else in life but his profession, hunting and catching spies.

He was instructed by his superiors to investigate and find a traitor who was about to give a list of Libyan chemical and biological warfare capabilities secrets to an American spy. Once caught he or she was to be interrogated to whatever extent was necessary. The traitor was to be tried as a criminal and executed for all to see.

Surprised by his entrance, Maryam reacted to the Major.

"Who are you? What are you doing in my office?"

"Professor, you know very well who I am and why I am here."

Bashak gestured to two of his guards to station themselves at the door. The third guard stood at the Major's side. That guard had a pistol pointed at Maryam.

Maryam protested with an offended voice.

"This is outrageous!"

Slapping the desk in indignation, she continued to chastise the Major.

"How dare you insult an academician of my standing? I demand you leave my office at once!"

The guard raised his pistol towards Maryam in response to her sudden and dramatic movement.

The Major coolly spoke to her, while inspecting the office furniture.

"Not yet. Enough of these games, Professor. I have a question for you? Why would an 'academician of your standing' go through the front door of the Revolutionary Command Council and go out the back?"

"And what business is it of yours?"

"Everything you do is my business, Professor."

"Would you risk visiting a Council member with a jealous wife and half a dozen gossips roaming around the halls?"

"Ha! I know you met someone, Professor. But it was not a lover. Sooner or later I will find out who it was"

Impatiently standing up he straightened his uniform coat.

"Professor, the game is over. It has taken me considerable time and effort to find you. Won't you please join me at my office for a discussion of your activities on behalf of the infidel capitalists?"

"Well! I don't know what you're talking about. You're certainly arrogant to accuse me of such a despicable act."

She coolly smiled and began to walk towards the door. In apparent resignation to fate, her fingers dragged along the bookshelf molding in a final goodbye. Instead of going through the doorway, she quickly wheeled around. She grabbed a copper-colored bust of Colonel Mohamar Quadaffi from a nearby shelf. With some effort she then pitched the heavy statue through the hundred-year-old glass window, diving out behind it.

Leaping ahead in time to the present, Maryam found herself once again falling off the bridge, floating to her fate. After what seemed like an eternity, her instantaneous recollection of the events of the day was broken by hard reality. She fell from the bridge to meet her destiny.

ELSEWHERE IN TRIPOLI

The group of Libyan government conspirators were secretly meeting in an abandoned, nondescript warehouse. Such a grouping of high officials would surely be noticed if they met in a government building. The gathering of men was addressed by their spokesman.

"We are here for the express purpose of discussing exactly how we are going to accomplish the assassination of a large group of diplomats, statesmen, political leaders, economists and generals like us. Let's not kid ourselves. We are members of a secret club formed for the perpetuation of our power and the destruction of western civilization."

The warehouse was huge. It was not a room so much as it was a steel cavern once used to store hundreds of tons of grain and its by-products. Last winter Libyan authorities were forced to use the last of these reserves due to dismal crop performance the previous year. Also, making matters worse was the international embargo of grain shipments and many other necessary commodities to Libya. The embargo had been imposed in response to the Libyan downing of a civilian airliner several years ago.

The room was pitch black except for one battery powered table lamp on a crate in the middle of the seated men. They were in a circle facing each other but unable to see one another's faces. By design, the shroud of the lamp limited the light. It was unnecessary. They all knew each other.

The light shone only to chest level. Some of the men were smoking acrid, Turkish cigarettes. They could see their breath puffing downward into the light, then rising upwards into the blackness. The drafty air mixed with the swirling smoke from their cigarettes. No one outside the group knew of their conspiracy.

Their voices echoed when they talked. The speaker, obviously in charge spoke in Arabic. "What I shouldn't have to mention but everyone knows, is that our individual financial stakes in the oil production profits is also being severely restricted by the embargo. This provides very strong incentive for us to stay together and take some sort of action to hopefully lift the embargo.

There is a traitor among us. I know he has leaked a list containing the names of everyone in this room. It doesn't matter how I know. Just know it to be true."

A concerned murmur went up from the group of men.

The leader quieted them, repeatedly raising and lowering his hands.

"Gentlemen, gentlemen. Quiet please. He knows who he is and soon so will I. When I find out, I will have him killed. Nothing must hinder our 'patriotic duty' to strengthen our country's exalted leader and punish the Western infidels for the starvation of our women and children!"

In the dark the men turned to look at each other's shadowed faces with suspicion. No one trusted anyone.

Another voice from the dark spoke. "This is very unfortunate for this to happen at such a late date. It may jeopardize all our plans, all our preparations, our lives!"

There was a slight pause. Then a third conspirator, a sick and elderly man spoke up. "We must redouble our efforts to ensure our plan is not compromised!"

The leader assured them. "Do not worry. I have every available resource looking into it. And all of you know how extensive my......resources can be. The traitor and the list will be found."

The men again nervously fidgeted in their seats and warily looked at each other, silently wondering which one of them was the traitor.

LANGLEY, VIRGINIA

CIA Communication Technician Patrick "Sonny" James heard the beep of the laser jet printer. This signaled the arrival of a priority message from somewhere in the world. Once the computer received the entire message, the machine flashed a red light notifying the technician that it was ready to decode the incoming cable.

"Okay. Let me run my speech for tomorrow's briefing by you. I'm getting tired of doing it. You know you've been doing it too long when you've memorized the whole thing. You know? Okay. Here's the introduction. See if this sounds okay: The Telecommunications Center or TCC is a large room about fifty feet by fifty feet. Its walls are lined with the most advanced high tech computer and communication systems available anywhere in the world. The room is immaculate. It looks more like a hospital clean room than a spy communication center.

This area is the electronic nerve center for the CIA. It has a backup power supply to run the equipment. The TCC is so important that even the backup power supply has a backup."

Sonny expertly pecked at the computer's keypad, instructing it to translate into English the garbled collection of letters, symbols and numbers that made up the one page of encrypted text.

He continued his briefing practice while processing the incoming message. "Although decryption seems like a simple process, these abbreviated actions are the result of many decades of research, mathematics, espionage and technological development.

People have died to protect these secrets. The powerful computers are used to send, receive and analyze encrypted satellite and other forms of communication. They process incredibly complex algorithms at amazing speed to keep all but the intended eyes from seeing the coded data."

The technician spoke to his only other colleague in the TCC, Carlos "Tex" Fuentes. Both were armed with fully loaded 9mm military issued pistols.

"Tex, I got a Flash, Priority One message on the line. Request verification."

"Verification? Affirmative. Stand by one, Sonny boy."

Tex went over to the coffee-drinking table and took a swig of some cold, three-hour-old coffee.

He grimaced.

"On my way."

As he watched Tex take his drink of coffee, Sonny continued his briefing speech.

"TCC personnel are strictly prohibited from drinking any sort of liquid or eating any food near the equipment. If anything were spilled into the computers or other electronic consoles, it could cost millions of dollars. Even worse if a message did not get received or sent in time it could cost someone their life while on assignment. It could also cause an international incident."

Without looking at the text of the message both of the men verified the date, time, message number, sender and addressee. Sonny typed this information into a computer logbook to officially record the receipt of this particular cable. They then both signed and witnessed their names and identification numbers.

A few seconds later Tex called the addressee's office.

"Sir, there's a Flash message here at TCC for you. It's from the Beirut Embassy Chief of Station."

Within a few minutes the addressee had arrived. The CIA case officer in charge of Daphne read the message. Manuel "Manny" Cordoba-Martinez thought to himself.

"Hmm. I think it's time to talk with Bud Harlington."

THE PENTAGON, WASHINGTON, D.C.

Army Special Forces Colonel Maxwell "Bud" Harlington passed by the escalator leading down to the Pentagon Metro or subway station. He continued down the Concourse striding by the various shops and stores. He didn't notice any of them. In all his years in the Pentagon he never had the time or inclination to go shopping there.

He continued up the wide floor ramp through a seemingly endless series of stairwells, turns and hallways, all of which looked confusingly alike. Anyone who spends any time in the labyrinth of the Pentagon soon learns to memorize the necessary alphabetized rings, hallways, routes and landmarks within the great building simply to keep from getting lost.

Eventually he stopped at a door with a shrouded keypad door lock. He punched in some numbers unlocking the door. It made a loud click. Once inside an entryway he then faced a heavy metal door secured with a safe's combination lock. He dialed the proper series of numbers: right; then left; then right again.

He spun the dial back to zero, flipped a toggle switch, then turned

the dial to the right to unlock the mechanism. The door buzzed loudly
as he pulled it open. He flashed his National Capitol Region identification
card to the armed guard stationed just inside the door. The guard
nodded and allowed the Colonel to pass.

Bud turned to go down the darkly paneled passage. As he walked
down the hallway, he noticed for the thousandth time the security
reminder poster boldly facing him. It showed a picture of a computer
floppy disk, a telephone and a classified document strewn on a desk.
The poster's caption mocked a popular movie.

"Lethal Weapon too. Be alert. Be smart."

Marching down the hallway he passed two more armed guards who
snapped to attention as he passed.

The senior ranking guard spoke.

"Good morning, Sir."

"Morning, Sergeant."

Bud rounded the corner avoiding his assistant, an ambitious young
captain. Bud tried to slip by the captain because he would always hand
him a stack of phone messages. Bud slipped quietly into his office.

He hung his officer's wheel cap on his hand carved, teak hat and
coat rack. It was a gift from a Malaysian friend. Bud's life was a collection
of friends both living and dead. For every thing he possessed
he had a memory and a story associated with it.

His gunmetal gray desk and two chairs were strictly government
issue. An oversized map of the world covered most of one wall. A
collection of awards, medals and career photographs covered another
wall behind his desk. This wall of accolades was commonly known as
the "I love me wall." On Bud's desk was a nicely framed photo of his
smiling wife.

He went to one of his safes and dialed the appropriate combination, then signed the access sheet. He took an official personnel file out of his vault and set it on his desk. The orange and white cover sheet attached to the front was marked "TOP SECRET."

It was Bud Harlington's job to match up the best intelligence operative with the mission objective requested by the Defense Intelligence Agency or DIA and the CIA. At this level there was very little difference between them. In reality, the DIA wound up doing the vast majority of the CIA's human intelligence work.

Bud was considered to be a master at selecting the right man or woman for the task.

His current job was the latest in a long career of sensitive intelligence assignments throughout the world. After twenty years "in the field" he was given a staff position in the Special Operations Command. Bud had a long and distinguished career with several tours of duty in Vietnam and elsewhere.

It was upon returning from a particularly successful raid in Laos, monitored by U.S. and Laotian Army brass, that a Laotian General schooled unusually well in western slang, nicknamed Captain Maxwell Harlington. "Hey Bud, you do good job." The name stuck and from that day on Maxwell would be known as just "Bud" Harlington. Over the years his natural abilities, experience and extensive field contacts made him a guru of covert and clandestine operations. Bud was the natural choice for his current position upon its availability.

He opened the personnel file titled, "MAJ. Nicholas B. Dentworth, US ARMY."

On a mission in Central America Bud first met then Lieutenant Nicholas Bartholomew Dentworth or "Nick." He had been recently recruited into the Army Special Forces, SF / Green Berets as a First Lieutenant. Dentworth had been a counterintelligence agent assigned to a Mechanized Infantry Battalion in Germany. There, he got to know some SF personnel pretty well.

After learning about the Green Beret program, Dentworth knew that was what he wanted to do with his Army career. After a long series of grueling schools, Lieutenant Dentworth found himself assigned to the Seventh Special Forces Group, U.S. Army Southern Command (SOUTHCOM) in Panama City, Panama.

It was 1978. America had a new President who was determined to show his good faith and support of democracy by helping to finance the revolutionary Sandinista of Nicaragua. The President viewed the Sandinista as the answer to the tyrannical reign of the Anastasio Samoza family regime. This dynasty had controlled the country for decades.

There were, however, voices within the U.S. Government and military establishments that suspected less-than-purely nationalistic motives on the part of the leftist Sandinista. The task came down to SOUTHCOM to complement the CIA's effort to try to uncover any evidence that would show the extent of communist, foreign control and influence over the Sandinista. This job eventually fell to Nick.

Relying on his natural instinct, intelligence techniques, and his fluency in Spanish, Nick devised and implemented an ingenious ploy to penetrate the Sandinista Political Headquarters. As a result he obtained authoritative documents showing extensive Cuban Intelligence Service involvement and direction in the structure and daily operations of the Sandinista.

Nick also found evidence indicating the receipt of Soviet arms shipments and their subsequent transmittal to leftist groups in other Central American countries. Bud and Nick had worked closely on this operation. It was quietly heralded throughout the intelligence community as a great success.

Bud recalled with a smile how, after this mission, he and Nick celebrated by getting a case of beer. They downed it in an hour. They got very drunk, very happy and very rowdy. It took eight Military Policemen to subdue them and cart them off to their quarters to sleep it off.

The Army post Commander declined to press charges. The Commander was also a Green Beret. He decided that their hangover the next day would be as just a punishment for their conduct as would be any jail cell or disciplinary action.

Over many years Bud tried to keep track of Nick's career and exploits. He viewed Nick as a fast tracker and rising star. He watched as Nick developed a reputation for being able to successfully retrieve or extract people, documents, items or information from hostile environments. Bud was impressed with Nick's professional abilities.

All SF soldiers are multi-skilled and are taught to be flexible, creative and adaptive to changing situations. Each soldier also develops specialties in which he has a particular forte.

Bud saw Nick again on a handful of occasions. They were able, as much as globe trotting agents can, to establish a mutual friendship and respect for each other's abilities. They had also downed a few cool drinks together in more than one hot and cold spot in the world. It was with an almost paternal affection that Bud read the TOP SECRET file on his desk.

Bud read an encapsulated autobiography required by all intelligence agent personnel files.

"Born in Tucson, Arizona, I attended public schools. My parents were hardworking and old fashioned. They raised me on the farm where they instilled traditional American ethics and values in me, their only child.

I learned Spanish growing up in Arizona. I attended the University of Arizona in Tucson because my family and I couldn't afford out-of-state tuition. I was a good student.

My last two years of college were paid for by Uncle Sam through the Army Reserve Officers Training Corps. This program was a sensible option and one that would shape my entire future. My father died of a heart attack just before I graduated from Officer Candidate School.

Filled with grief and pride, I was commissioned as a Second Lieutenant. I would forever feel a special sadness that my father did not see me become an Army officer. My aged mother now lives in the retirement community of Green Valley, Arizona."

Bud Harlington flipped through the obligatory and extensive career records without a glance. He paused at reaching Nick's latest official photo, now two years outdated. He saw a tall, fit and confident soldier.

The hot Central American sun had tanned Nick's skin and slightly bleached his light brown hair. His piercing blue eyes looked straight at Bud drawing his attention away from Nick's impressive uniform.

Grinning slightly, Bud moved to the back of the file where he found the summary of Nick's current status. He was still unmarried and assigned to a temporary teaching position at Fort Bragg, North Carolina. "Bragg" is the center of the Special Forces universe.

Nick's situation suddenly made Bud feel old and sedentary. Since being restricted to staff duties, he and his wife had settled down in the suburbs of Washington, D.C. with their two dogs Rocky and Uschi. Bud simultaneously thanked his lucky stars and secretly yearned to be back in the field where in his mind a good operative belongs.

Snapping out of his daydream he frowned and found Dentworth's phone number. He picked up the receiver and dialed.

Three rings later Nick answered. "Special Operations Instructor Cadre Office. This line is not secure. May I help you, Sir or Ma'am?"

"Nick it's Bud Harlington."

"Hey, how the hell are you, Sir?"

"Fine."

"Good. But I don't know nothin' about how General Taylor's daughter's panties got run up the Pentagon flagpole. I also don't know nothin' about the fifty cases of scotch missing from the Fort Bragg military liquor store."

Bud smiled and faked an impatient voice.

"Cut the crap, Major. I've got something to say. Are you tired yet of wiping kid's noses?"

Nick mockingly snapped to attention at his desk and barked. "Yes, Sir. Six months too long, Sir!"

"Good. Do you remember Manny Martinez?"

"You bet. He still owes me fifty bucks on the '81 World Series."

"He and another gentleman will be visiting you tomorrow for a talk. Take them somewhere nice."

"Somewhere nice, huh? Sure thing. The Pussycat Club. No, on second thought you're right. Manny is more the Lair of the Drag Queen type."

Bud involuntarily chuckled, caught himself and snapped at Nick.

"Dammit boy, you'll never grow up!"

"I hope not, Bud. Or I'll be chained to the beltway, dishing out Alpo and credit cards."

Bud scowled. He was slightly jealous at the remark.

With affection in his voice he counseled Nick.

"Be careful on this one, Nick. I mean it. If I had anything to say about it, I'd be out there myself watching your little chestnuts."

Nick was genuinely appreciative.

"Thanks, Chief."

Then he sarcastically added a thought.

"But, the last thing I need is another old rucksack to drag along."

Bud shook his head, smiled and sternly remarked to Nick.

"Damn you, boy."

Nick smiled, as he hung up the phone. "It's good to hear from you, Sir. Goodbye."

Bud ended the conversation. "Take care, son. Out of here."

A couple of Nick's coworkers talked amongst themselves.

"Didn't the Major seem distracted and preoccupied this afternoon?"

In fact, Major Nick Dentworth hardly slept a wink that night. The excitement and adrenaline of the upcoming mission was too powerful to be conquered merely by sleep.

Chapter Three

FT. BRAGG, NORTH CAROLINA

The pale, yellow, wood planked exterior of the structure Nick chose for the meeting looked like many of the other buildings on the army installation. It was that vintage architecture and style reminiscent of a pioneer, mining town that was seen at many U.S. Army bases around the world.

The wood buildings vary only in color from post to post. They are pale yellow, green, blue, pink or tan. No one really knows or cares to admit who the architect was. The structures are facetiously known everywhere as "splinter villages". Their outer appearance is deceptive, belying the fascinating things that often occur within them. Nick would meet Manny Martinez in one such building, number 2307.

At ten a.m., Nick heard the bell and looked at a closed circuit television monitor. He smiled broadly at the sight of his old friend, fifty-year-old Manny Martinez, as he peered into the camera. Martinez wore a tan trench coat and sported a pencil thin, black mustache. Nick thought it complemented his salt and pepper hair. It gave Manny the look of a distinguished South American diplomat.

Manny was shuffling back and forth from his right foot to his left. He was trying to ward off the cold air. Standing behind him was a man Nick had never seen before. He was a tall, thin, gaunt man in his early forties with baby fine hair and a receding hairline. To Nick the man seemed exceptionally pale, even considering the luminescence of the color security camera.

What Nick thought most peculiar was that the man stood absolutely motionless. The man appeared to be made of stone. He stared straight ahead at the door. The only sign of life was the steady stream of steam escaping from the nostrils of the stranger.

Nick spoke to the camera monitor. "Bizarre looking dude."

Nick noticed all this in the few seconds it took him to reach over and push the red entrance button that disengaged the electronic locking mechanism of the outer door. The solid click of the door lock signaled the two men to push the door open and step into the outer room. Manny was glad to get out of the cold. There, a second television camera and benign x-ray device scanned the men, as they entered the anteroom. The outer door locked behind them. Nick could see on the second monitor that Manny had a shoulder harness with a Browning high-power semiautomatic pistol in its holster. Manny also had a "Baby Glock" in a velcro holster wrapped around his right ankle. The stranger had no weapons at all.

Manny pushed the intercom button. "Mr. Martinez and guest to see Major Dentworth."

Nick pushed his intercom button from behind the desk. "Enter."

As the door loudly buzzed, Manny and his guest pushed their way through the door and went inside.

Nick came out from behind the desk a few feet from the door. He gave a hearty smile and a firm handshake to his pal. Manny and Nick slapped their hands together in a firm grasp.

"Geez, Nick, you look great. It's good to see ya!"

"Manny, you old scallywag. How the hell are you?"

"I'd like to introduce you to Mr. Kimberly Phelps, Special Assistant to the Deputy Director of Plans at Central Intelligence. He's borrowed from the Libyan Desk."

Nick shook Phelps' hand. He immediately noticed that Phelps' long, bony fingers had a weak, almost feminine grip.

Nick quickly slacked off his normally strong grip.

"Pleased to meet you, Sir."

Phelps had a waxy, yellow complexion. His thin lips curved into the slightest of smiles. His gaze seemed as cold as the weather.

Phelps eyed Nick over from head to toe.

"I'm pleased to meet you, Major. It's good to finally see you in person."

Nick, still with a frozen smile, looked at Manny then back at Phelps. Nick wondered what Phelps meant with his last remark.

"Yes, well, please follow me, gentlemen."

Nick led them down a typical government style, nondescript hallway. They walked towards a conference room. The only distinguishing features on the hallway walls were the cheap paneling and obligatory photos of the chain of commanders culminating with the President of the United States.

As he walked, Nick talked over his shoulder to Manny.

"After the tone of voice in your phone call, I thought it best to reserve the secure room instead of meeting somewhere else."

"Wise choice buddy. This one is really tight."

"God, it's good to see you. You look like you should be floating on a yacht off Costa Rica. What have you been doing since you retired?"

"Oh, a little of this, a little of that. Heard any good blues lately?"

"Oh yeah. I just got an excellent digital recording of Ike and Tina Turner playing Memphis in sixty-five."

"You're kidding! Where did you ever find something that rare?"

"I got a buddy who runs a blues club in Charlotte. He's got an inside track on finding hard-to-get European imports."

"Damn. That's great. If you find any good Howlin' Wolf collections, let me know, will you?"

They continued walking down the hall. The wood floorboards creaked under the short, indoor-outdoor carpet that was cheaply tacked down to the floor.

"Sure thing. And I'll make you a tape of that Memphis gig? You been pushing a pencil in D.C. since last year?"

"Yeah. But I'll tell you Nick. You think we had it bad? Every time I sneeze out in the field, Langley has a blizzard of paperwork and catches pneumonia. They're incredible!"

Phelps looked up at Manny and blinked his eyes at the last remark, as if he was making a mental note of the comment for future reference.

Nick took them into the conference room. He closed the door.

"We're completely alone except for the security guards down the hall."

Nick motioned the men to sit at a large oak table.

"Coffee to warm your gullet, anyone?"

Manny nodded and went to the coffee pot in the corner of the room. "Mr. Phelps?"

Phelps silently shook his head no and sat at the table. He pulled some papers from his portfolio case.

Manny Martinez had an interesting background. He was born and raised as a streetwise kid in Brooklyn, New York. In 1968, he was drafted into the Army. As a twenty-two-year-old Private he was known as the "old man" of his Airborne Infantry platoon in Vietnam. After two tours, he went to college on the GI bill instead of going back to the old neighborhood. After twenty-five years of duty in the U.S. and Central America, he retired as a Chief Warrant Officer Four, or CW4. He specialized as a case officer who used "trade craft" to supervise or "run" secret agents inside Nicaragua and Cuba. The CIA hired him one month after retirement, as a senior level case officer in charge of Central America. Manny had worked several times with Nick in Central America in the eighties.

Phelps spoke to both of them in a dry tone of voice.

"Gentlemen, may we begin?"

Nick looked at Manny once again with an unspoken understanding between them "What's with this guy?"

Manny rolled his eyes and took a seat across the table from Nick and next to Phelps.

In a monotone voice, typical of Washington bureaucrats, Phelps addressed Nick.

"Major Dentworth, this is about a matter seriously affecting the national security of the United States. The Director has authorized me to impart to you certain information regarding planned actions by Libyan military intelligence and their secret police or LIS."

Manny broke in.

"You see Nick, the Libyans are really hurting since we slapped the economic and military embargo on 'em. Sure, they've smuggled a little bit of arms and supplies into their country. But they've had a tough time selling much bootleg oil on the international market. Oil is their main source of revenue for their infamous terrorist activities. They've had to resort to bartering, borrowing or begging for money from their Arab and non-Arab allies. And for Quadaffi, the egocentric megalomaniac, it has been a hard pill to swallow.

Intelligence indicates that he thinks that no matter what happens the West won't lift the embargo. He apparently sees it as a personal machismo thing between the various heads of state in Europe and North America and his 'supreme holiness' himself. It's also, of course, slashing the hell out of the Colonel's personal wealth from what he thinks he deserves.

Their abysmal economic situation is increasing the unrest among his 'loyal' masses both in the city and in the countryside. It's not that his iron fist can't control them. It's more irritating to him that he is losing face among his so-called friends. From his perspective, he's got nothing to lose and everything to gain if he strikes out wildly at the West.

He thinks he's invincible since we missed him in the 1986 bombing of his palaces. There also is a not-so-quiet, fundamentalist movement behind the throne curtain. They're threatening to challenge his authority to rule Libya. This appears to be pushing him to slide towards the extreme, more under the influence of the Mullahs. He really doesn't give a hoot about Islam. He's lying with his enemies to keep track of what they're doing. He's trying to decapitate the head of the serpent from within its own coils, before it bites him."

Phelps glanced at Manny then spoke up, slightly annoyed at being interrupted. He was also irritated with Manny's plainly spoken explanation of the situation. "In the midst of all this, the Egyptian President is going to be hosting a G-7 Conference of the world's economic powers in three weeks time. Egypt in return will be granted official observer status from now on. The conference will be attended by Presidents, Prime Ministers, Foreign Ministers, Economic and Trade Ministers brought together from all of the participating countries. This will be an attempt on the Egyptian President's part to forge a stronger diplomatic and economic tie with the West and to develop his highly overpopulated and product-starved country. It would bring Egypt closer within the folds of the international economic community. It would also raise his prestige rating in the geographic region. This would increase his own power in Northern Africa and Southwest Asia.

At the same time he will be using the conference as a world media stage to offer newer, more far reaching cooperative, economic development ventures between Israel and Egypt. Together, they would in turn agree by treaty to recognize Egypt as an official financial trading partner. It would give a boost to the Egyptian Prime Minister's dramatic, new, economic reforms.

Israel Desk analysis indicates that the Israelis will accept the offer. Even without Egypt's bid to increase its power in the region, there's no love lost between the Egyptian President and the good "Colonel" of Libya. They've been squabbling over country boundaries for decades, sometimes in open warfare."

Manny then added to the scenario. "Here's the kicker, Nick. We've received reliable information from a credible source, deeply rooted high in Libyan government circles. That source said there is a secret group of Libyan hardliners. This group, within the military and LIS has been meeting and planning an inflammatory incident to sabotage the conference."

Manny took a sip of coffee and continued the story. "This secret group will make the incident appear to have been carried out by a coalition of extremist ethnic Jewish groups opposed to any alliance between

Jews and Arabs. That same source reported that the incident would be a huge bomb blast that would make the Beirut Marine Barracks bomb look like the popping of a champagne cork. We're talking mucho kilotons of ammonium nitrate here. "

Manny took another sip of coffee. "Not only would it be the most spectacular terrorist incident in history, it would eliminate most of the troublesome leaders of the Western world, for Libya. The bomb would be the heinous excuse for Quadaffi to use as justification for his argument that no peace deal is possible with Israel. He would also blame the Egyptian President, whether he survived or not, as a lackey, a fool, not worthy of respect or power in the region. Naturally, Quadaffi would stand up, offering his divinely inspired leadership of the true Arab world."

Manny drained his coffee cup. "He would effectively seize the reins of power and reestablish his own preeminence, if only in his own mind. By solidifying his controlling position in that strategically important area, he'd no doubt then pressure the US to negotiate the lifting of the embargo. All these things he thinks he can accomplish by having a few of his flunkies flip an electronic detonator switch."

Nick asked Manny a question. "Why are you telling me this? What do I have to do with it?"

Phelps answered for Martinez, trying to regain control of the conversation. "The President of the United States is sincerely committed in his support of a Middle East peace. As such, he, that is the United States, has a vested interest in seeing a stable political situation in that area. He wants one in which the reforms and joint development have a better chance of success. And, uh, he wouldn't want all of his friends and allies killed either."

"That's all very nice. But what does this have to do with me?"

Manny paused, then offered an explanation. "That same highly placed, government source somehow got his hands on a list of the members comprising that secret group of plotters. He passed it to a courier, a 'cut out.' But before the courier could get it to us, we lost contact. That's where you come in my friend."

Manny then looked directly into Nick's eyes. He spoke to him in a low, measured voice. "We want you to get that list out of Tripoli in time to expose the plot and prevent the bombing."

It was Nick's turn to blink. He looked intently at Manny's serious facial expression, ignoring Phelps. "I thought you said you lost the courier."

"I said, 'we lost contact with the courier.' We have no information that our courier or our source 'Daphne' is compromised, yet."

With a puzzled look on his face, Nick asked Manny a logical question. "Why don't the Egyptians take care of it themselves? They know the territory inside and out."

Phelps interjected. "One, we haven't told them about it yet, for politically sensitive reasons. Two, without knowing who to trust, who's on the list, they can't use their own contacts within the Libyan government."

Manny further added to the conversation. "You wouldn't be completely alone. We do have some resources, that would unquestioningly act on your behalf, should the need arise."

Phelps then cleared his throat and purposely avoided Nick's eyes. "But ,of course, should anything go wrong, our agency would have to deny any knowledge of you or your activities."

Nick sarcastically looked directly at Phelps."Of course."

Phelps quickly put on his transparent but well-rehearsed diplomatic hat. I would add however, that the Director is behind me, one-hundred-percent, when I say that we have complete confidence in you and your ability to successfully complete this job."

"Thank you, Mr. Phelps. It's comforting to know that one's work is appreciated."

With raised eyebrows, Manny looked at Nick. "So you're in?"

After a pause Nick answered him. "I'm in."

Although Phelps was apprized of the existence of Daphne, he had no need or right to know the details of the espionage agent communication techniques used between Manny and Daphne.

Manny politely pointed Phelps to the door. "Please wait outside the room for a while."

When the door was opened, Nick called for one of the security guards. "Sergeant!"

"Sir!"

The soldier knew what to do. He led Phelps to a lounge where he would have to wait for Manny.

Phelps sat down on the lounge's soft couch. He folded his long, spider like legs over one another and settled into it. Only the slightest movement of his flat chest betrayed that he was even alive. He looked like an expressionless, store front mannequin. The guard posted himself outside the lounge door. This was done partly to provide security for Phelps, partly to keep him from wandering around the building and partly to be available for any questions or needs he might have.

Manny then spent the next two hours going over the system set up to communicate with the courier before the disappearance. Nick absorbed everything, all bits of information into his memory.

After Manny finished Nick noted something to himself. "I will be operating in Europe, Egypt and inside Libya itself."

In the pit of his stomach he felt a strange sensation. "This will be the most risky and dangerous mission I have ever had."

Finally Manny finished. "O.K., Nick. Any questions?"

Nick thought for a moment. "Yeah, Manny. When am I going to get my fifty bucks you owe me for the '81 World Series?"

Manny chuckled.

"Nick, if you can pull this one off, I'll get you in the dugout of your choice and an autographed team bat from the winners of this year's World Series!"

Chapter Four

LANGLEY, VIRGINIA

Samuel J. Gibbons, the Deputy Director of Operations or DDO for the CIA, waited in the anteroom for the signal to enter the Director's office. He had been there on many occasions in the past. The waiting room was separate from both the Director's office and that of his able and pretty secretary. The wood paneling highlighted the two portraits of the Director and of Allen Dulles, the legendary past holder of that office.

Gibbons was there to brief the Director of Central Intelligence or DCI, the chief of the spy agency. Today's briefing subject was the Daphne case. Manny Martinez would also be present to answer any questions. Gibbons had overall responsibility for the success or failure of the operation.

As he sat alone outside the DCI's office, Gibbons mused to himself.

"What an awesome responsibility rests on the shoulders of the man behind that door. Career professionals within the intelligence community highly respect me and have twice proposed my name to be the DCI. But, each time, political appointees were chosen over me. But, why? I am the ultimate professional intelligence officer." This did not really bother Gibbons. Although he secretly wanted to be DCI. "I prefer to stay on the operational side of the house, rather than be consumed with administrative and political maneuvers." he thought to himself.

He was an old man now but was still active, alert and full of vigor. He had a small stature, full head of pure, white hair and thick eyeglasses. He looked more like an aging school teacher than an expert spy master. Despite his frail appearance he was widely acclaimed for his life experience, wisdom, intellect and past exploits.

As Sam waited he quietly wondered to himself. "How would I write a resume for the DCI's job? I am part of a surviving elite of the few active veterans left from the OSS or Office of Strategic Services, the World War II predecessor of the CIA. Shortly after its creation in 1947, I was recruited into the CIA. For over half a century, I managed the overthrow of dictators, the cultivation of spies, the fighting of insurgencies and counterinsurgencies all around the globe. I'm a fierce patriot, and a cool thinker in the midst of crises. As the DDO, I direct the most sensitive projects and human operations the Agency has."

Sam thought a moment about what he had just recounted to himself. He quickly told himself out loud, "Poppycock, Gibbons. You're not so special."

Daphne had become one of the most valuable sources Sam had ever encountered. Proof of this was the fact that only a handful of people even knew of Daphne's existence. All references to Daphne information were categorized "Eyes Only" for the DCI, DDO, Manny Martinez, Phelps, and now Nick Dentworth.

Manny arrived two minutes before the appointed meeting time.

"Sorry, Sam. Hope I'm not late."

"No problem. I was just organizing my schedule for the day in my mind. I'm glad you could make it. You know Nick and that other person better than anybody." Sam instinctively codified the name "Daphne" as an ingrained security measure.

As the DCI, his schedule had to be precisely planned and coordinated. Exacting punctuality was one of Peter St. James' strong points. Over his twenty-year Washington and intelligence career, he achieved his promotions within the CIA through a skillful use of power, political fund raising, connections and rumor had it, some shady persuasion.

He was known by friends and foes as a meticulous, political animal and calculating man. Some thought his ultimate destiny pointed towards the White House. His cunning, savvy and staunch cold warrior attitude had won favor in the successive Republican administrations of the eighties. He had been very active in the political campaigns of the last two Presidents, even though one was from the opposition party. It was no secret that his appointment as DCI was a reward for the massive funds he had helped to raise in those campaigns. In his current job, St. James comfortably combined his talents and character with his brains and judgment.

St. James called the meeting so that he could personally monitor the operation. He looked at his desk, his calendar, then his watch. He waited quietly as the last few seconds ticked toward the top of the hour.

He blinked and softly spoke to himself. "Now, I am ready for you. There is a place for everyone. And everyone has their place." He felt he was in control. That's where he liked to be. At eight-o'clock a.m. sharp, St. James buzzed his secretary.

"Show Gibbons and Martinez in."

The secretary rose from her desk and walked over to Sam and Manny. She led them across the room to the large oak doors. She spoke to them with perfect diction. "Gentlemen, the Director will see you now."

The office was expansive, and furnished in a stark, modern style. Black metal chairs, a chrome and glass desk coldly gleamed in the brightly lit room. Manny thought to himself.

"This office belongs in the penthouse suite of a Manhattan venture capitalist rather than a staunch old line cold warrior."

The office was devoid of any personal belongings. Not a trace of family pictures or a glimpse of humanity was seen anywhere in the room.

"Sit down, gentlemen." The Director waved his hand in the general direction of two chairs. St. James was a business only man. He did not waste any time with small talk.

"Sam, I understand that Daphne has come up with some interesting information. Your brief reference earlier seemed to indicate some sort of LIS plot to sabotage an upcoming conference?"

"Yes, Sir. That is correct. Our source has obtained a list of names of conspirators that come from high ranks within the LIS and military intelligence."

St. James then satirically offered a comment.

"What? The LIS and Army working together on something without quibbling?" Without waiting for a reply he asked Sam another question. "So where is this list now?"

"Well, Sir, we don't know exactly."

"What do you mean, we don't know? It's our source, isn't it?"

"Daphne's courier got spooked before getting it to us. The courier went to ground. We are, however, attempting to remedy the situation."

"What are we doing about this?"

"We'd like to send a man into Tripoli to try and meet with the courier."

"Continue."

"Manny, why don't you fill the Director in, as to the details."

Manny was relaxed. He was not intimidated by the powerful person before him. He cleared his throat, looked at his watch and began. "Sir, with your permission, our man will be leaving for Cairo in, two hours. Here's our plan …"

Manny generally described the series of actions to get Nick to Tripoli. Nick would notify Langley prior to and after the meeting with Daphne's courier to relay any results. Nick would monitor the established meeting arrangements to try to find the courier.

Manny's instinct talked to himself. "Don't unnecessarily divulge all details of Daphne, even to the DCI, unless specifically pressed to do so. My gut tells me to hold the emergency meeting instructions as a trump card, a protective measure for both Daphne and Nick." Manny as the case officer, had to do anything he could to protect them. Sometimes, it was a matter of life and death.

After Manny finished, St. James asked a question. "What are the risks?"

Sam answered him. "There is a possibility that the courier's meeting arrangements are compromised. Because of the seriousness of the conspiracy, there is a high probability that our agents if caught, would be tortured, interrogated and killed to eliminate knowledge of the bombing plot."

"And if we don't obtain the list?" Gibbons bleakly replied.

"We'd likely see the worst terrorist incident in history and an end to the Middle East peace process, such as it is."

St. James coldly analyzed the risks and rewards, causes and affects.

He thought of the possible futures of the Middle East.

`"I approve. But I want someone to watch him, someone unseen to be there if he needs help."

He then emphatically stated a demand. "I must have that list. Keep me informed."

Sam turned to Manny and simply instructed him. "Make the calls."

The room was very quiet with its acoustical, sound proof walls. Sam and Manny could hear the swishing of the suit fabric as they got up and left the office.

Alone, St. James slowly and silently rocked backwards and forwards in his well-greased swivel chair, staring out the window. He saw but did not notice the Virginia countryside. Grimly, he pondered the situation. His hands were together, touching his mouth as if to pray.

NORTHWEST WASHINGTON, D.C.

"Ding dong."

The door opened. Phelps smiled, looked around behind him then went inside. He locked the door behind him. He was at the apartment of his lover, a male lover. After two and one-half bottles of champagne, Phelps had finally exhibited some emotion. He was drunk. His masculine lover Tony, had been sipping the same drink for the last hour. Hardly able to stand up, Phelps tripped over the coffee table spilling his drink and himself over the carpet.

"Oops!" Giggling like a school girl, Phelps tried to pick up the glass. He licked the champagne from his fingertips with his pointed tongue.

"Here, Let me help you, sweetheart." Tony helped the giddy Phelps over to the couch and sat him down.

"Woops!"

Phelps slid off the couch onto the floor, using the couch seat as a backrest. Tony sat on the couch cradling Phelps' bony shoulders between his legs. Phelps slid down further between Tony's legs, facing out towards the burning fireplace. Tony started to massage Phelps' soft shoulders.

"Oh my, you're so tight. Has work been so stressful?"

Phelps pouted with his lips and talked in a tearful voice.

"Yes, it's been simply horrid. They're working me like a dog. First it's over to the CI … ."

Phelps stopped himself from completing the words "CIA Director's Office."

Tony poured Phelps another glass of champagne. Phelps temporarily amused himself by watching the bubbles rise. It made him dizzy.

"Then to Ft. Bragg, then back to Washington. Just no rest, no rest at all."

Phelps stared into his glass as he drank it dry. His head bobbed backward.

Tony continued to massage Phelps. "Poor, dear. Go ahead and tell me all about it. If you can't tell me your troubles who can you trust? Here, have another glass of bubbly. It will help relax you. Now, what's all this about Fort Drag?"

"Bragg, silly, Bragg."

Tony had succeeded in loosening Phelps' shoulders and tongue as he loosened his own belt buckle. Phelps leaned his head back on the couch seat and stared up at Tony's face. Phelps pursed his lips into a kiss.

Phelps, now thoroughly drunk started to slur his speech.

"You see, there's this good looking guy named Dentworth. He's got to get that list of names so the bomb won't go off."

Tony kneaded Phelps' shoulders lowered his mouth to Phelps' ear and softly spoke to him.

"Just relax. When you're limber, I'll give you a surprise. Now, what bomb, hon?"

Phelps smiled his most alluring smile for Tony, thinking about the promised reward.

Phelps wanted to please his lover, his master.

"Well, this list …"

Phelps did not know it but he was in the arms of a Libyan gigolo paid handsomely by the ultra extreme wing of the North African Liberation Organization's or NALO terrorist group. His job was to extract secrets from Phelps and to compromise him into cooperating with them. The embarrassment of Phelps' exposed homosexual relationship with a prostitute on Quadaffi's payroll would be too much for his CIA career to withstand.

Within a few hours, Phelps' story to Tony would be read in Tripoli by the NALO, a branch of the LIS. Tony will have dutifully transmitted the story. Phelps' indiscretion sealed his own fate and that of Nick Dentworth.

QUADAFFI AIRPORT, TRIPOLI

While in disguise, Maryam watched the people entering the main terminal from across the street. She was looking for a certain type of passenger. Eventually, she was rewarded for her long wait. An American businessman wearing an expensive, hand tailored suit strode into the building. She followed him. She was glad that quiet, capitalistic opportunity flourished in the face of an official embargo.

She caught up with him from behind. They were midway down

the long hall to the gate area. By design, she chose this spot to be as far as possible from anyone that could overhear their conversation. In her best American accent, she called to him.

"Excuse me, Sir."

He turned around.

"Yes?"

"I'm sorry to bother you. But are you American?"

"Why, yes. And you?"

She answered with her most friendly smile.

"Cincinnati. I hate to bother you. But I have a problem."

"What is it?"

"See, my best friend is having her birthday next week. And I've written this personal letter to go with this birth day card."

"Uh huh. How can I help?"

"With the economy as it is, there's no IPC stamps. And the mail is unreliable, anyway. Would you mail this for me when you get home or when you go to the next U.S. Embassy? I'd be glad to pay you for the postage. It would mean so much to her and to me."

Maryam flashed him another friendly smile.

"Well, I've just been visiting an unofficial business associate here in Tripoli. And I'm sending some mail for him. I guess one more wouldn't hurt. O.K."

Maryam's face lit up.

"Oh, wonderful! Thank you so, so much, Sir! She'll be tickled pink."

"No problem."

She handed him the "birthday card and letter" while she reached into her handbag, with her good hand, for some postage money.

"No need, Ma'am. One stamp won't break my bank."

Maryam smiled again.

"You're very kind. Thank you. You better hurry, so you don't miss your plane. Thanks again and God bless you."

The businessman had been around long enough to know that even if you do a favor for someone from Libya or anyone from the Middle East, you still check it out. It's better to be on the safe side.

Chapter Five

RONALD REAGAN INTERNATIONAL AIRPORT, VIRGINIA

"Chickeez, chickeez."

The camera's automatic winder quietly whirred as the photographer depressed the shutter button. The frame showed the frozen image of Nick carrying a medium sized shoulder bag at the airline ticket counter.

Over the airport loudspeaker, an announcement was made first in Japanese and then in English. "Now boarding MAL flight 1937 to Athens."

Nick carried the bag and his black overcoat. He was dressed in a tailored, navy blue silk suit with black wingtip shoes. His handsome features and penetrating blue eyes made him look like a model accustomed to posing for the pages of a men's fashion magazine. Nobody would expect that he was a seasoned soldier trained to eat snakes and bugs while in the steamy jungles of Central America. His hair was dyed dark brown to help him blend in with the population of Cairo. He tucked his bag in the overhead rack across the aisle from his first class seat. Nick took a brief moment to nonchalantly glance at each passenger as they walked past him to sit in their seat on the aircraft. He looked for anything in their eyes, faces or mannerism that seemed out of place, or that showed undue interest in him.

A very old man laboriously shuffled by. He seemed mystified at finding himself on this flying, metallic bird. He was accompanied by his fifty-two-year-old granddaughter. She was busily chattering to him in Arabic. The old man wanted to sit down and rest in the first available seat. But, neither he, nor his grand daughter had first-class tickets. They were assigned seats way back in the economy class section. She urged him to keep moving.

There were two college students dressed in traditional, Arabic, one-piece, white, cotton thobe. They were wearing it for their pious return to their homeland. There was no trace left of the wild drinking party they attended last night for graduating from university with honors.

A few apparent businessmen filed past Nick. One had deep, dark eyes that seemed to be burdened with a serious matter.

Nick thought to himself. "I'll have to keep track of him."

A very beautiful woman of uncertain nationality glided by him. She looked back over her shoulder and glanced at Nick, squarely in his eyes. Her eyes flashed a message that Nick had no need to fear. Anyone who made direct eye contact was unlikely to mean him harm. So far, he saw nothing to cause him concern. He settled in for the long flight.

Midway over the Atlantic Ocean, Nick closed his eyes and recalled the conversation he had with Manny prepping him for the mission. "Here are the locations, dead drops and signals used by the courier. Nick, you'll also have to memorize the decoded content of the last two messages sent by Daphne. The first message read, 'TAURUS, have list great import. Names LIS/ARMY G-8 conference bomb plot conspiracy. Must pass immediately. No time waste. No risk normal channel. Will adjust. Daphne.'

Nick remembered what he told Manny. "Two things troubled me about this message. First, is the phrase, 'No risk normal channel.' Does this mean Daphne mistrusts the usual means of transmittal indicating a potential compromise? Or, is Daphne trying to protect the receiver of the message? Second, instead of going through the alternate communication plans, Daphne ingeniously but uncharacteristically had the courier deliver a sealed envelope containing the coded message. Normally, the plan isn't changed unless something was wrong, very seriously wrong."

Manny explained what the courier did. "The message was delivered, by an American, to a Marine Officer at the American Embassy in Beirut. The man who presented it was a businessman who had just arrived from an unofficial visit to a business associate in Tripoli.

So, while doing his State Department recommended check-in at the Embassy, he asked for the Marine officer of the day. Then, he presented the envelope to him. The businessman said an American lady gave it to him while he was waiting for a plane in Tripoli. She asked to have it mailed for her with his other correspondence, as a favor to her. The address was an undercover post office box that we have in Baltimore. The Marine Captain had it X-rayed, then presented it to the Embassy Security Officer, just in case.

The security man recognized the address as one of ours and became suspicious. Upon opening it, the security officer thought it was some type of coded message. He passed it to the CIA Chief of Station (COS) in Beirut. The groupings of encoded, scrambled letters alerted the COS to the fact that it appeared to be some sort of secret message.

Another fact that struck the security officer was that whoever sent the message either was playing a joke, was an amateur, or someone who was desperate and didn't have time to mask the message in a more normal looking manner such as in the phraseology of a personal letter. Just to be on the safe side, the security officer decided to treat it like the real thing and rushed the message to Langley where it was decoded and delivered to the only agent handler for Daphne. That case officer TAURUS, is me."

"Yeah. But, the unusual tactic that Daphne employed to relay the message unnerves me. It was risky. Even more disturbing is the last communication received. 'No time. Must go under. They suspect I have list. Will await news from Alexis.' I now know that Alexis is not a person but a code name for the emergency, last resort dead drop or secret storage place. You said it's located somewhere in Tripoli, established between Daphne and you alone."

"Yeah. I went there and picked it out, myself."

"But you think Daphne might pick a different place? I know I would."

"Daphne has proven so valuable that the only other person that knows of Alexis is Sam. The only reason I even told him was because if something should happen to me, I want someone trustworthy who could help Daphne in an emergency."

Remembering all this while flying over the Atlantic, Nick now realized there were presumably seven people in the world that knew of Alexis. They were the DCI, DDO, Manny, Phelps, Daphne, the courier and himself.

Even though he had just started, Nick was already starting to feel the odds stacking against him. He tried to sleep on the rest of the flight, but could only manage to catnap.

CAIRO, EGYPT

Upon arrival in Cairo, Nick wrapped the strap of his flight bag tightly around his wrist to help avoid would be bag nappers from even attempting to steal his.

"The thieves in this particular airport are unusually bold," said the CIA travel briefer.

He made his way through the wave of Africans, Indians and Pakistanis trying to leave or emigrate to Egypt. They came to work the low level jobs even the Egyptians didn't want to take. The noise, confusion and cultural mix at the airport reminded Nick more of a clogged bazaar than a modern, international airport. Nick passed through Egyptian Customs without incident, the agent stamping his passport without even looking up at him. He quickly grabbed the next passport, urging Nick to move along. The Egyptian Immigration official inspecting Nick's passport was more inquisitive. Nick had a false passport using the name Nicholas Mezani. The official quizzed him. "What are your intentions in Egypt?"

Nick smiled and carefully and proudly replied in badly American accented Arabic. "I'm an American. I grew up with Egyptian grandparents and visiting family members in my house. I'm here to see the Pyramids and to visit my family."

The Immigration Inspectors visibly twitched at the badly spoken Arabic. He returned Nick's passport and sent him on his way.

The plan that Manny and Nick had worked out called for Nick to visit his "Uncle Ali Hassan," who lived in an apartment in a congested, downtown neighborhood. He would then go to a village called Mukhti Baya.

It was decided that Nick had to enter Libya "black," with no official status. He was supposed to have never been there.

"Your contact will transport you to Tripoli where you will meet the courier and obtain the list. After getting it, you'll go to Greece then on to England. Once in England, you'll be flown by a special CIA chartered jet back to the US. You are to communicate with Langley only before and after having obtained the list or in the case of an emergency."

Nick ran through the scenario time and time again committing every detail to memory.

Nick walked outside the Cairo Airport terminal to hail a taxi. A pudgy man with a flat nose like that of a bad boxer, leapt out of his taxi and scurried over to Nick.

"Marahaba, Kaifa halak? Taxi?"

Translated, it was, "Hi there, how ya' doin'? Taxi?"

Nick looked at the imploring eyes of the taxi driver. "Laa. Shukran," or "No. Thanks."

The dejected driver's toothy smile vanished as he sauntered back to his taxi cab.

Over the years, Nick had learned to be wary of overanxious taxi drivers and overly helpful citizens in a foreign country. They quite often turned out to be in league with criminal organizations or working for an intelligence service, helping to keep an eye on foreign visitors.

Instead, Nick took his bag which contained a couple of changes of clothing, his boots and a shaving kit and slung it over his shoulder. He then walked around the outside of the air terminal building and looked into the street. Stuck in traffic was an available taxi. Nick chose this taxi due to the unplanned randomness of its availability. It was not likely to be waiting for him. He dodged a couple of honking cars, bolted across the roadway and jumped into the cab.

As he did so, the traffic jam broke, allowing the taxi to drive on. He spoke in English. "Hotel Internazionale."

"Na'am," or "yes" replied the driver.

He was obviously pleased at this unexpected customer.

Nick next spoke in Arabic. "Gif hina!" or "Stop here".

He was about two blocks from the Hotel Internazionale.

He got out and paid the driver, adding a nominal tip.

"Shukran." The driver shrugged and drove away.

Even tipping was an art form. Nick had attended extensive cross-cultural communication classes to learn the normal customs, procedures and idiosyncrasies particular to many countries of interest to him. Shaking hands with your left hand instead of your right was an insult in some countries. Too little a tip or too much of a tip could offend someone depending on where you were. Just the right tip made you blend in as someone familiar with the locals. In the intelligence business, blending in was as important as breathing. If you stopped doing either, you would soon die.

During the few kilos and many turns it took the taxi to get near the hotel, Nick had casually been glancing out of the corner of his eye to see if he was being followed. He did not notice any of the same cars twice and he saw no erratic driving by Egyptian standards. He noticed no surveillance helicopters or planes visible from his vantage point. There was nothing apparent, except for the fanatical driving that characterized Cairo's "no rules" style of driving. Whatever happens is supposed to happen according to the Egyptians. It's the same throughout the Arab world.

"If there's a crash, there's a crash." There is one phrase that strikes fear into the heart of any visitor, enduring a harrowing taxi drive in Cairo. "Insh' Allah," or "It is God's will."

Nick thought back to a lecture he heard once at a Middle East cultural intelligence briefing.

"The Egyptians and most other Muslims believe they have absolutely no control over their actions, destiny or the likelihood of events.

Allah makes all things happen. Let's say another taxi driver crosses the center line of the street, trying to take a short cut across traffic. He drives straight into the face of oncoming cars and crashes and kills everyone. To Muslims and particularly Egyptian taxi drivers, there was nothing the meandering taxi cab driver could have done to keep from killing himself and his passengers. It was completely out of his hands. 'Insh' Allah'."

After walking a few blocks, Nick hopped into a slowing public bus. He went towards the middle of the vehicle and sat by the side exit. He was lucky. His was the only seat left. He rode with the bus for several blocks, again looking for surveillance. It was basically clean. It would have been tough to see anything anyway, because the bus was belching out thick, black, choking exhaust that obscured his vision. He shook his head and thought to himself. "Just what this air polluted town needs, another smoky bus."

He got off the bus in a market or "souk" district and pretended to shop. The souk he went into was one of many in the area. It was more like a wide alley in between two large buildings. Each side of the street was lined with dozens of booths and tables jammed with goods and wares to sell. There was a great clamor of voices offering and negotiating prices. There were three hundred people talking at once. They were all trying to be heard, make money, and get a bargain.

There were different smells for each person, a different spice for each nose. Five different types of music played happy and culturally unique tunes. Many nationalities had gathered there to barter. A throng of people moved all around him like ants at a picnic.

He looked at the reflections off shiny pots and pans on display, trying to ascertain if anyone matched his direction, or walking pace. Nick saw no one who appeared to be watching him. Nick tried to observe the crowd as they all looked at each other.

Then he saw a man in a gold colored, fez hat. The man's expression screamed out to Nick. "I'm nervous. I'm not looking at you. So, quit looking at me."

When Nick went towards a booth in the man's direction, he quickly turned away. When Nick took four or five steps towards the man, he retreated four or five paces matching Nick's distance. Nick walked passed the man and continued through the market. Nick let the man catch up until he was just a couple of steps behind him. Nick was reeling him in like a hooked fish. The man lunged at Nick. He didn't want to hurt Nick, he just wanted his wallet.

Nick spun around with lightening speed. He grabbed the man's right arm, and turned him around, twisting the man's arm behind his back. Nick's arm bar was painful to the would-be pick pocket. Several people took notice of the scuffle and stopped what they were doing. They all had serious looks.

Nick realized the man was just an inept thief. He cranked the guy's arm up one notch causing the thief to wince with pain. Nick then kicked the man hard in the buttocks, launching him into the crowd.

He scrambled to his feet and ran away to lick his wounds. Nick shook his head and smiled. The crowd burst out laughing, then went back to their noisy business.

Having studied a map and photos of Cairo, Nick knew exactly where his destination was. He took another passing taxi to within a few blocks of his "Uncle's" apartment. He then walked a repetitive route, back tracking from time to time as if he was indeed a slightly lost tourist. It was starting to get dark. Convinced that he was not being followed, he went to his "Uncle Ali's" apartment.

It was a square, two-story building located on Nasser Boulevard with a large, open air courtyard in the middle. The door numbers pointed him to number eighteen on the second floor.

Nick knocked. A man opened the door, taking a bite from a piece of some sort of jerky he held in his hand. The short, chunky man looked to be in his late fifties. He was almost bald and had a graying, bushy mustache. He wore a thick, red colored vest. Nick envisioned some caring, matronly woman with a ball of thread and some needles, busily creating the garment.

"Na'am?" The man had a kind face. Nick smelled the unfamiliar odor of a hot, fresh meal coming from within. For a split second he wished that he was actually visiting the foreign family.

"Ali Al Hassan?"

"Na'am?"

Ali answered with a noticeable concern in his voice.

His words were muffled by the food in his mouth.

He was eying the tall man in front of him with some suspicion.

"I am your American nephew, Nicholas Mezani."

This was one of Nick's few practiced phrases in Arabic.

"I guess Aunt Karima told you of my arrival?"

Ali Hassan's brown eyes narrowed perceptively. He stopped chewing. He talked with his mouth full.

"And how is Karima? Her operation went well, yes?"

"Yes. It went very well. She's at home now, knitting sweaters for the children."

"And Najib? How is he?"

"Very good. He's retired and enjoying his falconry."

With this exchange of pre-established sentences, both Ali and Nick knew that they were talking to their appointed contact.

"May I come in?"

Ali quickly gestured him in with a wave of his hand. He switched to English. "Please, please."

While standing in the doorway talking to Ali, Nick was temporarily bathed in orange light from inside Ali's apartment. As Nick started through the apartment door, he glanced to his right to see if anyone was watching him enter. As he did, he exposed a highlighted profile of his face.

"Chick, eez."

From the shadows across the courtyard, the camera's operator steadily pushed the button. The shutter momentarily hesitated while closed, due to the low light conditions under which Nick was photographed entering Ali's apartment.

Chapter Six

Once inside the apartment, Ali was immediately warm and friendly towards Nick. "Please, your coat, please."

After hanging Nick's coat in the closet by the door, Ali led him into the kitchen. "Come, come."

On the way to the kitchen, Nick looked around the small apartment. The entryway welcomed him with a wooden sign that was inscribed in Arabic. "Allah's blessings be upon all who enter our home."

He passed by the dimly lit sitting room. The end tables had old, intricately woven yet yellowed doilies. On the wall hung a three-foot square tapestry of an illustrated page from the Koran. It was magnificently ornate in its use of gold leaf calligraphy so celebrated throughout Muslim history. The background was royal blue, with red, green, and yellow figures depicting an ancient scene of daily life. The apartment hallway had three doors. One was open revealing a simple but tidy bedroom.

The kitchen was bright and full of pleasant, unfamiliar odors. Nick decided his nose was smelling the residue of fried potatoes in olive oil, with perhaps cilantro flavoring the dish. Shining pots and pans hung on the wall. Something was sizzling on the gas stove in a skillet. Ali pulled out a chair for Nick at the small table set for two.

Bending over the stove, stirring a pot, was Jasmina Hassan, Ali's wife of forty years. Ali beckoned Jasmina to the table. She put the stirring spoon in a bowl on the counter top next to the stove, wiped her hands on her apron and turned to meet Nick.

Nick immediately thought that her brown eyes, although clear, seemed to intimate an inexplicable sorrow. Her graying black hair was wavy and brushed in the proper Egyptian style of her generation. She was taller than Ali and squarer in the shoulder. Her steady, deliberate motions exuded patience and persistence. She had the qualities of someone who had survived very difficult times. She had lived in a society where women are second class citizens in public and burdened with managing most of the affairs at home.

Ali introduced Nick to his wife. "Jasmina, this is Nicholas Mezani. He is from America."

Jasmina strongly took Nick's hand and spoke to him in Arabic. "Pleased to meet your Mister … Mezani."

It was quickly apparent to Nick, that this was not the first of such strangers to knock on her door. Jasmina looked Nick over from head to toe, then spoke.

"Sit down. You must have some of my Kubba and baklava."

Nick took his seat but looked down the hall towards the door, still slightly uneasy. Noticing this, Ali reassured him.

"Relax. You are safe here. And Jas makes a wonderful baklava. The sweetness just melts in your mouth."

Nick smiled and sat back in his chair. His stomach reminded him that he had not eaten since six a.m. that morning. Jasmina put pita bread on the table and placed a generous helping of Kubba and a cold salad before Nick and Ali. Jasmina's husband scooped up the first bite and shoveled it into his mouth.

"Mmm, good. Try." He then tore off a piece of bread and bit off a chunk to compliment the salad.

Nick quickly enjoyed the tasty food, mopping up the last of the sauce with a piece of bread. "It was terrific." He then spoke to Jasmina, who was checking on the cooling baklava.

"Ya Jasmina Hassan, this is the most delicious meal I have ever eaten."

Jasmina smiled, came to Nick, patted his cheek. She turned and talked to Ali, this time in English. "Very nice boy Ali, very nice."

After finishing their meal, Ali and Nick moved to the sitting room. Ali turned on a dim lamp. He then poured each of them a cup of strong, Arabic coffee, gawa, from a porcelain pot. It lay on a small coffee table in front of the couch. Ali sat in his over-stuffed reading chair. Nick sat on the couch. Nick directed a few more words of praise towards Jasmina and her cooking talents. He then turned back towards Ali.

"We have some business to discuss. You and I need to go on an officially authorized survey trip at the Libyan border. I'm told you already have the necessary documents." "But why do you go on a survey trip?" "It's just to get us close to the border."

"Why?"

"I have to cross into Libya, completely undetected."

"Let's see. With the new travel freedoms, there's no problem getting near the border. Which crossing point?"

"The closest one to the Mukhti Baya area."

"Ah. I know the area. There is a checkpoint very near there. Good. Now that's settled. Let's enjoy the coffee. It goes good after baklava."

They both took a sip and sat back in their chairs to relax.

Ali jumped out of his chair, startling Nick. "I almost forgot."

He went over to his intricately carved writing desk and moved its chair, He pried a floorboard up underneath the table and pulled out a package wrapped with butcher paper. Ali replaced the floorboard and repositioned the chair. He opened the package on the floor, with his back to Nick.

Ali turned and spoke to Nick. "They instructed me to give you this." Ali leveling a Browning, 9mm, fifteen shot, semiautomatic pistol at Nick's chest.

Nick gulped the coffee, his heart pounding hard. He calculated the distance to Ali and judged his chances of leaping to Ali's right. He'd have to kick the gun from Ali's hand without getting shot. At the same time, Nick felt that perhaps "Jas'" dinner may have been intended to lull him into a false sense of security to lower his guard.

A millisecond before Nick was going to lurch for the gun, Ali sensed the impending action. He flipped the weapon over. He tossed it to Nick. Nick's reflexes took over, catching the gun and instantly pointing it back at Ali.

Very apologetically, Ali stammered. "I'm, I'm sorry. I never had a need to learn how to handle guns."

Nick intently stared at Ali. He then brought the package over to Nick. It contained three magazines, fifty bullets and a silencer. Somewhat relieved, Nick expertly dismantled and reassembled the weapon, noting to himself that all pieces seemed to be in working order. He also noticed something else.

"Hmm. The weapon is clean, unmarked, untraceable, with no serial number."

Nick then looked at Ali. "How did you get involved with my people?"

Ali's face became sullen, as he went to the mantle over the sitting room fireplace. There, the look on his face bore the resigned and fatalistic burden carried by people who had been subjugated for decades. He took down a framed photograph and handed it to Nick. The photo was of a young man in his early twenties, smiling broadly and standing between Jasmina and Ali. They had their arms around his waist. The young man had a strong resemblance to Jasmina. Nick looked at the photo for a few quiet moments.

Ali broke the silence. "That was our only child. His name was Wadid. He was just about to graduate from the university. Years ago, the Egyptian secret police arrested him for treasonous crimes against the state."

Ali paused a moment, then continued. "You see, Wadid was a poet. He had a gift for writing poems filled with great truths. His heart was pure gold. Unfortunately, some of his poems discussed the hopeful joining of the Arabs and Jews in a peaceful union. Wadid was pressured by the authorities to denounce and give up his poems and manuscripts. Instead, Wadid had a friend smuggle the poems to the West where they were published. He was arrested, interrogated and tortured to death in the underground jails of Cairo."

Ali cleared his throat, then continued. "I was so distraught, I found myself crying in the streets and coffee houses. It was risky. The police could have taken me too, for 'spreading such lies'."

Ali clenched his teeth upon saying these last words.

He composed himself, obviously still extremely angry.

"An American overheard me one day, sadly telling my troubles to a friend. The American privately offered me a way to strike back at the monsters that killed my only son. I have worked from time to time with 'your people' ever since. A year after they killed Wadid, Sadat and Begin signed a peace treaty, bringing my son's poems to life, even in his death."

Ali's voice hardened. "But in the basements of Cairo prisons, the same monster still lives. That is why I help you."

Nick was genuinely affected. "I am truly sorry."

Ali nodded in acknowledgment.

"And Jasmina?"

"She knows only that I help the West. She is torn between the pain of losing her son and the risk I run for both of us in having you here. You are not the first."

Ali glanced affectionately at Jasmina in the kitchen. She was habitually washing the dinner dishes.

As Nick listened to Ali's story, he was nimbly loading fifteen bullets into each of the three magazines, all by feel, without looking. He then slipped one of the loaded magazines into the 9mm and chambered a round.

"Ker chunk."

As he did so, the metallic sound of the spring loaded slide putting a bullet into the breach of the barrel caught Jasmina's attention in the kitchen. She turned her head, pointing her ear down the hall. Then, she slowly turned her attention back to dutifully scouring a pot in the dirty, soapy water. She apparently resigned herself to the events unfolding in her sitting room.

A somber Ali informed Nick of the immediate future. "We will be leaving at five a.m. tomorrow morning. I suggest we go to bed early in order to be rested for the journey."

He took his emptied cup to the kitchen sink. Nick agreed.

Nick wiped the thin film of gun oil off the weapon with a handkerchief as Ali left the living room. Without thinking about it, Nick's training kicked in. He wiped his fingerprints from the coffee cup. Ali returned to the sitting room and showed Nick to the bedroom where he would sleep the night.

As it was a two-bedroom apartment, Nick realized he had the eerie honor of staying in Wadid's former room. Adding to the ghostly atmosphere was the fact that the room seemed to be preserved exactly as Wadid had left it over twenty years ago. It was as if he was going to bounce through the door, his door, at any minute. Nick thought that the couple with which he had just shared bread, must still be in great pain at the loss of their son, to take the risks they have for so long.

Nick put his bag on the chair at the foot of the bed and climbed under the blanket, fully dressed. The last thing he did before turning off the light was to put the loaded pistol on the night stand next to his head, within quick reach should it be necessary.

Chapter Seven

Nick awoke to a soft knocking on the door. Jasmina had dutifully risen early. She quietly spoke to Nick.

"It's four-thirty a.m. and breakfast will be served in fifteen minutes."

Nick got up, wiped the sleep from his eyes and grabbed the shaving kit out of his bag. He went across the hallway to the apartment's only bathroom. He splashed his face with icy, but murky water and shaved, wondering when he might get his next chance to clean up.

In special forces work, one is sometimes in the field for days at a time, trekking across rugged landscapes. If you were very lucky, you might be able to wash up a bit by wallowing in a stream long enough to rinse the first layer of filth off your sweat and mud encrusted body. Nick felt lucky to take advantage of the simple luxury of a shave.

He returned to the bedroom and gathered his things. He packed his bag again, placing his weapon and accessories on top of his neatly folded clothes. He remembered with some amusement an old girlfriend teasing him for folding his dirty clothes.

"Crazy Army discipline!"

He zipped his bag, shouldered it and went down the hall, into the kitchen.

Ali was already at the table eagerly spreading marmalade and honey on his breakfast roll.

"Good morning, Ali and Jasmina." She was packing food for Ali and Nick's "surveying" trip.

"Good morning to you. I hope you slept well."

"Yes, Ali. I slept like a rock."

"A sleeping rock? Ha. Americans are so funny."

"Mmm. Smells wonderful, Jasmina."

She silently smiled her thanks to Nick. She was afraid of what might happen to Ali.

After a light but filling meal of meat, rolls and piping hot coffee, the men prepared to leave. Once in the sitting room, Jasmina nervously wrapped Ali's scarf around his neck and buttoning his tunic. "You'll catch a cold if you don't wear a scarf."

"Oh, Jas. You act like I'm made of glass."

"You're not as young as you think you are, Ali Hassan."

"You're like an old ... Oh, stop fussing!"

Jasmina stopped. She bent over and whispered something in Ali's ear. His eyebrows raised and his eyes widened. "Oh? Oh!"

Almost apologetically, Jasmina turned and smiled warmly at Nick. Ali, looking a little embarrassed, shooed her back to the kitchen.

"Go on now, or I'll take you up on your offer, before I go." She disappeared, then quickly returned. She handed Ali a basket of food and bottled water. "A little something for the trip. Be sure to make the boy eat."

Ali looked inside and saw containers of lamb stew, pita bread, fruit, two thermoses of coffee and some bottled water.

Kissing her on the cheek, Ali put on an exaggerated face of disappointment. "Thank you dear. But where's my Arak?"

Jasmina scolded Ali, chasing him down the hall. "Oh you. You and your Arak!"

Ali explained what it was to Nick. "Arak is a very tasty and potent Lebanese liqueur."

"Yes, I know."

Ali walked out the front door, but not before swatting Jasmina on her behind.

Nick was delighted by the playful spat between two colorful people in an otherwise depressed and stressful lifestyle.

He privately told Jasmina a parting word. "Ya Jasmina Al Hassan, thank you. Your meals and kindness must have been sent directly from Allah."

She smiled again.

"Very nice boy. You speak Arabic so well."

Her voice took on an anxious tone. "Please bring my Ali back to me. And you come back and see me. I will make you my famous lamb and vegetable soup."

She watched Ali go with a concerned expression on her face. She had a dreadful feeling unlike anything she had before.

Ali gestured to Nick from the front landing that it was time to go. Nick waved goodbye to "Aunt Jasmina" and trotted to catch up with Ali.

Nick mused to himself. "It' refreshing to see real people in the sometimes unreal world of espionage."

Barely five in the morning, the courtyard was deserted. Nick looked around searching for anyone peering through parted curtains. They passed unnoticed into the street, where the early morning light was just beginning to melt the shadows. Ali quickly wiped the dew off the windshield of the boxy sedan. As Ali approached his car door, ready to take the driver's seat, Nick put up one finger, cautioning him to wait a moment.

Nick popped the hood of the car and carefully raised it an inch or two. He looked into the engine compartment for any dangling wires or extra devices. All looked normal.

Ali watched him with some confusion as Nick checked the under-carriage and wheel wells for any sign of tampering or explosives. He then looked under the dashboard and front seat for any extra electronic boxes or pressure sensitive plates. Ali sighed with relief after Nick's "O.K." hand signal.

Ali nervously got in the car door and hesitantly took his seat. After all these years, he still wasn't used to all the cloak and dagger ways of his double life. He started the engine and sighed with relief when he heard only the intermittent rumbling sound of the engine. He let the car warm up as he put the food basket and some survey equipment in the back seat.

They drove out of the city south, then west on the main road. They traveled for hours, heading towards the Egyptian-Libyan border. Ali pointed out points of interest along their route. As they passed an ancient Moorish castle on a hill, or railroad tracks and tunnels Ali explained how they were used for the transport of soldiers and military material, bound for the North African front during the Second World War. He added that the same roads and mountain passes were also used two thousand years earlier during Rome's domination of the region.

Nick wondered to himself. "How many soldiers have marched through these valleys? It must total millions through the millennia, from the birth of civilization to the Cold War."

Ali also told Nick Egyptian stories and legends associated with a valley or village they passed on their route.

Ali proudly talked to Nick. "I had a construction worker career of twenty-six years. My wife and I have been living off our savings and a small state pension. I was laid off by a commercially efficient Singapore-Egyptian joint venture company. They bought the truck transport portion of my company. Egypt started looking for outside business opportunities in the mid-eighties. But my story, told a million times in the lives of my countrymen, is better than living under the oppressive control of a police state."

The veiled reference to Wadid's fate did not go unnoticed by Nick. After five hours on the road, they pulled off onto a wide spot on the roadside and stopped for lunch. They were both hungry after their long ride.

During their roadside meal, Ali turned to Nick. "Where is your wife and children? Don't they worry for you?"

Nick was used to eliciting information from others. He avoided divulging information about himself and was taken aback by the direct question. "I'm sorry?" He stuttered involuntarily, shoving some bread into his mouth, stalling for time.

"Your wife, your children?"

"I don't see a ring. But a man like you must have a beautiful wife and children, yes?"

The faces of former loves flashed in Nick's mind, but the face of one woman lingered. She was a twenty-two-year-old Second Lieutenant, at the time he knew her some years ago in Germany. He had met her in a Munich jazz and blues club. In his dreams, whenever he was lonely, the image of this woman, Georgina Matlock, always came to mind.

The relationship he had with Georgina was the closest he had come to marriage. She, too, was an Army intelligence officer assigned to Munich. An otherwise blooming relationship died when Nick left his duties as a counterintelligence agent and entered SF. The separation from Georgina at the time, had been painful. He took some comfort in the thought that she was guaranteed a successful career, with her sharp mind and fluency in German, Italian, Russian and Arabic. She could have gone to work for the United Nations.

At the moment, Nick was pressed for an answer to Ali's personal question. He lied. "They're back in the U.S.."

"When this is over, you will send me your address. I will make some toys for your children."

Due to the nature of the work, Nick realized it was, unfortunately, a rare occurrence to develop any real, foreign friends. Most foreigners he had known became sources of intelligence information, never anything more. Besides, every five years he had to go through a security clearance update procedure. It would be difficult to explain the exact nature of any foreign friendships.

He breathed a little more life into his lie. "The kids would love that, Thanks."

Ali nodded his approval and put the remaining food back into the picnic basket.

On the road again, Ali spoke up again. "I first came to the border area as a construction materials truck driver. My job was to drive me-chanical parts to the border troops, for use in their Army vehicles.

The roads, although passable, were often closed due to bad weather or disrepair. I learned many of the back roads that led to the frontier. I often had to wait for my return loads of broken auto parts. I was often invited into the guard stations for coffee or tea. I heard their gossip and heard them talk about their security. I learned many things about how the guards operate the border ground sensor system and how they do their patrols.

I heard that at each shift change, the guards monitoring the ground sensor display panel shut the system down for a moment. They do it sector by sector, within a twenty-mile area. The border defenses were, at least briefly turned off. After about ten seconds, they would turn each back on again, one by one.

They still do the same thing. They never change."

Nick listened carefully, taking mental notes. Although Ali did not know why, Nick reasoned that the guards did it to eliminate electronic signal stagnation. Nick knew this principle applied to motion sensory equipment, much as it did to surveillance camera systems.

Nick explained. "That's interesting. If a video camera is left on in the same position for a long period of time, it may visually burn that image onto the monitor screen. This could render it useless or impeded in detecting motion.

Similarly, if ground motion detectors are left on, they'd ultimately burn an electronic image on the sensor panel circuits, effectively creating a blank sector in which no motion could be detected. That's why they turn it off at shift change."

Ali nodded with interest. Nick remembered a security survey he did on a military police station, some years ago. The signal stagnation was very bad on their post surveillance cameras. Nick stood and waved his arms in front of one camera while the Military Policemen at the station swore to him over the radio that no one was being seen on that camera's monitor.

Ali explained his take on the situation. "To cross the Libyan border's electronic sensor field you'll have to find a ground sensor a safe distance from the guard shack. Hold it to feel the buzz of electric current running through it. When the buzzing stops, you'll know you have a few seconds to sprint the one hundred fifty feet or so to the imaginary border.

But, there's a problem. Just like there are sensors in Egypt to prevent unauthorized entry into the Libya, there's also sensors for one hundred fifty feet on the Libyan side to alert the guards to any attempted exits from their country. Each side's sensors are set to pick up motion one hundred sixty feet toward the border, with a ten-foot overlap in coverage."

The CIA had briefed Nick about the sensors. "For at least three miles on each side of the border crossing checkpoints, there's a road for use by patrol vehicles. The sensors have line of sight capability. If you can find a ravine or depression ranging across the border, you could conceivably beat the system by going under it. If you crawl below the signal's geometrical plane, you can avoid detection, because the sensors will not detect motion below that level."

A CIA weather officer had reported to Nick, "Due to the heavy rains over the last days, the known ravine crossing points have significantly been altered by erosion. It is raining right now. If you're going to avoid the sensors, you'll have to find your own ravine to cross through the Libyan sensor field."

EGYPT/LIBYA BORDER

Nick and Ali drove for many hours, stopping only to fill their gas tank from the Gerry cans of petrol Ali normally carried in the trunk. By late afternoon, they finally reached the border area of the Egyptian desert.

Ali turned off the main road about two miles from the guard station. It took him through a maze of small sand hills, that hid them from any long distance sighting by the border guards. He took a rough, secondary road which twisted and turned until it stopped in a flat, sandy clearing. The desert area covered with barren sand dunes, blocked the view of the guard shack. It was approximately a mile and a quarter from their location.

The smooth, undulating appearance of the landscape made it difficult to judge direction and distance. Nick had been on other desert operations during the Gulf War. He looked at the sinking sun, seeing West. He saw the shadows cast on the East side of the dunes. The contrast between the beige pastel of the sand, the purple shadows and the deep blue sky was beautiful to Nick.

Ali pointed out the general direction of the guard station.

"The guards shift change will occur in one and a half hours, just after nightfall."

Nick looked at his watch and saw that it was five-thirty p.m. He had until seven p.m. to recon or search the border area for one of the above ground sensors that was near a ravine or wadi. Nick was starting to feel pressed for time.

"Break out the survey gear so we can play out our role, should soldiers or other officials find us."

"We are perilously close to the Libyan border. Remember, If stopped for some reason by unexpected guards, my official survey permit and Interior Ministry authorization should at least give us a legitimate reason to be in the area. It's a thin but simply believable cover story."

Nick's honed navigational skills then took over. He mentally calculated his desired path of approach. He surveyed the terrain, the rolling dunes and horizon. He used his watch as a backup compass by aligning the numbers with the sinking sun, determining which direction was north. He then began walking toward the border, with Ali trailing close behind.

After ten minutes of brisk walking in the sand, Ali stopped Nick.

He was audibly out of breath. "How far are we from the border?"

"It should be just on the other side of this big dune." After catching his breath, Ali nervously spoke to Nick. I'm not sure how to get back to the car."

Nick looked at his watch again, then turned to Ali.

"Do you see that tallest sand dune, there to the right, the one that looks like a camel's hump?"

"Yes."

"Just keep on walking toward it and you'll run right into the car." Ali earnestly took Nick's hand. "I don't know what you're going to do and I don't want to know. But, whatever it is, do it well and above all, be careful. I want to see your children someday."

Nick warmly returned Ali's handshake. "Thank you, Ali Hassan. I look forward to your meeting them. Thank you for your help. Goodbye."

Nick then disappeared behind a dune and was gone.

Ali turned, located the camel's hump again in the distance. He began his labored hike back toward his vehicle, wheezing as he walked. After awhile, he dropped the survey tripod, shedding the extra weight. As he trudged through the sand, he murmured to himself. "I'm getting too old for this."

Nick progressed quietly through the sandy terrain until he could see the patrol road that passed by the guard station. He stopped and estimated that he must be about two hundred feet from the road.

"That means I must be about forty feet from the sensor line." He walked forward around thirty feet, then stopped again. He cautiously started to move laterally, pacing out one hundred steps. He gradually moved his search line closer to the one hundred fifty-foot boundary. He allowed a little buffer each time he took a forward step. Nick had to be careful not to set the sensors off. If he did, guards would come. He and his mission would be put in peril. He inched closer to the sensor line.

On the third pass, he found a sensor. It sprang out of the ground on a six-inch shaft too low to crawl under.

He thought to himself. "No way of digging under it. I'd still have to cross the sensor field. And the sand would fill in as fast as I dug it anyway."

At the top of the shaft was a square box containing the actual sensor. Nick carefully placed his hand around the bottom shaft. He was pleased to feel the slight but distinct vibration of electrical current, just like Ali had told him. "Ali, you da man."

Nick then looked around for the closest depression, ravine or wadi, a river bed, that might allow him passage, through the Libyan sensor field. There was nothing close enough to this sensor to safely try to cross. The evening shadows started to grow longer and darker. The lingering warmth of the sun was starting to burn the skin on his neck. The rain had stopped earlier in the day. There was no trace of it now.

He moved further to his left until he found another sensor. He felt for the buzz. This sensor was also working. He looked to his left. He saw a drainage ditch, trickling with what must be the remnants of run-off rain water. There were a few plants and shrubs desperately clinging to life in the shifting sand. It was a miniature version of a desert oasis. It was about sixty feet from the sensor.

So as soon as Nick felt the current stop, he would have to sprint through the deactivated Egyptian sensor field and leap into the drainage ditch. Nick could see that the ditch abruptly turned twice, winding its way through the Libyan sector. Past that point, he could not see its path.

Nick then dug himself a curve in the side of a sand dune to hide until nightfall. He covered himself with sand, almost completely concealing him from view. Only his head showed. He waited very still. Sometime later, he pulled his arm out and looked at his watch. The incandescent dials showed five, fifty-five p.m. Some feet from him, Nick noticed a small pair of glowing red eyes, reflected in the bright moonlight. He would have preferred a new moon with no light whatsoever. But the heavens don't always cooperate with creatures of the night, as Nick thought himself to be.

The light revealed to Nick that a curious little reptile had come to see him, the new animal hiding in the area. Nick blinked, wondering if his eyes could be seen by the local inhabitant of the desert. The inspecting desert lizard quickly looked him up and down. Apparently, he was satisfied with his presence. It darted away. Nick could barely hear the soft sound of displaced sand as the lizard ran farther into the distance.

Nick emerged out of the sand and crawled, on his belly, over to the sensor. It was still buzzing. Nick knew that he had between ten and fifteen seconds to make it safely to the ditch. With his bag diagonally strapped around him, his weapon tucked inside his belt he patiently waited, then waited some more. It seemed to take forever.

"C'mon, c'mon already. Let's get this show started."

Suddenly, the buzzing stopped, just like Ali had told him. Nick jumped to his feet and ran fast. He hurled himself into the ditch, quickly belly crawling, around the first bend, just like he had learned in the Basic Combat Training portion of Officer Candidate School. There he froze with horror.

Unseen from his original vantage point, in between the first and second bends of the ditch was a pile of sand, debris and a half buried, old tire. This blocked the ditch and consequently reduced the runoff water flow to a mere trickle.

Seven seconds gone.

Nick popped his head up, trying to control his panic and looked for an alternative. He saw what looked like the top portion of a drainage pipe crossing under the road inside Libya. It was hard to tell for sure in the dim light. He had to make a decision fast. In a couple of seconds he would be stuck in the middle of two zones, not knowing if the Libyan sector was activated or not. Ten seconds gone.

Nick judged the corrugated drainage pipe to be jutting out about ten feet from the road. He had to act and risk setting off the sensors, or wind up stranded and exposed in the ditch until the next shift change. He was not sure when that next shift change would occur. Ali only knew of this six o'clock p.m. change. And there was no sensor to hold onto, to know exactly when to run.

He sprang to his feet and somersaulted over the debris. He jumped up and ran as fast as his legs would take him toward the pipe. He ran as if his life depended on it, for it surely did. It took him a few seconds to get there. He pulled himself inside the pipe. The movement of Nick's foot briefly set off the sensor which had been activated one second before.

Nick hoped he had made it in time. There was nothing worse than not knowing. He clambered further into the pipe pulling along some dead brush that had been washed from the nearby mini oasis, just outside the pipe during the last rain. If a patrol did come and shine a light into the pipe, Nick hoped the small, dead shrubs at his head and feet would adequately hide him. He lay down on his back to make himself less visible. At the very least it might provide a momentary distraction. As a last precaution, he pulled out his 9mm and placed it on his chest. He waited to see what card fate would deal him next.

Inside the nearby Egyptian guard station, the young soldier monitoring the ground sensor panel saw the sector twelve light flash for just an instant.

In Arabic, he spoke out loud. "I've got something here."

The Sergeant looked at the young man, then at the board.

"I don't see anything.""It flashed, just for a second."

The Sergeant told the shift officer. The Lieutenant strolled over to the panel. He instructed the monitor operator.

"Clarify your observation."

"Sir! Just as the sector twelve sensors were being reactivated, I saw the light briefly flash."

The officer sipped tea from an unusually dainty and finely painted tea cup. A friend of his from his days at Oxford University in England gave it to him as a going away gift. The officer fondly recalled his collegiate years and the fun times he had, each time he drank from the cup. He asked the soldier, "Doesn't that normally indicate a small to medium sized animal?"

"Yes, Sir!"

The officer paused for a moment, running a forefinger around the gold painted rim of the graceful cup.

He then gave an order to the shift Sergeant.

"It may very well have been an animal, but there aren't that many beasts in this desert. And the timing is a little strange. Send a patrol out just to make sure."

"Yes, Sir!

Corporal, take your patrol to sector twelve immediately and report what you find by radio." The Corporal scrambled out of the station, collecting two men, their AK-74 rifles and a patrol truck.

Nick could hear the approach of the truck from a distance. He thought to himself. "It's taken them about two minutes to respond to the scene."

The truck stopped right on top of him over the drainpipe. He heard the squeaky brakes roll to a stop. Nick quietly flipped the safety off on his pistol, wondering how much noise the silencer-equipped weapon would make inside a metal drainpipe. He had never killed anyone from inside a drainpipe before.

He also tried to count the number of footsteps crunching on the road rocks above, to determine the number of responding soldiers. He watched the bouncing beams of flashlights in front and at the rear of the pipe. Footsteps approached from his feet. Nick held his breath, remaining absolutely silent, while pointing the barrel of his gun at the drainpipe opening.

A large, black, desert beetle, six inches long, lost its grip on the curved roof of the pipe. It fell directly on Nick's chest, landing on its back. Although startled, Nick remained absolutely motionless. After struggling onto its eight, scratchy feet, it lumbered up onto Nick's neck. It stopped, changed directions and crossed diagonally over Nick's face. It continued over the top of his head, and down under his collar at the back of his head. Nick didn't dare move. After a momentary stop, the beetle crawled off of Nick and made its way further down the damp drainpipe.

The soldier's flashlight seemed like a floodlight as it poured into the pipe. Nick waited for the furtive sound and movement which would indicate a man un-shouldering his AK-74 assault rifle. Nick's heart was pounding. His adrenaline pumped. Every sense was on heightened alert.

The beam peered into the darkness, picking up a faint reflection of something, the soldier thought. To Nick it seemed like a stadium spotlight. The patrol soldier stuck his head into the pipe to get a closer look. He saw the shiny glint of something, wet and reflective. He started to enter the pipe for a closer inspection.

Nick started to slowly squeeze the trigger.

Just then, one of the other soldiers called out to the one entering the drainpipe. As the soldier retreated with his light, Nick heard one of the other soldiers talk in Arabic.

"It's nothing. The Lieutenant's just paranoid."

The soldiers patted each other on the back, cursed their commanding officer.

The truck doors closed and IT drove away, back to the guard station. Nick's eyes began to sting. Beads of salty sweat had found their way down his face. He breathed a thankful sigh of relief. His body went limp. His mouth was cotton dry.

After assuring himself the patrol had truly gone, Nick crawled to the other end of the pipe, the one inside Libya. He couldn't see it. But a Libyan guard post was across from the Egyptian one. At the pipe's edge he peered outside and saw, in the sandy dirt to the left of the opening, a metal wire casing exposed to air. He followed it with his eyes forward and to the left.

He saw that the wire casing led right to a sensor located about eight inches above his head and three feet to his left. He figured he could not crawl by it without risking discovery. Nick reached up to feel the familiar buzz of current in the casing. He began to plan.

If he waited until the next shift change he could then sprint past the Libyan sector sensors while they too, were temporarily deactivated. It meant waiting unknown extra hours. As tired as he was, Nick felt lucky to have to lie in a gritty, grimy drainpipe for several cold hours.

Once again he reviewed his mission instructions. After a while he started to feel drowsy. Nick slapped himself in the face. He could not afford to fall asleep and risk missing the sensors shut down. There were too few seconds to make it to safety. He had to force himself to stay awake.

"Stay awake dummy! You're only gonna get one chance at this."

For a while, he quietly sang to himself to keep from getting sleepy. "Goodbye, Ruby Tuesday. Who could hang a name on you?"

He started to drift off. He slapped himself hard, four or five times. "Once I'm up and moving, I'll be fine."

He forced himself to concentrate on creating a mental crossword puzzle. He thought of specific words and their definitions. "O.K. How will the letters intersect?"

The mental exercises kept his mind busy, his eyes opened, his concentration focused. After working on the puzzle for a while, he again reviewed the details of his mission.

At 0400, after what seemed to be six weeks, the buzzing stopped. Nick wasted no time. He bolted from the pipe, like a track sprinter out of the blocks. He cleared the sensor zone and disappeared behind the dunes in about eight seconds. Once he had definitely passed the sensor zone by many yards, he stopped and crouched low to the ground. He listened for any sounds of pursuit. The only thing he heard was the cheerful chirping of insects. If the insects would have stopped, Nick would have worried, fearing someone close behind.

Mukhti Baya was a couple of miles west of the Libyan border on the road from the guard station. Nick did not use the road. He traveled through the wadis and behind the dunes as quickly and as quietly as possible, far off the road.

One of the first lessons in combat patrolling is "never use the enemy's roads." In this case it was not so much to avoid land mines, but was more to avoid unnecessary risk of exposure or questioning. He was, after all, never there.

As dawn approached, Nick could see the few twinkling lights of the town of Mukhti Baya.

Chapter Eight

MUKHTI BAYA, LIBYA

Located in the desert, dry and plagued by sand storms all year round, Mukhti Baya in winter was windy, harsh and cold, far from the image of a picturesque Arab village. Nick could see the dominating spire and gold-gilded domes of the two mosque minarets. They belied the town's primary use as a crude oil tank farm and drilling rig storage facility.

The East Germans built two-story tenement buildings. They circled outward from the town center and gave way to a cluster of tiny houses. They more closely resembled Quonset huts, where the state cooperative farm workers lived. The dirt roads were a mixture of hard sand and small pebbles. In the far distance, six small, oil drilling wells were visible, but silent. If the embargo was gone, they would be continually billowing out choking black smoke. Otherwise they would have a perpetual flame burning brightly, twenty-four hours a day, seven days a week.

Nick's instructions were clear. Manny's voice echoed in his brain. "Go to the first of two mosques and look due north. At the end of the road you'll see a school. Behind the school is a small adobe style cottage. The woman that lives there is the village schoolteacher. She is your contact. She will take you to Tripoli."

Nick looked at his watch; it was seven-fifteen a.m. The sun was peeking over the surrounding hills. He looked around and saw no one on the streets. He found the school and the cottage behind it. He knocked on its front door. It faced the sunrise. He heard muffled movement inside and knocked again. Footsteps shuffled unevenly as someone approached the door from inside. Nick thought it ironic that he now had to depend on a complete stranger for his safety. His training and experience prepared him to be self sufficient, relying only on himself and trusted teammates.

The door opened. The woman inside was dressed in a heavy housecoat. She yawned briefly, blinking in the morning sunlight. She closed, then opened her eyes. As she did the day's first sunlight struck the schoolteacher's face. The yellow light showed bright blue eyes squinting to make out the figure silhouetted before her. Her skin had a healthy glow. Her hair was long and blonde, slightly disheveled from the night's sleep. Blonde hair and blue eyes in a country where black hair and brown eyes are the norm is remarkable.

Nick was absolutely stunned. He felt himself go pale, his heart began to pound, again. His eyes were deceiving him, or he was seeing the double of Georgina Matlock. His memory raced through a hundred souvenirs of his time with Georgina.

The schoolteacher raised her hand to shield her eyes from the bright sun.

She asked the visitor a question in Arabic.

"Yes, who is it?"

Nick could not immediately respond to her. When her eyes focused on the man outside on her porch, she stumbled back two steps and accidentally knocked over a flower vase on the small table next to the door. She did not know why but the sight of this particular man really startled her. Her mind was also racing.

He spoke to her in Arabic. "Im sorry?"

Hearing his voice, she looked at him again and gasped.

"Who are you?"

Hearing her voice, Georgina's voice, his mind twisted in the clash of emotions and fate. Fighting back his emotions, he concentrated and faithfully parroted the practiced Arabic sentences he had learned for this moment.

"I'm here about the schoolhouse repair job. Is it still available?"

The schoolteacher struggled to comprehend what this man was asking. It was not because it was not clearly stated but because what he was saying was something she was not prepared for. The words Nick said were the first of a conversation that would identify him as an American intelligence agent.

The striking similarity of this man to one American she knew years ago and the fact that he was reciting the words of a contact signal, unnerved the woman. She was known in the village as Leila Haddad. The man repeated the questions as if she was not yet fully awake.

Fighting to compose herself, she remembered her designated response. "Yes, it, it is. But you, you, you would need your own tools."

She cursed herself for the slight quiver and nervous stutter in her voice. She had not expected this situation to occur for years to come, if ever.

Nick responded. "I have my tools, but no place to live. Can you direct me to where I could stay?"

The schoolteacher recovered and continued in a steadier voice.

"There are some empty rooms in town, but you'll have to talk to the housing official for permission. Let's talk about wages."

She cautiously motioned him inside, opening the door wider for him to enter. All the while, she stared at him, searching his face for some sign of recognition. Nick came in, looked around, and sat in a chair at the table.

She drew a chair opposite him, started to speak, then paused. She apologized in Arabic. "I'm sorry, you remind me of …"

Nick interrupted her and spoke in German. "I speak German better than Arabic. Have you ever traveled to Germany?"

Their anticipation grew as they both grappled with the illogic of their circumstance. "Ya."

Nick looked her square in the face.

"Do you have any relatives named Matlock?" Georgina's eyes instantly began to tear up. In an unsure voice, she switched to English. "Is it you?"

Nick stood up. "Georgina?"

She stood up. The force knocked the chair to the floor.

She came over to him. She sighed.

"Nick?"

He nodded.

"It can't be. You're dead!"

"I was still alive when I checked this morning."

"I mean, I heard you had been killed. They told me …"

"I'm always the last one to learn these things. I should have been about forty times. But I'm still here. I guess I'm meant to pay more taxes."

They embraced each other, tightly hugging wrapped in each others arms.

They both simultaneously spoke to each other. "I can't believe it!"
They stopped, laughed and talked again in unison.

"In stereo!"

They laughed and hugged each other again.

Nick looked at her.

"How? When?"

Georgina blinked her eyes in amazement. "I can't believe I'm seeing you, here, now."

"This is too weird." Nick flashed his broad smile at Georgina. His white teeth emphasizing the dirt he had acquired on his cross border excursion.

A little part of Georgina melted at his smile. A dull pang of what could have been vibrated through her body. She gazed at him and with a smirk.

"You stink. There's the water basin. We don't have plumbing around here, but there's water trucked to us in those cans."

She pointed to a ten gallon can sitting next to the basin.

"When you're clean, then we can talk."

Nick dutifully obeyed, grabbing his shoulder bag on the way. As he passed by Georgina, he gently squeezed her shoulder. He glanced back as her hand briefly pressed his. He shook his head in disbelief. He shook his head and chuckled.

"Oh, man!"

As he splashed the water on his face, Georgina sat there motionless. She stared at him, seeing nothing but the past. She still couldn't completely absorb the fact that she had just welcomed an old lover into her home, inside the barren desert of Libya, years after parting. She was here as part of a deep cover intelligence assignment.

In a daze, Georgina quickly dressed for her teaching day. She poured two cups of chai and set them on the kitchen table, the only table.

Within a couple of minutes, Nick came to the table dressed in a change of clothes he had brought in his bag. He sat down, took a deep drink of the tea.

"Aaaaah! Thanks. That hit the spot."

They silently looked at each other for a few seconds, their hands wrapped around their teacups. Their eyes searched those of the other.

Nick broke the silence.

"How did you get here? What happened?"

Georgina, still needed to reassure herself that it was truly him and not some type of bizarre trick.

She asked him a question. "What was the first gift you ever gave me?"

Nick was slightly surprised by the question. "What?"

"What was the first gift you ever gave me?"

Nick thought for a moment. "A gold, heart-shaped locket with our picture inside it."

Georgina smiled. Finally convinced that it really was Nick, she put a finger to her lips. She got up and went over to the radio on the wall shelf. She turned it on and raised the volume of the traditional Arabic music playing. The song was a celebration of the generosity of Qadaffi's rule. The singer praised the wisdom of his development of the countryside, turning it into a Muslim, socialist paradise. The singer noted his courage, even in the face of economic starvation by the Western devils.

Georgina went to a small wall cabinet and opened it. She took out a worn, scarlet red, felt pouch. She walked back to him and placed the pouch on the table. Its contents spilled out. Among them was the locket.

She pulled her chair next to his, cupped her hands over his ears and whispered to him.

"I'm only a schoolteacher here. But no one trusts the police or their next door neighbor. About a year or two after you left, a man from across the pond at CIA, came to me and offered me a job."

Nick marveled at how sweet and hot her breath felt on his ear.

She continued. "I was a First Lieutenant at that time. He said, 'Lieutenant Matlock, there's a special program sponsored by my agency tailored for intelligence trained officers with linguistic skills such as yours. Why don't you come to my office where we can privately talk about it.'"

Georgina drew back slightly from beside Nick.

An edge crept into her voice. "So I did. At the time I had nothing to keep me in Munich."

Nick blinked at the subtle reference to him and what they had together.

"He offered me a job, a long term job. I would pose as an Italian and teach Italian and Arabic to the kids in an oil town like this one. They had me resign my commission and hired me as one of theirs. They sent me through their training school, 'The Farm'."

Nick nodded, recalling how he had been recruited.

Georgina leaned even closer to him.

"They set up an elaborate life history, a cover story for my new identity. After months of study, practice and testing, they sent me here to teach the schoolchildren. I was to be a 'sleeper' agent, living here for years, unnoticed, until one day a man would show up at my door. We would exchange the simple set of words that we did at the door. They said that I was to assist this man with whatever he wanted me to do."

Although she had no fancy perfume, the natural smell of her hair and the close warmth of Georgina's breath in his ear, made Nick's knees weak. He flushed with sentiment. It was intoxicating. He wrapped himself in her remembered scent.

After she finished talking, Nick suggestively joked with her. "Whatever I wanted you to do?"

"Yes."

Nick gave her a devilish smile. "Well ..."

Georgina returned the smile and punched his shoulder.

She rose.

"I have to go to work now. Make yourself at home. There's food in the kitchen. You can cook can't you, Mister?"

He pompously answered her. "It's Major."

Georgina raised her eyebrows as if impressed. "Major Dentworth."

"Oh, I can cook all right."

"Ha, ha, ha."

Nick smiled as he watched Georgina's hair flowing as she swept out the door to the schoolhouse out front. She was even more beautiful now than she was in Munich. It was not just the age. She now seemed more of a woman than the girl he knew years before. He was a little surprised that she would end up as a deep cover agent.

"God, she's beautiful!"

Nick was astounded that after all these years, the fates and Uncle Sam had brought him to her once again.

Nick scavenged in the kitchen cupboards and gathered some food. He found some Italian canned beef, canned milk and wondered at the thriving black market that flourished everywhere. He made himself some breakfast and ate.

He took his chai and walked around her little house, looking at her new life here in the "Land of Sand," Libya. There were three rooms; a kitchen, a bedroom and a sitting room. The furnishings were very plain and functional. She had a few decorations on the wall to liven things up.

Nick thumbed through her wardrobe in her closet. He noted it to be mostly Italian with some local garb.

"Good attention to detail."

He reminded himself of the times he used to go shopping with her in Germany. Like most men, he did not really like shopping for hours at a time. He did enjoy spending time with her, so he would grin and bear it.

He browsed through her rather sizeable collection of books in both Italian and Arabic.

"Nothing in English. Nothing to give her away."

Then, he went out into the sitting room where he found a photo album embossed with "Leila Haddad." Nick sat down, put his cup on the only table and opened up the album. There he saw old faded photos of aged men and women with Italian notes in yellowed ink identifying the people.

"Fake grandmas and grandpas."

A progression of photos showed a young girl growing up. There were other people in the scenes as well. Nick was impressed. Even the little girls resembled Georgina.

"The CIA had certainly done their homework well on this one."

As he saw photos of the girl maturing into a woman, Nick noticed that it actually was Georgina in her late twenties, possibly early thirties. Once again his mind drifted back to the days and nights with her. He remembered taking some goofy pictures with her in one of those instant photo booths. He still had one of those photos stored somewhere in his gear, back in the States.

He compared this false history or "legend" with what he really knew of Georgina's background. Nick recalled a conversation he had with her, what seemed like a million years ago.

"Tell me about when you were a little girl." "I was one of two twin daughters, a career Air Force brat. I was very close to my mother and sister. I moved every few years with my family as Daddy was assigned from country to country."

"Where'd you learn the languages?" "I spent the most years in Italy where I learned the language from my Italian friends. In high school and college I also took German, Russian and Arabic. I was pretty good when it came to learning languages and got good grades. It was difficult to tell I wasn't a native. I could have worked at the United Nations as a translator right out of college."

"Why didn't you get hitched?"

"I almost married a college sweetheart but was jilted a week before the wedding. Cold feet, I guess"

"And the Army?"

"Against my father's wishes, I joined the Army and went to the Defense Language Institute at the Presidio in Monterey, California. There, I improved my Italian and Arabic until I was really fluent. I was the top of my class. Lucky, I guess. I was first assigned as a voice intercept translator. Then, I became a counterintelligence officer in Germany. And well, you know the rest."

She met Second Lieutenant Nick Dentworth, also stationed at the same Army post. They dated, had a sizzling romance and then parted when Nick joined SF.

He again heard her voice, from earlier this morning.

"At the time, there was nothing to keep me in Munich."

His face grew grim. His eyes saddened.

He found a photo showing a man as groom and Georgina as bride. There were other photos dated throughout the last several years of the man in work clothes and in the uniform of a Libyan Army officer. There were happy photos of the two kissing at parties and with friends. Nick realized that these photos had to have been taken while she was here in Libya.

Then he turned the page. In a typical Arabian eulogy fashion, there was an enshrined photo of the man, in uniform. Underneath the photo were words for which Nick needed no translation.

"Bassam Al Haddad, died 28 September, 1985."

The slightly crinkled stain of what must have been Georgina's, or Leila's, tears dotted the page.

Nick felt sad for, yet perhaps a little jealous of the Libyan. He, if only for a short while, was able to happily wed and live with Georgina. Nick closed his eyes and bitterly thought of how things might have been if only he would have stayed in Munich. He wrinkled his forehead in regret, as he looked at photos of her life without him. So many lost years.

The food settled in Nick's stomach. The events of the morning settled into his mind. Nick soon succumbed to exhaustion after his long journey. He leaned back into the sitting room chair and soon fell into a deep sleep.

Chapter Nine

It was not until he heard the turning of the front door knob that Nick startled himself from his slumber. He instinctively jumped from the chair and headed for the wall partition dividing the sitting room from the front doorway. He silently put the photo album down on the floor behind him and positioned his hands so as to be able to grab and snap the neck of whoever the first unlucky attacker might be.

If it was a soldier or the police, Nick would snatch whatever weapon the hapless victim had in his hands, before his lifeless body hit the floor. He would then use that weapon to take out the next two or three men who entered. He was like a poised, black panther in the jungle, ready to spring at his prey. Nick awaited the unseen intruder.

"Nicholas?" It was Georgina's voice. She turned left into the kitchen area, looking for him.

No one was behind her.

Nick saw her back as he cautiously peered around the wall. He suddenly felt almost ashamed that his subconscious had allowed himself to mistrust her. He actually thought, if only for a moment, that she may have turned him in. Perhaps it was that he was just waking from sleep. Or maybe it was just the strain of the mission. In any case, he sighed with relief as he picked up the album and stepped over to the window.

"I'm in here."

"Oh, there you are." She moved into the sitting room.

Nick playfully gestured to her. "How was your day at work, honey?"

Georgina's bouncy pace quickly slowed as she realized Nick had been looking through her photo album. Her apparent reaction to him holding the album verified to Nick that Bassam Haddad truly was a real and special person in her life.

"I stumbled onto the album and out of curiosity, I looked through it. I'm very sorry about your husband. You two must have been very happy."

Georgina, or Leila, smiled graciously and sat down. There was a short silence and then she spoke. "He was a good man. He was the best mechanic in the village. But like most men in this country, he was affiliated with the military reserves. At first, it was just to help fill the loneliness. And to a certain extent, it was to help my ... situation here. But then I kind of grew into him. We had a few years and a few good times."

She paused. "Then he was activated and sent to some country in Central America. They never told me which one. He was a military advisor, there to help train some rebel group how to keep their trucks running. A lucky hit by government troops with a captured rocket-propelled grenade, found its mark and set his truck on fire. Only one of his men made it out, but he died a few hours later of severe burns. Since then, the townspeople have taken me under their wing. Most families here have lost someone, either to war or to the secret police."

Her voice grew quiet. "He was a good man."

Nick sympathetically added his true sentiment. "And a lucky one."

Georgina gratefully smiled and changed to an upbeat note.

"Let's have some dinner, then you can tell me how my life is going to forever change."

They had a modest but tasty meal of meat, bread and soup. He turned on the radio. They put on their coats and went outside to quietly talk. The evening air was chilly but pleasant. The last few birds were heading to their nests for the night.

Nick looked into the darkening night sky. He searched his mind for what he should and should not tell her. "I have to get to Tripoli within three days so I can take care of some business. But I don't speak the language. I need you to take me there. Traveling in two's is more convincing."

"You want me to drop everything here? What would the village, let alone the police think if I just disappear?"

"Please Georgie. I really need your help. It's more important than you can imagine."

Georgina thought for a moment, inwardly smiling at Nick's use of Georgie. It was an endearing term he used to call her at romantic moments a thousand years ago.

"Well, I guess I could make a trip to Tripoli to obtain some new textbooks for the children. I'd have to arrange, at great difficulty mind you, for a substitute teacher."

She was toying with him now.

"But then again, there's really no one qualified to teach the students. They can be so demanding."

Nick dropped to one knee and in an exaggerated voice begged her. "Please, Georgie. It will make me happy. And besides, I'm a Major and you're not. And you're supposed to do what I tell you."

She leaned down with her face close to his. "If you would have done this some years ago, you wouldn't be in this fix now, would you?"

She coquettishly smiled, and brushed a lock of hair off his forehead.

She strutted back into the house sighing her resignation to his wishes. "O.K., O.K. Mr. Major. Tripoli it is. Tomorrow we'll go by truck."

Nick followed her inside and into the sitting room. She flopped down into the chair, throwing one leg over the arm. It was an entirely American thing to do. She seemed to be reacquainting herself with her own past. Nick sat down on the sofa and stared at her. Her legs were enticing and open. The top button of her blouse was undone, exposing the soft skin of one breast. Her lips were angelic. Her eyes demonic. Her hair was tossed over her shoulder. She stared at him. Her glance never wavered.

He physically convulsed with the pain of loneliness and lost chances.

Georgina noticed the pained look on his face. "What's wrong? You're looking at me like a college sophomore."

"I'm thinking of you like a college sophomore."

They both looked into each other's eyes, trying to suppress the desire they felt welling up inside.

The constant, Arabic music blasting over the radio suddenly pierced the mood. They chuckled together as they both silently recognized their brief but immodest thoughts.

Then, in an effort to relieve the tension and at least one basic urge, their hunger, they moved to the kitchen. They prepared the next day's meal, ahead of time. Nick helped by drying the washed dishes. They whispered old jokes and stories, laughing until they cried.

"Well, Nick, I have got to get to bed."

She brought out some sheets and blankets and tossed them on the couch. The moment seemed a little awkward for both of them.

She nervously backed into her bedroom. "Well, good night."

A few minutes passed. Nick knocked on the bedroom door then pushed it open. She was sitting at a small dressing table, looking at Nick in a mirror nailed on the wall in front of her. She was brushing her hair before sleeping, like women do all around the world. She was dressed in her nightgown and robe.

Nick tentatively approached her. He took the brush from her hand and began to slowly brush her long and silky hair. Georgina closed her eyes, then opened them again. She tried to read Nick's intentions from his brush strokes.

Truthfully, she couldn't tell what her own feelings were either. Part of her resisted and part of her leaned back into the long, rhythmic strokes. The magnetism was undeniably there, as overpowering as it was in the old days.

It could have been cut with a velvet knife.

Nick softly spoke. "This makes ten thousand and one times that I have cursed myself for letting you go. Every day since then, I have been incomplete and alone. I just wanted you to know that."

With her eyes closed, Georgina found herself turning to meet his lips in anticipation of a long awaited kiss. Instead she found him turning away, heading toward the door. His eyes were closed tightly with deep regret.

Georgina puzzled at the depth and contradiction of this man. He was a trained commando and intelligence agent. He could kill without mercy with his bare hands, when it was necessary. Yet, here he was vulnerable, remorseful and emotional.

Georgina sighed and shook her head. She turned off the light, removed her housecoat and crawled into bed. She curled up with her pillow and eventually drifted off to sleep. She thought of Nick, what he had said and how he hurt for what they had lost.

Nick fell on the couch with a plop. He stared at the ceiling, trying to sort out his feelings. Part of him wanted to take her in his arms, and make passionate love with her. Part of him wanted to retreat into his familiar and painfully comfortable cocoon of loneliness. He cursed himself for putting the only woman he ever really loved in harm's way. He quietly made a promise to Georgina.

"If we both get through this coming ordeal, I will never, never, never leave you again."

Chapter Ten

CIA HEADQUARTERS

St. James' secretary buzzed the intercom. "An Alpha Two call for you, Sir, line three."

An Alpha Two call was the second most important call the CIA Director could receive. Alpha One was a direct line to the President of the United States. Alpha Two was a completely secure, private line used only by the DCI. On it he could talk by satellite to anyone in the world he chose to give the coded telephone number to.

He picked up the receiver. "Yes? Who is this?"

"It's Jetta. He's inside, made contact and will be on his way to the capital."

"Good. Follow him. Make sure he gets there. See who he meets. Get the package and bring it to me."

St. James spoke with an air of authority. It was very clear to the caller that it was an order, not a request.

"What shall I do with them?" "You know what to do. Use all your influence to make this happen."

St. James issued the last command, then had Jetta repeat his instructions. Jetta acknowledged the directives.

"I understand."

"It is absolutely imperative that I get that list."

"Yes, Sir."

"That will be all."

He hung up. St. James would have no loose ends to jeopardize this very important chance. He looked intently at the U.S. flag next to his desk. He fingered the corner of the flag, crumpling it into his fist.

MUKHTI BAYA, Libya

Nick and Georgina set off on their three-day trip to Tripoli in a truck borrowed from the local oil storage facility. Georgina talked to the facility's manager.

"You know, we hardly have any school books from the Institute for Technical Education. I need a truck that will make it to Tripoli and back without breaking down."

The manager sympathized. "I have two kids of my own in the village school." He winked at Georgina, broke the rules and gave her their best truck.

"If anyone questions me about the truck, I will claim that someone from the Ministry of Security requisitioned it for official purposes, about two weeks ago. I will not remember the officer's name or where he was taking it. It would be lost in the bureaucracy of mismanagement."

Everyone in Quadaffi's socialist paradise understood the confusion and incompetence of bureaucracy. After all, the authorization system, as it had evolved in this country was premised on incompetence.

Georgina thanked him and drove the truck to her cottage. Nick watched her arrive through a crack in the folds of the sitting room curtain. He grabbed his bag and the one Georgina had prepared for herself. He went out to meet her. Nick jumped in the driver's seat as she scooted over to the passenger side. Georgina would be the navigator. In several Muslim countries it was not customary for women to drive. In Libya, women perform many key jobs that in the West, are typically held by men. Yet, they are still frowned upon for exhibiting certain kinds of independent activities.

About five miles outside of town, they approached a security checkpoint. Georgina told Nick what she thought. "It's strange to see a checkpoint here. The only other time I can remember a road block here, was when an incident occurred along the border. It was believed that a small band of separatists clashed with an LIS border patrol, but got away. In their typical, overkill fashion, the village was put under curfew for two weeks. Each car was stopped and searched. Did you do anything to cause this?"

"I hope not."

As they pulled to a stop at the portable road gate, Georgina whispered to Nick.

"Act as if you're deaf."

Two soldiers motioned the truck to stop and moved to each side of the truck cab. Each soldier asked them for identification papers. Georgina promptly produced her papers. Nick smiled and nodded to the soldier. Again, he asked Nick to produce his papers. Nick smiled again, shook his head slightly and pointed to his ears. The soldier angrily shouted his demand a third time, gripping his sub machine gun.

Georgina interrupted her answers to the soldier inspecting her papers. She leaned across to the other soldier.

"Please. I'm sorry. I should have told you. He's a carpenter in my village. He's deaf."

She gestured to Nick, to show the soldier his papers. Nick nodded, pulled out his papers that Manny had fabricated and presented them to the soldier. The man now relaxed the grip on his weapon.

The documents were expertly forged by the CIA, using paper from the same rolls used by the Libyan authorities. The stamps used the same ink and depth of impression. The soldier looked at the documents and then at Nick. Nick smiled again.

In a perfect local dialect of Arabic, Georgina asked the soldier a question. "This is unusual. What's going on?"

The soldier returned her papers.

"We got a report that black marketeers were smuggling goods on this road. We're just doing routine checks."

Although outwardly calm, inside, Nick was nervous as he received his papers from the soldier.

With a grunt the soldier waved them through the checkpoint. As they picked up speed, Nick impatiently asked Georgina a question.

"What did you say?"

With a straight face, Georgina replied. "I asked what gives? They said they were looking for a Yankee spy, sent here to subvert their Islamic worker's paradise."

Nick's head thumped the rear window as he mockingly leaned back in exasperation. Giggling, Georgina relented. "They're looking for black marketeers, dear, black marketeers."

The two drove for many hours, stopping only for petrol, food and the necessities of life. It felt like they were driving the Paris to Dakar cross country rally. One tried to sleep while the other drove the truck, on four hour shifts. Georgina drove only during those long stretches where it was unlikely to meet anyone who would care if she was behind the wheel. The city folks were more sensitive towards strict, Islamic customs than were the few country inhabitants they encountered.

Several hundred miles into their journey, they stopped in the town of Jabar. Nick told Georgina to park the truck for several days in a place where it would not cause suspicions. She parked it in an alley behind an old basket maker's shop. She took some paper out of the glove box and in Arabic wrote a note.

"Engine breakdown. Will return in two days to repair."

She placed the sign in the front window.

"Now what, Major?"

"We're making pretty good time. We take the train the rest of the way."

Manny had given Nick information and options on how to get to Tripoli. They walked around the corner to find a ride to the train depot. Nick did not notice the sedan, covered with dust, slow to a stop two streets behind them. The occupants were very good at avoiding detection. Inside the car, behind darkened windows, Jetta clicked the shutter of the camera.

"Chickeez."

Jetta and his men had been loosely surveilling Nick and Georgina throughout their trip. Jetta had used a combination of vehicular and aerial surveillance. He also used his knowledge of the most direct route to the capital. Jetta's position allowed him to exert considerable power and authority over operational men and equipment.

After a typical two hour wait, an unsuspecting Nick, Georgina and three of Jetta's men got on the train to Tripoli. The trip lasted a long time. Nick and Georgina hardly spoke during the trip. They fitfully slept instead, exhausted by their cross desert trek. They awoke, still groggy, just as the train arrived at Tripoli's main station. As Nick and Georgina stepped off the train, a nearby camera clicked again.

"Chickeez."

With today's sophisticated surveillance techniques and technology, it is almost impossible to detect or foil a coordinated effort by a competent intelligence service. Even the best spies need to invoke meticulous patience, training and a good dose of luck to shake a surveillance.

St. James had told Jetta each step of Nick's plan, as he had been briefed by Manny. Under those circumstances, there was nothing Nick could have done to lose Jetta's agents or avoid this camera. It would have taken a miracle. But Manny had not arranged for that.

Chapter Eleven

TRIPOLI, LIBYA

In the city, Nick and Georgina took a bus from the train station. She whispered to him.

"Do you have any preference as to where you stay, Nick?"

"Somewhere downtown."

"Then follow me." She knew the city and its bus routes well. He followed her directions, changing buses from time to time.

They eventually made it to the city's center, where they found a transient workers' hotel. It was a kind of private hotel, subsidized by the Transportation department. It was officially referred to as a hotel of the Ministry of Structural Engineering.

They went to the registration desk and found the clerk. Georgina did the talking.

"One room please."

The clerk was leaning against the desk. He was thoroughly occupied with reading an article in the newspaper. He never looked up from the page. "Papers."

She offered her work permit authorization. Without watching, he pulled a receipt from under the counter. He placed it on the desk pad, reached for a stamp and imprinted the receipt. He turned the newspaper page to the right, to finish the sentence he was reading. He reached behind him to a wall rack of thirty keys. Only two of forty were missing. He unhooked a room key and tossed it on the desk in front of him. His eyes moved to the top of the next column in the article. He moved in slow motion as if handling a vial of nitroglycerine. Nick and Georgina looked at each other, amused by the man's lack of enthusiasm. A few moments of silence passed. Then the clerk slowly looked up from his reading and stared at them.

They facetiously interpreted his look, "Welcome, folks. O.K., I'm finished now. I hope you two enjoy our accommodations here. Just let me know if there's anything I can do to make your stay here more enjoyable. Thank you for your business. Have a wonderful day!"

Nick thought of a second interpretation.

"Well? What are you looking at? Go!"

In either case, the message was clear. As they walked up the stairs, Nick whispered to Georgina.

"So, is there anything special you'd like from room service? Sky's the limit."

The cramped room had very few furnishings, just like the thirty-nine other rooms in the prefabricated "instant" building. The thinly papered walls had become yellowed and flaked over time. The only distinguishing feature of the room was the two bulb chandelier hanging from the center of the ceiling. There was a twenty-year-old radio on the small desk for entertainment. It was more likely to be there for propaganda bulletins.

"Charming, Georgie."

She immediately fell on the wrinkled bed sheets. Within a few moments she was asleep, exhausted by the long trip. Nick decided to let her rest. He had mixed emotions. He knew that eventually, he had to send her back to her village. "I'll deal with that later."

With Georgina asleep, he decided to get on with his mission. He walked down the hall and found a janitor's closet. He looked for anything he could use to make a mark on a light pole. He found some plumber's tape in the hall's janitor closet. It was behind a bottle on the shelf that was full of some sort of toxic liquid, dripping onto the floor.

Nick had kept track of where downtown was, compared to his hotel. He walked downtown to a pre-designated intersection, picked some time ago by Manny and Daphne. He had quickly memorized portions of a downtown map. The cross street was in the museum district of Tripoli. He looked toward the northeast corner of the intersection and found the bus stop. Behind it was a black wrought iron light pole with a handbill pasted to it. The handbill trumpeted the "Islamic purity" of one of Quadaffi's son-in-law, appointed to head the Ministries of the Interior.

Nick looked hard at the people milling around the area. Everyone seemed normal. Yet, something told Nick to be particularly alert. A few people briefly looked at him, curious at his height. He went over to the light pole and leaned against it, as if he was waiting for the bus to arrive.

After a minute or two, he glanced up at the handbill and pretended to read it with some interest. Inside his jacket pocket, he clutched the six-inch piece of tape. He reached up and smoothed the lower left hand corner of the poster. As he did, he placed the tape diagonally across the corner.

Nick again heard Manny's voice. "This is the first of a series of signals used to prompt Daphne's courier to start the Alexis meeting arrangements. Each day at ten o'clock a.m. you should check the light pole to look for the courier's response signal.

The Tripoli Museum of Archeological History is just around the corner from the bus stop. Although near the light pole's intersection, it is the next location to be used according to Alexis."

Nick went back to the room and watched Georgina sleep. He remembered the old days with affection. It felt so strange to him.

"Just the other day, I was at Ft. Bragg, teaching Green Berets and commandos from other services how to blow up bridges, rescue hostages and defeat jungle booby traps. Here I am now, in a Tripoli flop house, gazing into the sleeping face of the only woman I have ever really loved and lost. But here she is. I can see the gentle rise and fall of her breathing. It's something I haven't done for what seems like a lifetime."

Nick reached down to brush a lock of hair from her face. He stopped himself, still not able to emotionally connect with the former love of his life. Even in sleep, her pouting lips drove him crazy. He stared at her for almost an hour.

Rested and aware of someone's presence, she stirred. She slowly opened her eyes and smiled. She propped herself up on her elbow.

"Where are we going to now?" "We, are not going anywhere. You are going back to Mukhti Baya."

Her mood suddenly changed from soft to harsh.

"Oh, no I'm not. I've seen you this far and I'm not just going to disappear back into the woodwork. Hell, you don't even speak the language. How long would you last? You're illegally here to begin with. I'm staying."

"There's no reason for you to stay. You got me here and that was all you were required to do. I'll soon be done here and gone."

Nick felt slightly guilty that he was once again telling her that he would be leaving her.

The point was not lost on Georgina. She was thoroughly angry at him. "You bastard. You drop into my life out of nowhere, after fifteen years or so. You expect me to drop everything, take you wherever the hell you want. Then, you say 'Thank you Ma'am. You can go home now. That's a bunch of crap!"

Nick was surprised to hear such a string of angry words from her. "You know that's not why. It's dangerous and there's no need to expose you to this. I'm not going to argue with you about it."

"Expose me to what?" She said this with an air of exasperation.

"To why I'm here."

Reflecting on her angry outburst, she decided to soften her tone and try a different tactic. "Listen. I've trained my whole life to work on this."

"I'm sending you back."

"They didn't say there would ever be another time when I would be called upon to assist someone. That means I don't necessarily have to go back there."

Inside, what Georgina wanted was to stay with Nick, no matter what was going to happen to them. She continued. "I've outlived my usefulness there. I'm ready for a change anyway. I need to move on. And you need me whether you admit it or not. I've spent a lot of time here. I speak the language. What if you get stopped? How many times can you play the deaf and dumb act?"

Her logic was hard to ignore. So were her flashing eyes. He thought for a moment in silence. Contrary to his better judgement, he made a decision. To let her stay. "Okay. But only until the next part of this gig."

She knew she had won him over, again. "Well, we have a museum to see."

Nick and Georgina went to visit the archaeological museum. Although she didn't know why, she figured it had something to do with the reason he was in Tripoli.

They took a taxi to the area. It was 9:55 a.m. Nick glanced up at the handbill on the light pole. Over the top right corner was a six-inch piece of tape diagonally placed parallel to the one he had placed there only hours before.

Nick thought to himself.

"That was fast. This guy must really want to get together. Or is it a trap."

This was the response signal from the courier, to continue to the next step in the Alexis instructions.

Instead of going directly to the museum, Nick told her what they would be doing.

"We're going to do a little sightseeing walking tour through the district."

"You're the boss."

Nick closed his eyes, remembering the map and photos he had studied. He envisioned the starting point and initial direction, then set out. Over the next two hours, Nick and Georgina walked her through a complicated maze of memorized turns. They went from street to street, intersection to intersection. They went north, south, east and west.

Jetta's unseen men took careful notes, making sure they were not noticed, as Nick and Georgina walked. Also, unseen was someone else. Daphne's courier had timed the route that the contact would follow walking at a normal pace. She knew the walk was supposed to start at ten o'clock a.m. Similarly, Maryam went to several prearranged locations along the same route. Eventually, by seeing the same person at the different locations, she was able to identify Nick or Georgina as the contacts. She was slightly concerned about the presence of a second person. That was not part of the plan.

Once sure, Maryam went to the endpoint, which was the archeological museum. Already inside, she saw Nick and Georgina enter the museum. Their cheeks were flushed with their exertion in the streets of Tripoli. Nick knew the courier should have identified him from the walking route.

"The courier should already be here. Who could it be?"

They walked through the museum admiring the artifacts and models of ancient civilizations. These were uncovered in the deserts and hills of Libya, by local scientists and some Soviet "archeological advisors," who also just happened to be petroleum engineers. As they walked, Georgina would periodically make comments in Arabic, about an object or artifact. Nick would dutifully nod from time to time, responding to her statements in a language he didn't understand.

The museum was laid out in such a way that a complete tour ended at the rest rooms and exit. Maryam was only a few yards from Nick, positioned there so as to be a couple of minutes ahead of his exit of the museum.

Nick heard Manny's voice. "Alexis' instructions say for you to visit the rest room before leaving. You are to go to the third basin from the left, reach under the counter. You'll find a piece of paper detailing the time and place to meet the courier."

Nick instructed Georgina.

"Wait for me by the exit and immediately leave for your village, if there's any trouble at all."

Nick entered the lavatory and noticed he was not alone. After relieving himself, Nick washed his hands and face, delaying a bit, until the only other man had left.

131

Nick approached the rest room without hesitation. Maryam, was expertly disguised as a man. She was already inside. As Nick entered, she was leaving. She passed right by him on the way out. With her broken arm, she painfully reached up and subtly adjusted her fake mustache upon leaving the men's room. She timed the message pick up, so as to have it there for only a minute or two before Nick retrieved it. This would limit the chances of the paper falling out, or being discovered. Maryam left the building as soon as she came out of the men's room.

Once alone, he quickly reached under the wood veneer top of the third basin and felt a lip of wood. It went the length of the cabinet. He moved his fingers under the lip but could not feel any paper.

Nick began to worry as he wondered if he had been set up. He looked at the door hoping no one would enter. He expected men to rush in and arrest him at any second. He racked his brain, retracing his actions, trying to decide if he had somehow made a mistake in the sequence.

He impulsively ran his fingers further down the lip, under the fourth basin then under the fifth and last basin.

"There it is!"

He felt a piece of paper and pulled it out. He relaxed and thought back to one of his first classes of intelligence agent training. The old, experienced agent on the teaching platform emphatically spoke to the student agents. "No government operation by definition ever, I repeat ever, goes exactly as planned. Half of them are blown by Murphy's Law. If something can go wrong, it will."

Nick read the message printed in English.

"Krasivwye Cemetery, seven a.m. tomorrow."

He put the paper in his pocket and went out to meet Georgina. She was anxiously waiting for him.

On the way out of the museum he thought to himself.

"Interesting that the name 'Krasivwye' meant 'beautiful', in Russian. It must be a carryover from the days when the Russians were still buddy-buddy with the Libyans."

Just around the corner of the building was an alley. They walked into it.

Nick pulled out the paper.

"This is why I'm here."

He unfolded the message, took a cigarette lighter from his pocket and ignited the flame.

"I always carry one. You never know when you'll need fire."

He lit the corner of the paper. Whoosh! The paper erupted into a ball of light and disappeared into thin air, like a magician's flash paper. There was no smoke, no ash and no smell. It simply vanished.

Georgina startled at the sight. "Great. What are you going to do next? Swallow a sword?"

Nick was pleased with himself. "Abracadabra, Alakazam."

He took a ceremonial bow.

As they made back to the hotel, the camera clicked and clicked again.

Another man, in a broad brimmed hat, also watched them walk. Mack, as he was known, worked for Manny Martinez. He was directed by Manny to watch Nick. He was to see Nick contact the courier, and do what he could to ensure that Nick safely got out of the country. He would keep Manny informed of events as they occurred.

Ten minutes after Nick and Georgina left the museum, several cars full of LIS security men screeched to a halt outside the building. They poured inside looking for Maryam. They had been tracking her for days. They always seemed to be just-one-step behind. The LIS men fanned out from room to room, exhibit to exhibit. They ran with guns in hand. They met again in the center of the museum.

Bashak asked his men an urgent question. "Well?"

They all shook their heads "no."

After determining that she once again had evaded them, Major Bashak threw his glove down in anger on the museum's polished marble floor.

"Damnation!"

Through hard work and some "lucky tips" from Military Intelligence, Bashak was closing in on Maryam. He felt sure that she should have been at the museum. He knew who the courier was, but could not catch his treasonous compatriot. Bashak thought back to the incident at her university office.

The most recent lead provided by the military was that the traitor would be meeting an American spy somewhere in Tripoli.

Bashak talked to his men. "No effort will be spared. Men will be detailed to every area of the city, twenty-four hours a day until the she is found."

As a personal backup plan, Jetta was utilizing Bashak to help find the courier. He was the military intelligence man. He was feeding certain pieces of information to him. He tolerated his LIS competitors only so far as they were useful in helping him to find the courier.

From St. James, Jetta had learned that the meeting would be in Tripoli. St. James had pressed Manny for the details of the plan.

"So where exactly are they supposed to meet?"

However, an overly cautious Manny did not name the museum.

"Sorry, Sir. I'd have to check the file and get back to you on that one."

Nick and Georgina stopped at a city park. As they walked along together through a nearby parking lot, Nick checked the door locks of several cars until he found one that was unlocked.

"What are you doing, Nick? I hope you're not going to do what I think you're going to do."

He opened the door, popped the hood and quickly hot wired the car to start it up. Georgina reluctantly acted as a lookout for the car's owner.

"This is not a good idea, Nick. Nobody steals cars in this country. It's just not done."

"Precisely. The confusion will last for hours. In a while, we'll bring it back. Besides, an object lesson in American street smarts will do them some good. A friend of mine that grew up in New York taught me how to do this." That friend was Manny Martinez.

"I don't believe you're doing this. But, that's O.K. With you, I know it could be worse."

"I'm not doing this. We're doing this. And we're not here. Remember?"

Georgina shook her head and got in the car. Nick drove around until they found a bookstore.

"Go in and buy a map of the city and the surrounding area." She did and then got back into the car.

"O.K., now what?"

Nick told her where he needed to go. Libyan maps, were purposely printed with errors and omissions to confuse any perceived enemies. As Nick's navigator, she lead him to a state oil refinery twenty miles south of Tripoli.

"Turn here. This should be the one."

They found the assigned, dusty road Manny had told him about.

135

"Turn left here, honey."

"Right."

"No, left."

Nick smiled.

"Right,"

"No, I said left."

"You're too easy. You've been gone too long."

They proceeded to the second road intersecting it on the left. It was in a sandy, scrub brushed area. The ground was covered with hard dirt and small bushes.

Nick drove the car around the first bend in the road, until he came to a two branched tree that had been struck and burned by lightning. There were several palm trees. He stopped the car and got out. "Wait inside. I'll only be a couple of minutes."

He walked north for several yards over a small hill, hiding him from her view.

He located a small, dry watering hole, found the north end and went to the tallest palm tree. He dug at its base. His strong hands easily displaced the hardened sand and rock. A few inches in the ground, he struck something hard. He uncovered and lifted up a square case. The box contained a high tech, worldwide satellite communications set. This device was the latest in equipment used by secret agents in hostile environments to securely communicate with their headquarters, anywhere in the world. It had been placed there by a CIA agent some months before for just this type of situation.

As he undid the clasp, there was a hiss of pressurized air that escaped as the sealed container was cracked. He switched the satellite feed transmitter to the "on" position. He pushed the "check battery" button showing the device to be almost fully charged. It showed that the battery had lost some charge over the time that the communicator had been stored underground.

He then pushed the "ready" button on the small lettered keyboard and typed "Comsat2Priority1Execute." He pushed the "enter" button. When the satellite had successfully linked up, a green light came on. Nick now typed his message.

"Desert Rat to Taurus, MSG-Meet set for morrow at Krasivwye Graveyard Stop No problem yet Stop Good choice helper Stop Next talk post meet End."

Desert Rat was Nick's code name while on this mission.

Nick then tapped the "transmit" button.

The encrypted text was instantly shot into the sky. It was received by a classified communications satellite orbiting twenty-two-thousand miles above the earth in space.

A millisecond later, the transmission was sent to the CIA TCC where it would be quickly routed as a TOP SECRET cable for Manny Martinez.

The technology involved in sending high speed "burst" satellite messages from anywhere in the world, was a closely guarded secret in the Special Forces and intelligence community. This sort of high-speed computer processing technology was revolutionizing the spy communications business. That advanced technology made it extremely difficult for the Russians or anyone else to intercept messages in flight.

Nick waited for the "transmission completed" light to come on, then repackaged the transmitter. He buried it, lightly sprinkling debris and dirt over the area until it looked undisturbed.

Back in the car, Nick kissed Georgina on the cheek.

"What's that for?"

"Yankee ingenuity strikes again"

An hour later, they had parked the car back where they had stolen it. The car's owner never even knew it was gone. He had been sitting at a park table with one of his friends, engrossed in a three-hour domino match.

AL AHRAM MOSQUE, TRIPOLI

Jetta was called before the highest ranking General in the Libyan Army, a four-star Colonel General. It was a very unusual order to meet so surreptitiously in a basement of a closed mosque. He would not dare say no to such an official. This General was also one of the conspirators at the warehouse. He had learned from his friend and counterpart at the LIS of Dentworth's mission. He was going to have his best men assist in finding the list and the traitor. One of those best men was Jetta. He stood at attention in front of the General.

"At ease. I have called you here, to take on a very important mission. It is one that will protect our nation's innermost secrets."

The General handed Jetta a file. "Open it."

Jetta complied. Silently shocked, he looked at an official Army personnel photo of Major Nicholas Dentworth.

"He is on his way to Tripoli, if not already here."

Jetta looked up to meet the General's eyes as he continued.

"He will try to steal our most sensitive chemical secrets. You are in charge of many men and the best equipment. Find him, follow him, get his contact here and bring me what he came for. He's a dangerous man. Any questions?"

"Yes, Sir. How did you find him, this Dentworth?"

"We have a well-placed asset in Washington. This person keeps us informed of CIA activities, here in Libya. Now, do you have any other prying questions, Colonel?"

"None, my General."

"Dismissed."

Jetta snapped to attention, saluted, turned and hurriedly left the mosque basement.

Jetta thought the situation quite ironic and grinned to himself.

"Allah, smiles upon me. Surely he sees how clever I am. Stupid, General."

Once Jetta left the basement, the General motioned to the tall, dark man hidden in an alcove of the dark room. The man walked up to the General and clicked his heels to attention.

The General flatly instructed him. "Follow him and keep me posted. And don't get noticed."

The man crisply saluted, then left the basement without uttering a word.

Even the General wanted a backup. Until the traitor amongst the group of conspirators was discovered, he did not trust any of his agents. It would not be the first time loyalties had been tested.

Jetta quickly made his way to a telephone to immediately call St. James. He took a small computerized device out of his pocket and placed it on the speaking part of the hand set. He dialed a long series of numbers, bypassing the international operator. Once he heard the ringing of the phone, he flipped a small switch on the device. It was a sophisticated phone scrambler, secretly given to him by St. James. It was the best equipment the CIA had.

St. James answered the phone.

"Yes?"

"I was just ordered to find and follow your man. He showed me his name and photo. The General himself showed me his file."

St. James was angry.

"How'd he find out so fast?"

"I don't know. Someone in your house, who knows your people."

"My people? Hmm. It's no matter. Now you'll have the authority to do whatever you have to do. You won't stand out as much. Just make sure that the General doesn't get in your way. Keep me informed."

Chapter Twelve

TRIPOLI, LIBYA

Back in their worker's hotel room, Nick and Georgina prepared a simple meal. Still, it was better than the average citizen would enjoy. They had purchased an assortment of meats and vegetables for highly inflated prices. It was from the illegal, but tolerated, publicly displayed, black market.

Unfortunately, they could not go out and enjoy an exotic evening on the town. Tripoli can be a very exciting town, if you know where to go. When on a mission of this importance, Nick did not dare chance the possibility of being caught up in an unexpected problem, traffic accident, or police inquiry. He and Georgina stayed in their room for a quiet evening together. They stared at each other in silence while they ate. Both wondered what the other was thinking.

After dinner, they sat down and again talked of the old days. "Remember in Munich, we went to that Bavarian folk festival? Who was with us?"

"Phil and Nana, wasn't it?"

Nick nodded his head in recollection while he laughed out loud.

"Yeah, yeah. And Phil got so drunk that he stripped naked. What did he do? Oh, yeah. He grabbed that old man's accordion, jumped up on the table and sang Nazi drinking songs at the top of his lungs. He hit every possible, wrong note on the instrument."

"I thought Nana was gonna die."

"So did I until she stripped and jumped up there with him. Damn, she was fine!"

"I noticed that you noticed."

"Just enjoying her dance, dear. Just her dance."

"Yeah, right. Mm hmm." She punched him in the shoulder again.

"Ouch! Every time you punch me, your knuckles get sharper. Let's change the mood with a little music, shall we? I don't want to get beat up." Nick found some melodic Arabic music, on the radio. Although, he didn't understand the language, he could tell by the male and female singers and their tone of voice, that the song told a great love story.

Respectfully bowing, Nick extended his hand with drama.

"May I have this dance my lady?"

She curtsied and smiled. "I would be delighted, kind Sir."

Nick took her in his arms and they danced around and around the tiny room. The music rose to a crescendo, culminating in a feverish finale. They both laughed as they swirled and circled, trying to keep up with the frantic pace of the music.

As the last note sounded, they tripped on the corner of the bed. Nick only halfheartedly stopped himself from falling backwards on the bed. She landed on top of him. The end of the song found them looking into each other's eyes.

She lowered her face and brushed her lips against his. He drew her beautiful face in closer with both of his strong hands. They could no longer resist. They no longer wanted to. Their lips met, their passion was set ablaze. Years of being apart enhanced the intensity of the moment. Nick longingly remembered her caress and awaited her touch. Her body quivered with anticipation.

They desperately wanted to taste every inch of each other's body. He darted his tongue in and out of her ear, tickling her senses. She giggled in delight. He brushed his lips down the nape of her soft neck. He tenderly kissed her. Then, they kissed each other hard. Their tongues wrapped in a loving dance.

Their clothes hurriedly came off, as their raging desire consumed them. Georgina started to rip Nick's clothes off his body, desperately yearning to fuel the fire of their passion. The heat of the moment intensified as their hands eagerly explored each other's contours.

Her fingertips gently touched a couple scars Nick had earned. One was from a gun battle. The other was from a hand to hand fight in the jungle night. His presence indicated who the victor was in those encounters.

Nick stopped her. "Slow. I want every touch to be searing with pleasure."

Nick rolled Georgina over onto her back, exposing the curves of her shapely figure. She was even lovelier than he remembered. He kissed her breasts while she panted with impatient expectation. His tongue roamed over her entire body, tasting her moist and salty skin until he lingered between her thighs. He repeatedly teased her, driving her body to demand that he instantly make love to her.

Into the night, they passionately loved each other time and again. One time they cried. The next time, they laughed. It was as if they were making up for so many lonely nights, so many years gone by. They warmly held each other and slowly slipped into sleep. It felt so good.

They awoke face to face before dawn, tightly holding each other. Nick smiled and marveled at the softness of her breath against his skin. Their sexual desire was also awakened to the pleasures of the new day. Nick had never felt so satisfied. Once more they made love, reinforcing last night's bond. They finished with a kiss and a vow. "Promise? Never to be apart again."

"I'll never leave you again."

They both nonetheless felt slightly strange inside when making this promise. They did not know why.

By the time they had washed and dressed, it was time to go to the appointed meeting. Again giving in to her persuasion, against his gut feeling, Nick allowed her to accompany him. If he had one weakness, it was her.

"You go to the train station immediately afterwards. Once we get to the meet, you wait in the taxi for me. You have no need to know who I'm meeting."

He silenced her protest with a kiss.

A faint voice inside wondered to himself. "Am I going to regret this, taking her along?"

His training told him that he should have cut her loose after she got him to the capital. Deep inside, he knew that. Technically, she was just another government asset used to accomplish a part of his mission. That, she had done. But she was so much more to him now.

As they arrived at the Krasivwye Cemetery, the night mist still clung to the ground. It was an eerie sight, more reminiscent of an eighteenth century ghost story, than of a modern espionage meeting.

The taxi driver shivered as he watched Nick open the gate. It creaked loudly. Its hinges were rusted over many years of disuse and neglect. Since it was not a cemetery used very often by the Muslims over the years, not a lot of attention had been paid towards upkeep or maintenance. It was filled in the sixties and seventies, mostly with the bodies of East European and Soviet advisors and their families.

The one main path led into a particularly dense cloud that covered the graveyard. A path was barely visible in the smokey mist. It seemed to audibly call him, offering a supernatural invitation to step into another world.

On his left, he could barely make out a gigantic stone angel trumpeting the arrival into heaven of the soul that rested beneath it.

"Kind of strange seeing an angel in an Islamic country."

On his right was a small tomb with a vase sitting in a niche atop the door. It contained one withered flower placed weeks ago by some mourner paying their respects. Nick had been in cemeteries before. But, none had ever made him feel the grim emptiness of death like this one did.

The crunch of small gravel pebbles under his shoes sounded like thunder in the quiet of the early morning. It was the only sound he heard. The mist shrouded even the distant early traffic sounds. No bird had stirred yet to chirp its greeting to the new day. No branches rustled in the wind.

Nick thought to himself.

"What a deafening silence."

In the distance, through some trees, he could see the burnt orange sliver of the rising sun, occluded and cold.

Nick kept walking. "Crunch, crunch, crunch."

Something small and furry scurried across the path in front of him. This was apparently the only other living creature in the place. Or was it? He kept walking, watching, listening.

145

When he was about a hundred paces into the graveyard, he heard the crunching of gravel about twenty feet behind him, walking in his direction. Nick reached inside his pocket and gently flipped his semiautomatic pistol to the "safety off" position. He was careful not to make a sound.

He cautioned himself.

"Don't get yourself killed, not here, not now. Manny would probably have a stroke laughing at the irony of getting whacked in a cemetery."

He stopped walking.

The person behind him, half hidden in the fog, also stopped. Nick continued down the path, then stopped again, under a tree. The person behind him kept walking towards him. As the person approached him from behind, Nick slowly turned around, his weapon leveled at the follower.

Maryam had recognized him as he walked by a tomb, behind which she was hiding. As the shadowy figure emerged from the fog, Nick aimed at center mass, the chest area. He noticed that the courier's gloved left hand was empty and swaying with a natural gait. The courier had no weapon in hand.

She talked to him in slightly accented English.

"You won't be needing that for me. Thank you for coming." "You're a woman."

"Does that surprise you?"

"I just didn't expect ..."

He suddenly felt a bit foolish at his brief chauvinism.

"It is no matter. Alexis does not judge on the sex of her visitors."

The fog started to lift. Nick's surroundings started to lighten a little. His suspicions did not. He kept the 9mm pointed at her.

"Don't worry about me. If I was your enemy, you would already be dead."

Nick noticed that the woman's right arm was suspended in a home-made sling, made from a waist belt.

"You are hurt. Has there been a problem that I need to know about?"

"Oh, this? A slight disagreement over where I'd be spending my winter vacation." She had the slightest hint of sarcasm in her voice.

"Your English is very good. Where did you learn to speak so well?"

"I was trained as an international exchange student in Tblisi, at the American Service International School. We had some of your country-men, who believed in our ideals, teach us in preparation for our service overseas in the U.S.A."

"And how did you like my country?"

"It was bountiful. The rural people were kind. But, your cities were too violent."

Nick halted the pleasantries, somewhat satisfied with the genuine-ness of the woman.

"And how is Daphne?"

"Daphne is very concerned with the coming events and for our safety."

"Is Daphne in imminent danger of arrest? If necessary we can ar-range for you and Daphne to get out."

Maryam woefully shook her head and spoke in a sad voice. "It's too late for me. But, for the moment, Daphne is safe."

"Do you have something for me?"

She cautiously glancing around her.

"Have you ever heard of our famous poet of the nineteenth century, Farid? He wrote with his soul full of things that needed to be said. Even in death, he calls on the conscience of the Libyan people."

She paused for a moment, recalling a passage Farid that he wrote a hundred years ago. Her eyes swept the graveyard.

"He was half-Italian. He is buried here."

She gestured broadly.

Nick began to become impatient at the talk of dead poets at a time when he was standing in a Tripoli graveyard with a spy whom he still could not completely trust. He wondered if the LIS be far behind.

With her left hand, Maryam removed the hat she had worn to ward off the morning chill. The suddenness of her action made Nick's finger squeeze the trigger ever so slightly. But, he quickly relaxed his grip. The sun was beginning to burn off the gray mist. He took a better look at her face in the morning glow.

She was a good-looking woman. Nick estimated her age at fifty. She had strong cheekbones and almond brown eyes that pierced like the stare of a Siberian tiger. He imagined her to have come from a countryside background, where hard work lasted from dawn to dusk. Her hair was medium length, dark brown with streaks of gray.

Her eyes had the steady and confident gaze of a veteran soldier, or a learned university professor. Little did he know he was right on both counts.

Nick interrupted his musings to concentrate on the business at hand.

"That's very interesting. But, where's the ..."

Nick was silenced by the sound of running feet coming at them. They heard a few voices and saw dark blurs moving through the headstones towards them. Nick immediately crouched down behind a nearby grave stone to lower his profile.

He cursed at Maryam. "Damn you!"

The woman pulled a Makarov machine pistol out of her coat and instead of pointing it at him, swung around to face the direction of the running feet.

She talked to him in an excited voice, "They're here for me. Run!" She then opened fire on the nearest shadow advancing at her. The loud report of the weapon was answered by a hail of "splats." They were the sound of a gun with a silencer attached. She kept firing at any and all pursuers. Bullets were ricocheting in every direction, off the cold, gray stones.

Nick heard the distinct sound of "thud" immediately followed by "splat." Then, he heard "thud, splat" again. Maryam dropped to the ground hard.

The thud indicated that she had been hit. The splat came a fraction of a second later.

Nick noticed that the gun was now in her injured right hand. She was leaning up on her left hip, still firing at the attackers.

Maryam looked at Nick with a fearsome intensity. She yelled at him.

"Run, you fool. Run!"

At that instant, Nick saw a bullet pierce the woman's head above her right ear. It exited over her left ear with a much larger wound and a splash of blood. She collapsed. Her head struck the ground. Her eyes were open in death. Her motionless face softened, with all traces of pain finally gone. He almost felt sad at not knowing the name of this woman who had risked so much.

Nick had been in fire fights many times before. Each one was different and unique. He noticed that the fusillade of lead had centered around the area from where the woman had fired her machine pistol. Whoever the pursuers were, they concentrated their fire at the threat, and not directly at him. Since Nick didn't shoot his weapon, they did not fire at him.

He could hear shouting, cursing and moaning from the attacker's direction. Although he did not understand Arabic, he deduced what one man yelled. "Cease fire! Cease fire!"

When the bullets stopped flying, Nick took his chance. He somersaulted over the headstone closest to him. He sprung up and began to run in a zig-zag fashion through the cemetery, to make himself a more difficult target to hit. He went away from the armed men and the front gate.

His mind screamed. "The front gate! Georgina is in the taxi by the front gate!"

His primary concern had to be to stay alive and not get captured. He could not think about Georgina now. He had to survive without being arrested or shot. If he failed, he would be unable to complete his mission. He would certainly be of no use in helping Georgina.

The men saw Nick running away and chased after him. One of them apparently in charge yelled to the other men.

"Don't shoot him, damn it! We need him alive."

Nick ran until he thought his lungs would explode. The men started to gain on him. On the run, he turned and fired a two shot burst at them. His pursuers dove to the ground. That gave Nick more time to put some distance between him and them.

He turned and fired two more shots, then another two. Nick counted that he had ten more bullets and an extra magazine in his jacket. He fired four, two shot volleys, then two more after a short delay. He heard two men go down. One cried out in pain. One just quietly tumbled to the ground.

Nick ran, changed magazines and chambered a round all at the same time. Momentarily losing his concentration, he tripped and fell against a small statue of someone that looked like Napoleon. He felt a sharp pain and brushed his hand over his brow. He looked down at his fingers. There was blood. He had cut his head over his left eye.

As he got up, he noticed the next grave with "FARID" on it. Nick did not wait around to read poems. He hurdled rows of headstones and ran out the back gate of the cemetery.

A taxi roared to a stop in front of him, almost running him over. Georgina was driving it. The taxi driver was gone. Without a word and gasping for air, Nick dove into the front, passenger seat. Georgina was already speeding up as the door slammed shut. Trying to catch his breath, he looked back to see if anyone was following them.

"How?" "I forced the driver out at brush point."

Nick was puzzled. He looked down and saw a hairbrush on the seat.

"I shoved the handle of it into the back of his head, telling him it was a pistol. He ran screaming from the cab. I did it when I heard the cars coming through the mist. They can't be far behind. I hope you got what you came for."

"They killed my contact before she could tell me."

"She?"

Georgina looked at him.

Nick yelled.

"Watch out!"

Georgina swerved to miss the white car that seemed to appear out of nowhere. The car almost t-boned them on the driver's side. The hard, banking swerve forced Georgina to take a secondary road.

She dead reckoned her way through an obstacle course of tight turns and narrow streets. Whatever she did, she could not shake the white car now trailing close behind. Eventually, she found a main road. As soon as she turned onto it a black car fell in line and began to chase them. A third, blue car pulled up along side of the taxi. A man pointing a gun motioned for them to slow down and stop.

Georgina nodded and started to slow the taxi.

Nick blurted out to her. "What the hell are you doing?"

"Watch this."

The blue car sped up to get in front of Nick and Georgina. She punched the accelerator to the floor. The taxi lurched forward, smashing into the rear of the blue car. The impact cracked Nick and Georgina's windshield.

Not expecting the impact, the blue car with the gunmen, popped up and over the curb, struck a traffic sign and a kiosk selling tea. It careened back into the street and hit another vehicle. It bounced into the air and fell down again, its engine stalled.

The remaining cars following the taxi were more wary. Now there was a helicopter flying overhead, heard but not seen. Georgina, starting to panic.

"They have choppers, cars, radios and men. How can we possibly get away?"

"Just keep driving. We need time to think."

It was not to be. An old woman with a net shopping bag was on her way to get an early spot in the long cue at the bread shop. She feebly stepped out to cross the street, completely oblivious of the trio of cars speeding towards her. She never looked to the side. Her bony neck was too stiff. She painfully tried to turn her attention to the noisy cars.

Through the damaged windshield, Georgina's eyes met those of the old woman in an instant of horror. Georgina cranked the wheel and hit the brake as hard and fast as she could.

Their taxi spun out of control as it was rear ended by one of the pursuit vehicles.

Nick heard a short but piercing scream of terror from Georgina. The next thing he saw was darkness.

Chapter Thirteen

NASRAT HOUK, NORTH OF TRIPOLI

Nick groggily awoke to find himself lying face down on a cold and damp cement floor. After awhile his eyes reluctantly focused enough to see that he was in the middle of a darkened prison cell. He looked up and mentally measured the dimensions of the cell to be about twelve feet cubed. There was a small barred and glassed window set in the back wall at about ten feet high.

He slowly turned his head toward the door. As he did so, his stiff neck and aching head responded with blinding pain.

He almost yielded to an enticing wave of unconsciousness. He physically resisted, forcing himself to focus his senses on the dark shadows in the corner of the room.

"Think Nick. Think!"

The swelling around his eyes made it difficult to open them very wide. "C'mon, c'mon open your eyes!"

He vaguely remembered being beaten and thrown into the cell, more than once. "How long have I been here? How many beatings?"

He stopped asking. It hurt too much to think. But he knew the more he forced himself to concentrate, the clearer he would get.

His nose detected the distinct and pungent smell of aged urine and feces. His ears could hear a muffled dripping sound which he guessed must be coming from a drain located in the floor directly beneath the window.

As Nick shook the cobwebs from his mind, his eyes were adjusting to the dark. While he stared into the black corner, he increasingly saw the outline of what appeared to be something white. He painfully got to his hands and knees and began to crawl toward the whiteness in an effort to investigate.

He mumbled out loud. "What the hell is that?"

As he approached to within three feet, it now seemed to be triangular in shape. He stopped to rest. He could now make out the outline of a bench. Nick then realized there was a person on that bench. With great effort, he crawled closer. Each small step felt like he had traveled the length of a football field.

As his eyes further adjusted to the dimly moonlit cell, he clearly saw that the person was a woman. She was lying on her side facing him. She was dressed only in her bra and panties. Her left arm was placed across her breasts and on the bench. This concealed most of her bra. The triangular white garment he saw from the middle of the cell was her panties. His heart started to beat faster as he placed his face close to hers. Nick surveyed her face with his fingertips.

Suddenly his mind silently cried out. "Georgina!"

He could hardly believe it. Although shallow, he could feel her breath. "She is alive after all. The bastards! They lied to me."

He remembered being tortured to the chant of "your woman is dead, your woman is dead."

He swiftly but gently passed his hands over her entire body.

"No broken or protruding bones. No severe bleeding. But you do have a slightly swollen left ankle and minor facial contusions."

Nick could feel her shivering in the cold prison air. He realized that she might go into, or may already be in hypothermic shock.

He also noticed that he too, was shivering and that he also was in his underwear. As there was nothing to cover her with to guard against the cold, Nick knew his only option was body heat. He knew from his alpine commando training that under these conditions, he had to maximize both his and her natural body heat.

She was still unconscious and he was barely awake. He slowly, stiffly, painfully climbed up on the bench with Georgina, so she could benefit from both the limited heat conduction of the metal bench and the shield of his body. Nick placed her legs between his, her hips against his, her chest against his. He placed her hands under his armpits, his under hers and his cheek against hers. He immediately felt her still unconscious body instinctively gripping him tighter, responding to his warmth.

He was briefly reminded of the humiliating, but life saving, alpine training, during which he had to do the same thing with a Green Beret "A" team partner. Nick and Sergeant "Red" O'Hara uncomfortably clasped at each other in a shovel dug, snow cave on a blizzard blown Alaskan mountain. That was many years ago. This was now, crude, dangerous, raw and very cold.

Even as Nick felt the incremental warmth from Georgina's partially clad body, his mind drifted. He dreamed of other times. They were times when they held each other in the night, under very different circumstances. Those were days of laughter, passion and happiness. In his mind's eye, Nick saw past summer afternoons and living room picnics spinning around in his delirium. He heard her laughing, giggling as if in an echo chamber. "Stop it, silly. Stop it. That tickles! Stop it some more."

Georgina and his memories softened the edge of the prison cell temperature, as he drifted off into a much needed sleep.

These few minutes of physical exertion were more than enough to overcome a man with a concussion and a pain racked body.

Five seconds later, something happened. "Splash!"

Nick's reverie was abruptly interrupted when the cell door was flung open. It smashed against the interior wall with a thunderous roar. Nick was jerked out of his brief sleep by a bucket of freezing, putrid water thrown on both he and Georgina. Nick was yanked off the bench by a giant, bearded man.

The man resembled Black Beard the Pirate. He was six feet four inches tall, two hundred sixty-five pounds of muscle. His hands were the size of catcher's mitts. His grip was like that of a steel vise. He had curly black hair and a shaggy black beard. His eyes were fiery and dark. Although beards were not regulation in the Army, here in this unconventional place, regulations had little effect. The guards exercised unorthodox measures. They looked like thugs in sloppy uniforms.

Nick was hurled out into the hallway. He unsuccessfully tried to glance back at Georgina.

She made a surprised gasp as the icy water instantaneously revived her. She tried to hold onto him when Nick was pulled from her grasp. She was violently pushed back down by a second man.

This guard was smaller, less than six feet tall and skinny by comparison. As he pushed her down with his billy club, the small guard let out a contemptuous snicker. He licked his lips as he admired her bruised but nonetheless voluptuous figure. He started to approach Georgina to maul her shapely curves for a quick and cheap thrill. He wanted to inflict yet another indignity on his prisoner and satisfy his hormonal urge.

The big guard strongly gripped Nick's left arm, handling him like he were a rag doll. The giant bellowed for the smaller guard to grab Nick's other arm. He was visibly frustrated. The smaller guard wiped the drool of his mouth with a swipe of his shirt sleeve. He left the cell, slamming the locked door behind him.

Georgina tried to yell something at the guards. Instead, she sputtered and coughed, still caught off balance by the effect of the cold water. She eventually caught her breath and assessed her situation. First, she noticed that the sun was just starting to show through the window, meaning that she had been unconscious or asleep for many hours.

As Nick had done, she quickly checked herself for serious injury. She felt a throbbing pain in her left ankle and a slight sting on her face, dismissing both injuries as unimportant. She slowly rolled her neck and flexed her leg and arm muscles. She noted that she surprisingly still had good strength.

"Could be worse. I'm glad that I've kept up a physical workout program." As a testament to her discipline, she had developed a firm but feminine, muscular figure. Many women and men for that matter, yearned for such a figure. She tried to piece together what had happened over the last several hours.

"Let's see. We were in a car crash. I was knocked out. I awoke in this cell, or one just like it. Then Bruno and Pee Wee showed up."

She had named the giant guard Bruno and the small one Pee Wee.

"They dragged me down a hallway into a room, ripped my clothes off and threw me in a chair. They asked me a bunch of questions, told me Nick died in the car crash and that I might as well tell them where it is. Where what is? They beat me up with a phone book and old Bruno punched me and knocked me out again. I got cold water splashed on me, when they pulled …"

Georgina's eyes filled with tears, when she realized that they must have pulled Nick from her a moment ago. It happened so fast. "It was him. Wasn't it? It must have been. Who else could it have been? He's just got to be alive!"

She desperately questioned herself, trying to decide whether she felt something familiar about the man they had just ripped from her arms. It was all so confusing. "But then why did they tell me he was dead? Asses! I've been in tough spots before. And by God, I'm going to think Nick and I out of this one."

In a fit of anger, she forced herself to stand up. She tenderly limped around the dark cell trying to find something to help her get out.

"I just know he's alive. I feel it!"

She wanted to grab Nick and get away from these barbarians. The only thing she found was a large, yet quite agile cockroach that ran across her hand, as she searched along the wall. She recoiled in disgust and sat down again on the bench, disappointed and angered at the sparseness of cell furnishings. There was absolutely nothing in the cell.

In the hallway, the small man grabbed hold of Nick's hand as the big man hurled him down the hall at a brisk pace. The guards dragged Nick like a sack of potatoes. Nick's legs were still weak, straining to both support his weight and maintain his balance. This task was made more difficult by the ever present banging in his head.

Each time Nick stumbled, the guards squeezed harder, to forcefully propel him down the seemingly endless hallway. After the darkness of the cell the bright lights in the hall were blinding. It took all Nick's strength to look up from the floor as he was dragged along.

He noted something to himself. "Five doorways on each side of the hall."

After passing the fifth one, he noticed that on the left, there was an open door. He squinted, trying to make out the interior of the room.

His eyes saw only a little bit. "Office and window."

Through the window, he saw the orange glow of a sunrise. Nick remembered the window in the cell.

"It too was on what must be the eastern wall."

As he was taken past the open office, the hall ended. A door opened and he found himself once again in the beating room.

He was dropped into a hard wooden chair with no arm rests. The chair was situated in front of a desk. Behind the desk was an executive rocking chair, with red leather padding and puffy armrests.

A smash to the side of his head blurred his vision of the plush chair. The room started to spin. Nick tightened his stomach muscles trying to lessen the impact of the now expected onslaught of blows. Nick counted this as the fourth beating since he was captured.

From the direction of the open office, he heard the sound of hard healed boots slowly and methodically crossing through the hall and into the beating room. The two guards clicked their heels to attention at the entry of the boots, signifying that an officer or superior had just arrived.

A man in his late thirties, medium height and build, with thinning black hair and a tight frown sat down in the plush chair. He had a scar from the corner of his right eye to the right corner of his mouth. He was dressed in the uniform of a LIS Major.

The Major looked at Nick and burst into a smile talking in heavily accented English.

"Good morning, Major Dentworth. Yes, I have found you in our files. I am LIS Major Bashak. I trust you are enjoying your stay here?"

Nick replied, swallowing hard and forcing a grin.

"Your accommodations are superb, but your masseurs a bit heavy handed."

The Major stopped smiling, then nodded to Bruno. He struck Nick again on the side of the head. The Major held up his hand as the giant was about to hit Nick again.

The Major got up, walked over to Nick and leaned close into his face. Nick smelled the acrid smell of stale Turkish cigarettes on the Major's bad breath.

He spoke in a dry manner. "You disappoint me, Major Dentworth. I show you my hospitality by reuniting you with your woman. You repay me by insulting my staff. I was hoping our gesture of good faith would convince you to tell me what I want to know."

"And what pray tell would that be?"

The LIS man's face turned red, obviously suppressing his anger at Nick's defiance.

The Major barked out his question again, literally spitting with each word. "Where is the paper?"

At the enunciation of the word "paper," he clenched his teeth. His madman's eyes glared with the maniacal expression reserved only for those that truly enjoy inflicting pain on another helpless human being.

Nick hesitated, then taunted him. "Perhaps if you could be more specific about what is on this piece of paper I'm supposed to have."

Bashak stood back from Nick, slowly stepped around his desk and sat down. The methodical squeaking of the rocking chair's springs was the only sound in the room.

In an almost hysterical voice, he gave his order to the guards. "Teach him a lesson!"

For the next ten minutes, they alternately beat him into unconsciousness and woke him. Ten minutes is a long, long time when you're getting beaten. Bashak left for a while, but returned as a bucket of cold water was dumped over Nick's head to, once again revive him.

The Major again stood before Nick and turned his head, as if he had a nervous twitch. He admiringly gazed at the job his guards had done to Nick. He praised his guards for their thoroughness. "Not bad, gentlemen."

He leaned over and softly, but menacingly whispered in Nick's ear. "Major Dentworth, professional courtesy aside, the pain and misery I could inflict upon your body is nothing, compared to the torture I could visit upon your soul by applying my, how should I say? ... my information extraction methods upon your beautiful lady friend. Even if she knows nothing, I would systematically dehumanize her until you tell me what I want to know."

Nick's heart sank. He was totally convinced that the Libyan was devoid of humanity and undoubtedly a sadist. He would not hesitate to torture Georgina to death, if he didn't tell him about the list.

In an effort to buy time, Nick apparently gave in to the Major. "We'll need food and clean water. We haven't eaten in a long time." Nick tried to show a hint of submission in his eyes.

Bashak's face suddenly broke into a broad smile. He was pleased with his own persuasive manner.

He clapped his hands together once, turned to Nick and sighed. "Major Dentworth, I'm surprised to see you give in so easily. I suppose every warrior has his Achilles heel. Yours just happens to be the girl."

He looked at Nick with a leer in his voice. "And yours is a particularly tender weakness. Is it not? I think this is wise. We shall talk again, I hope for the last time, after you have enjoyed one of my gracious meals. That will be all."

Bashak nodded to the guards. Bruno then picked Nick up with one arm. Pee Wee hung onto Nick's other arm. Both guards quickly and roughly escorted him back to his cell, the same cell in which he had left Georgina.

On the way back to the cell, Nick made careful mental notes. "In addition to the five cells on each side of the hallway,

I saw on the way to the interrogation room, there are five more cells on each side of the other end of the building. This would make the interrogation room the south end of the building."

Nick saw a possible exit ahead of him at the north end, adjacent to a cell or room with a few male voices coming from inside.

"Probably more guards."

He also saw the clubs hanging from the belts of his escorts.

He was again thrown inside the cell. As he tumbled to the middle of the room, the door sounded like the sealing of a tomb.

Chapter Fourteen

Georgina rushed to pick up Nick as he lay in a crumpled heap on the cell floor. She helped sit him on the bench.

A light bulb in the center of the ceiling suddenly flickered with a short circuit, then clicked on. It bathed the room in a sickly yellow glow. A few multi-legged creatures scrambled for the relative safety of the room's dark corners. Georgina cradled Nick's aching head.

A tear from her eye dropped onto his face. "Thank God you're alive. They told me you were dead. I love you so."

With that, Nick cautioned silence. He raised himself up and put his finger to her lips. He pointed toward the cell door to indicate his suspicion that those outside the door were listening to them in the cell.

He was right. The guards were listening and recording every word that was said in the hope that in a weak or unsuspecting moment, the captives might reveal their closely guarded secrets. Nick didn't want to add fuel to the fiery threat of torturing Georgina by showing how very close they were to each other.

Burying his face in her matted hair, he whispered to her.

"They're listening to us. They're going to bring us food and water. I pretended that I will cooperate with them. Don't worry. I'm not crazy.

I noticed that the hallway was empty when they took me to the Major. There are ten cells on each side with an exit at the end of the building. The guards carry clubs. Let's eat, drink and then escape. We're dead if we stay. What do you say? Are you in?"

She whispered back to him. "You bet. I'd love to knock that yellow toothed grin off that little weasel of a guard."

Nick smiled as the door unlocked with a heavy metallic "chunk." Nick quickly hung his head and drooped his shoulders, to convince the guards he was weaker than he actually felt. The giant gave Nick a large, shallow-rimmed metal dish full of some sort of stew, beans and bread along with a large mug of water. Pee Wee gave the same to Georgina. The guards almost threw the meal at the prisoners with disdain.

A little stew from each plate splashed onto the cell floor. A few bugs started to go for it. But Nick shooed them away with a wave of his hand. Nick immediately scooped up the dropped food with his fingers and put it in his mouth. Georgina started to do the same thing, but changed her mind after remembering her encounter with the cockroach. They devoured the meal quickly. They literally licked the plates clean. Every drop of water was gulped.

CIA HEADQUARTERS

Manny Martinez had received a report from Hatim, his agent that he sent to watch over Nick.

"I followed him to the graveyard. I don't know if the transfer of information took place with the courier. But, Nick and the woman were captured."

"What? Oh, God."

As Manny informed St. James, he decided that St. James seemed to take the news a little too well.

Manny grimly laid out the situation and options for St. James.

"I believe that torture, interrogation and certain execution await our two agents."

"Do we know where they're being held?"

"Yes, Sir. They're at a certain field prison, just north of Tripoli. But …"

St. James interrupted him.

"Set up your new escape route, Mr. Martinez. I didn't get to become DCI without having a few cards up my sleeve. They're not officially dead yet. I need that list!"

Manny was puzzled by St. James' reaction to the news of Nick and Georgina's capture. Manny went to his office and immediately contacted Hatim.

"Loosely watch them. Just be around if they need help. And make a separate escape route for them. Hatim, something is very wrong. I don't know what it is. Be extra careful."

NASRAT HOUK PRISON

Fifteen minutes after finishing their meal, Nick and Georgina were already feeling an energy rush from the food. The guards entered the cell to retrieve the plates and mugs.

Nick and Georgina sat on the bench with their empty dishes in hand. The guards approached them, grunted and pointed to the dishes. Nick raised the metal dish with what appeared to be a weak arm. Just before the giant took hold of it, Nick shot off the bench and used the dish to hit the big man at the bridge of his nose, instantly breaking it. Nick returned a favor and firmly clapped his hands against the giant's ears. Bruno saw stars and the room spun for him, this time. The stunned behemoth's eyes watered from the pain, obscuring his vision in the dim light.

Georgina did the same, but was not quite as accurate. Her blow landed just above Pee Wee's right eye. Nonetheless, the blow stunned him, and blood poured from the wound, blinding him in that eye.

Nick stepped to the giant's right side and yanked the club from the belt hook. With a practiced skill, he took the hardwood club, and using it as a battering ram, jammed it into the giant's solar plexus, located just below the sternum. This knocked the wind out of the mammoth but did not stop him from grabbing Nick's hair. The giant still managed to almost lift Nick off the floor. Wincing with pain, Nick hit the giant's knee with the club, shattering it. The guard tried to groan but only managed to open his mouth. He could not even breathe.

The big man's grasp weakened. Nick jerked away, losing a tuft of his hair. He spun around and delivered a skull cracking blow to the back of Bruno's head. The now lifeless hulk crashed to the ground. Although slowed a bit by Nick's physical condition, all this happened in a few seconds.

Georgina was wrestling with the smaller man over his club. Pee Wee yelled for help as he elbowed Georgina in the face, giving her a bloody nose. Nick jumped towards the smaller man, wrenching his head backwards in a deadly twist. Georgina grabbed the club in her left hand and swung it across her body with all her might. It smashed into the man's mouth. As his yellow, bloodied and broken teeth flew to the floor, he collapsed next to the bench. His head dangled from its broken neck, like that of a ringed chicken. Nick grabbed Georgina's hand and they ran out of their prison cell, clubs in hand.

Just outside the prison, a team of twenty black faced commandos approached the compound. A roving prison perimeter guard was silently garotted, his weapon taken from him before he could pull the trigger. Another prison guard met a similar fate. A third lost his life as a knife was thrust upwards into his brain, through the opening in the back of the head, where the spine meets the skull.

The rest of the commando team quietly ran to the prison building housing Nick, Georgina, and the sizeable contingent of guards and soldiers. Only a slight sound from the shifting of their equipment and boots on the ground was heard. They prepared to enter the building.

Now in the hallway, Nick and Georgina encountered two guards that had been alerted by the unusual noise in the cell and Pee Wee's cry for help. The guards menacingly walked towards them, clubs in their hands. They yelled back to their room by the north exit.

"Hey, guys! Bring the guns. We got us a couple of heroes here."

At the far end of the hallway, Major Bashak appeared in his office doorway to see what all the commotion was about. Nick and Georgina glanced at each other, nodded, then charged at the guards with their clubs. They knew that every second of surprise might help them in their unlikely bid to escape. Just as they were about to clash, they felt two deafening explosions, then heard them.

The north door blew off its hinges and landed ten feet inside the doorway. The guard room next to it erupted in a flash. Two guards, killed on their way into the hallway, tumbled against the far wall, propelled through the air by the force of the explosion.

At the same time, Major Bashak's office was destroyed by a commando's satchel charge that burst through his office window. The explosion blew Bashak into the hallway. He staggered to keep his balance. His life was saved by reacting quickly to the alarm. Shaking off the effect of the blast, he unsnapped the flap over his holstered semiautomatic, Soviet issue, officer pistol. He pulled it out and pointed it at Nick.

Immediately following the inwardly directed explosions, commandos somersaulted into the hallway from the north end. They came up on one knee and instantly took aim down the hallway. Nick and Georgina were in the middle of the hallway, stunned by the concussion of what was happening around them. They were shaken but unharmed by the assault.

Nick immediately dragged Georgina down to the ground as Bashak fired at him. The bullet whizzed over Nick's head. The commandos in front of Nick riddled Bashak with bullets. The two guards with clubs were next to die.

Nick knew he and Georgina were helplessly next in this unexplained carnage. He held Georgina's head to the ground and looked up. He could feel the dizzying effects of the stun grenades, but was determined to watch the scene.

Bashak's bullet, meant for Nick, had hit one of the commandos at the north end in the jaw. Nick saw the smoke from the explosions clearing. His ears still rang from the concussion of the blasts. Through the clearing smoke, Nick saw the commandos fanning out through the rooms.

Two black faced commandos walked past Nick, their black boots thundering close to his face.

"Bang, Bang!"

A guard who survived the raid was put out of his misery.

Nick wondered to himself. "No survivors, Except for us?"

The two commandos came back to where Nick and Georgina lay. Standing over them, the commandos motioned them to get up. They said something. Nick could not understand what he said. Still feeling the effects of the stun grenades, Nick noticed the man's lips moving, but could not understand their simple English command. "Get up."

Nick quickly recovered and surveyed the carnage.

Again, he wondered to himself. "Who are these guys?"

His mind reeled with the question. In ten seconds the commandos had killed approximately fifteen men and had blown up the building. These men were now motioning him to come with them. Was he imagining a smile on their faces? "Are they friendlies?"

Nick was not going to argue. He knew he would go with them one way or another. He himself was trained well in hostage rescue operations. In fact, he had commanded a raid not unlike the one he had just experienced. At that time, he was on the other end of a gun.

As he turned to view the scene one last time on the way out, Nick noticed that the wounded commando had been removed. All spent bullet casings and traces of who attacked were gone. Even the boot prints left in the settling dust were brushed away. All that remained were dead LIS men.

Outside, Nick and Georgina were pushed inside a panel van with blackened windows. Three soldiers, armed to the teeth, were silent guards. One soldier wrapped a blanket around Georgina. Nick was also given a blanket for warmth. They drove for about thirty minutes, making many turns, changing directions often. Nick surmised from the series of turns that they had headed south. He knew they were in a big city, probably Tripoli, because of the rising traffic noise.

The commandos were quiet during the ride. They didn't make a sound.

Nick thought to himself. "These guys are pros. They follow strict orders, regardless of who their victims are. But who they are and why they have rescued us, puzzled me. Their skill indicates Russian trained men."

When the van stopped, Nick and Georgina were hustled into a

building. They were seated at a table and told in Arabic not to move or they would die. Georgina translated for Nick.

"Pretty tough talk from people who just saved our lives."

"What did they say?" Georgina told him.

"Libyans?"

"Yes. Why would Libyans save us from Libyans?"

"Good question."

What Nick did not know was that the men belonged to a special, Russian trained, Libyan Army terrorist-hit team.

Chapter Fifteen

Their rescuers, pointed guns at them, as they sat.

Their benefactor entered the room. "Welcome my guests. I've been expecting you." He cheerfully spoke in English, with a British-accent. "You must be famished. The LIS can be such a bad host from time to time. No manners, brutes really. Wouldn't you agree? I'll have some food and drink brought to us directly."

The man instructed one of the guards standing at the door with machine guns. "Go get some clothes, a tray of sandwiches and some hot tea."

The other guard did not speak. He did not have to. His formidable physique and the array of weapons he had on his body translated lethality in any language. He struck a more threatening pose when the other guard left.

"My guard cannot understand us. However, as capable as you are Major Dentworth, he would not hesitate to kill you both with but the slightest glance from me."

"I've seen the efficiency with which your men dispatch human lives. What are you, Libyan Spetsnaz?" "But of course! You must have many questions. Forgive me. I am Colonel Ahmed Hussain of Army Intelligence."

Colonel Hussain was compact and of medium height. He had very curly, but fine red hair. It was very unusual in an Arabic country. His eyes were sea green and exuded confidence. He tried to affect the image of a British aristocrat by adopting an accent and hand gestures. His over exaggerated politeness hid a confidence in himself. It only served to draw attention to the absurdity of his masquerade.

Hussain continued, talking to Nick. "My men rescued you from the clumsy but persuasive hands of your LIS interrogators. Unfortunately, we find ourselves sometimes competing rather briskly in professional matters. But to you, young lady, I commend you for evading our notice all these years. What are you, American, Italian? Your agent handlers did a most marvelous job." With an ominous tone of voice he added one last thought.

"Until now."

Jetta was the code name given to Hussain by St. James. Hussain was a senior officer in the Libyan Army Intelligences' Illegals Directorate. This part of the organization was responsible for secret agent networks around the world. There, Libyan agents pose as local citizens, resident aliens and students in foreign countries.

In his important, commanding position within this unit, Hussain could use resources with little or no accountability.

This unit is also the Libyan version of America's Green Berets. They weren't of the same quality or training, but they were effective in working in the Middle Eastern countries. They worked closely with Palestinian commando units of the Fatah and the Palestinian Liberation Front. This same unit had received extensive training and real world experience working with the former Soviet Army's "Spetsnaz Razvedka" or Special Forces Reconnaissance units. Spetsnaz' main mission is as a commando raid team. But they also run secret agents around the world.

Hussain's group also received such agent training from Spetsnaz. So among the various Arab countries that worked with the Soviets, the Libyans have been very active, choosing to use their expertise to carry out numerous terrorist operations throughout the globe.

Hussain achieved his significant rank in Libyan Army Intelligence by proving himself not only on terrorist operations, but also within the Army elite.

He once had to establish his command authority by fighting an experienced Sergeant in hand to hand combat. It was a brutal fight. In the end, from his hospital bed, the Sergeant conceded Hussain's authority. They subsequently became very close friends and comrades in arms.

Several years ago, while St. James was the Chief of Station for CIA in London, he was able to recruit, then Captain Hussain as a double agent. Hussain had become disgusted by the rivalry between the LIS and the Army, over the political split within Quadaffi's ruling party. During a big operation in the early 80's, they had exposed some of each other's agents. It was an effort to embarrass the other, to win favor with the country's leader.

Five of Hussain's best agents and friends, were quietly recalled to Tripoli and executed as sacrificial lambs. Angered and confused, he offered his services to a rising American agent, whose ambition equaled his own. That American agent was St. James. He has privately run this important double agent ever since. Once Hussain crossed the barrier of treason, there was no turning back. Urged to continue his upward spiral within the ranks of the Libyan military, Hussain had become St. James' ace in the hole.

A knock at the door signaled the delivery of a tray of finger sandwiches, cheese wedges and hot tea.

"Please." Hussain gestured towards the tray of food.

Nick shook his head "No."

Georgina let out a slight gasp as Hussain extracted a bayonet from his desk drawer. He threw the knife, whizzing it passed Nick's head. It firmly stuck into the wood, wall behind him. Nick didn't flinch.

"Not exactly made for cutting cheese, eh?" Hussain smiled, took a smaller knife from his desk. He cut one of the sandwiches in half.

Hussain took half of the sandwich and ate it. Only then, did Georgina reach over and take the other half of his sandwich and a cup of tea.

Hussain smiled his approval and continued talking. "Where was I? Oh yes. I'm sure you're wondering why I saved your life. It is because you have something I want very much. You see, I have received orders just like you, Major. I too am to acquire a certain list of names. They are to come from you. In the absence of your cooperation I am, to put it simply, kill you."

Nick retorted with steely eyes.

"If you kill me, you won't get the list."

Hussain leaned back into his chair. "To the contrary, Major, I would learn the whereabouts of the list. You must understand. The LIS has comparatively simple interrogation techniques. In the field, my men don't have the time or temperament to engage in long term deprivation tactics to learn what they need."

Hussain leaned forward, looked at Nick. He spoke in a low, menacing tone. "They are trained to exert the maximum amount of pain in the shortest possible time, get the information and move toward their objective, for the glory of almighty Allah. I would much rather have you tell me where the list of traitors is, so that I may achieve my objective that much sooner without any, how should I say it, unpleasantness."

"And what objective is that, Colonel?" "To save lives, Major, to save lives."

Such a noble sentiment coming from a man with a great, demonstrated power of inflicting death made Nick doubt Hussain's sincerity.

"How do I know that you're not on this list? How do I know you're not just going to burn it and kill us if I gave it to you?"

"You don't."

"You said you were under orders. Whose orders?"

"Even if I chose to tell you, I think you'd be surprised at my answer. But after all, you're not in a position to have such questions answered. Are you?"

Hussain arose, walked over to a painting of a mounted Arab horseman in full battle dress, angrily swinging a sword over his head. The Colonel studied the figure with his back to Nick. He asked Nick something in an inquisitive voice. "Your contact in the graveyard spoke with you at length. What did she say?"

"We talked about Arab literature and how wonderful my country is."

Nick spoke with an air of confidence. He began to realize how little Hussain knew.

Hussain turned to him. "Major, I'm growing tired of your unresponsiveness. I am a busy man. Where is the list?"

"I don't know. The LIS goons killed her before I could find out. Your men, doing their most efficient best, would still get the same answer. I don't know. I would probably make something up, just to stop the torture. I really don't know."

"I wish I could believe you. I truly do. It will be such a pity to kill two agents of such caliber."

"She knows nothing of importance. You should let her go."

"It's no matter. I'll know soon enough. Take them away."

At that very moment, Nick began running over in his mind the conversation with the woman who died for him, before his eyes. "Have you ever heard of our famous poet of the nineteenth century, Farid?" Her voice echoed in his brain.

"He wrote with his soul full of things that needed to be said. Even in death, he calls on the conscience of the Libyan people. He is buried here."

"Here! Napoleon!"

Without showing the sparkle in his eye, Nick made up an escape plan as he went.

"Wait! Colonel, I have no doubt in my mind that your men would extract all information from us, so I'll just tell you the truth, on one condition."

"Splendid choice. What condition?" "That, as one Special Forces officer to another, you give me your word of honor that you will guarantee safe passage out of the country for me and my colleague."

Nick told him knowing full well that Hussain had no intent of keeping any such promise.

"Done. Now, where is the list, Major?"

"I don't know, exactly."

Hussain sighed with impatience. "Major, I don't have time."

The wheels in Nick's head were turning faster and faster.

"Please, let me finish, Colonel. My meeting with my contact in the graveyard was just to send a message to my people advising them that I had the list and that I was getting out. I had already been passed the list by the courier. Since you were following us, you must have seen us at the museum."

"I know everything you've done since your arrival, Major Dentworth."

Nick made a mental note of that last remark.

"What you apparently didn't see was me hiding the list at a make shift dead drop that I impulsively chose while on my counter surveillance route after the Museum pass."

Hussain looked incredulously at Nick.

Nick continued. "That was not a planned route. I don't know that part of town, nor the street names in it. I don't know the language either. But I think I could find it by recreating my route by sight."

"If I find this is but a feeble attempt to trick me into providing you an opportunity to escape, I will have your eyelids removed so that you must see the torture I will inflict upon your colleague."

With the reference to her, Georgina blinked. She had been quietly sitting while the conversation between Nick and Hussain had unfolded. She remembered that Nick told her the woman was killed before she could tell him where the "list of traitors" was. So, without letting on that she knew something was up, she listened with interest to the tale Nick was weaving. She did not know what he had up his sleeve. She did know that whatever it was, they would somehow escape, or die trying.

"I propose that you and your men take us along that route."

"You will go, she will stay as insurance."

Nick lied. "I need her. We talked as we went along. The things we said as we walked will help me remember."

"If I don't have that list by the end of your counter surveillance route, you'll both be dead within the hour."

Nick thought to himself. "You fool. You're falling for it. You are as stupid as you look. Or you must be desperate."

"There will be no need to kill us once you have the list. We'd be no threat to you then."

He knew the Colonel had no intention of letting them go, but he continued the charade. Nick thought to himself. "Time, more time."

"Understood."

Inside Hussain was wary of Nick's proposition. But time was running short. The conference was in four days. He needed to get the list first to St. James, then to his General. If the captured American spy was telling the truth, he would have the list within hours. If he was not, he would have them killed anyway after torturing the information out of them. In any case, he would send his best men on this job. "Dentworth, you will not escape."

Nick reached for the food tray. "I'll have that sandwich now."

Chapter Sixteen

In Tripoli, everything is either under never ending construction or in need of repair. Things are made cheaply, with shoddy materials and workmanship, especially buildings and streets. With no hope of a decent wage, there is no incentive to work. In the comrade's Islamic paradise, there is a worker's saying, "They pretend to pay us, we pretend to work."

In the late morning, before the habitual three-hour lunch break, the street was bustling with activity. Any comings or goings could easily be lost in the flow of people and vehicles.

Luckily for Hatim, there was only one open road leading to the impressive, three-story, courtyard residence. It served as a high security Army intelligence safe house in the middle of the capital. The only other road to the place was temporarily closed while the intersection was being repaired. It had been closed for three weeks. This meant that he only had to watch the one street to see any vehicles exit or enter the safe house, where the two American agents were being held. Hatim had a plan to rescue them. For it to work, he needed physical access to the Americans. He had to know what vehicles they were in.

Hatim had, over several years, painstakingly recruited a support network of thieves, pickpockets and assorted unsavory characters from the ranks of Libya's disgruntled ethnic minorities and underground crime societies. Both groups resent the control exerted and prejudice shown by the secret police in the Arab dominated country. In intelligence work, one sometimes had to overlook the unscrupulous character of the people used to get a more important or beneficial job done.

Hatim had to pull out all the stops this time. He compiled quite an array of thugs, drivers and assassins. Most of them would be in prison or executed in any civilized country, if their crimes were known. He and his band would follow from a distance until they could carry out his plan.

Through binoculars, Hatim saw a procession of three cars came out of the courtyard. They came through the gate and turned onto the road. The lead white car had four sentries; the middle, gray car had a driver and Hussain in the front seat. In the back seat, Nick and Georgina sat next to each other, flanked on each side by a guard. There was no room between them. The third black car had four more guards for rear security. Nick and Georgina had been provided gray colored workmen's jump suits and jackets.

On arrival in the museum area, Hussain motioned his car over to the side of the curb. They all got out and began walking the counter surveillance route.

A few people were braving the chilly weather, walking from building to building. Both Nick and Georgina were escorted by a guard who thrust a hidden pistol into their ribs. The black car drove slowly, several yards behind them. The white car sped ahead to make sure the way was clear.

A block and a few turns later, Nick turned to Georgina.

"We were talking about the museum, then we turned left, no, right at the mosque."

Georgina nodded and played along.

"Didn't we go down that long street next?"

"Here."

Nick pretended he had found a loosened brick, behind which he claimed to have hidden the list.

"Here it is! No wait. It's not the same one. But it looks just like this one."

Hussain spoke. "Don't try to confuse us. We have the exact route you took. You will turn here and go down this street."

Nick was just trying to improve his chances for escape, hoping to find a chink in the armor. So far, he was pleased. He had managed to maneuver his and Georgina's way out of a small fortress crawling with commandos and to be walking down a Tripoli street with only three to six men to worry about.

He thought to himself. "The odds are starting to come around in my favor."

Some of the museum district buildings on the streets of that part of town were giants made of marble and other stone, crafted in the grandiose style so often seen in the former Soviet Union.

As they turned the corner to start down the long block, Nick again thought to himself. "All I need is some sort of diversion."

Hatim also saw them start down the block. He quickly huddled with his men.

"O.K. Now we're going to have to make a few changes. Listen up. After I tell you what to do, you'll have to hurry. We don't have, check that. They don't have a second to lose."

About halfway down the block, the white car sped ahead to check out the next block. Two old women approached Nick, Hussain, Georgina and their two commando guards. The "old women" split up to go on either side of the group to pass by. As they hobbled by, one of the women gracefully reached up to readjust her scarf. On the way up, her hand swung over to the guard nearest Nick. The woman scratched the guard's neck with a needle dipped in a highly toxic poison which instantly causes paralysis and death. The assassin scratched the guard's carotid artery on his neck to hasten the process heading toward the brain.

The other "woman" scratched the hand of Georgina's guard. The two commandoes fell. Their knees quickly buckled. Only Hussain and the guards in the cars remained as an obstacle to their chance of escape.

Fast to realize what had happened, Nick turned around and kicked Hussain's knee with his heel. Then, he raised his foot, striking him in the groin. The colonel fell to the ground, doubled over in pain. Nick used a Kung-Fu disarmament technique to take Hussain's pistol from him before he had a chance to point and fire. Georgina picked up the pistols dropped by the other guards and pointed them at Hussain.

Nick cautioned her. "No. Don't shoot him, yet. He could be valuable."

The black car behind them came to a screeching halt. Nick turned to face them, expecting them to fire at him at any moment. The car doors burst open. At that instant, a speeding car crashed into the front of the black car. The impact knocked two of the guards unconscious. The man in the front passenger seat was dazed, but managed to stumble out of the car. He headed for Nick, who was about twenty yards away. The driver was killed in the collision, crushed by the collapse of the steering wheel. In the confusion, traffic was completely stopped.

Ahead of Nick, a large East German made semi-truck backed out of an alley, blocking the entire street. The diesel engine idled in place, as if waiting for something, or someone. The truck hid Nick and Georgina from the white car, which watched the scene with surprise from down at the end of the block. They were too far away and powerless to help their boss. They were blocked by traffic.

At the same time an unmarked panel truck backed up from the alley across the street. The back doors flew open. Standing at the back of the truck, holding the doors open, was Hatim.

"Come here! Hurry. Hurry up!" He motioned Nick to quickly come closer. Hussain was helplessly lying on the ground unable to get up. His knee was possibly broken.

Nick reached down. "Sorry, Colonel."

He knocked Hussain out with the butt of the pistol. Hussain sneered at Nick as he was hit.

Nick and Georgina cautiously but rapidly approached the rear of the panel van, sticking the pistol in Hatim's face.

Looking in Nick's eyes and ignoring the gun barrel, the man spoke to Nick in perfect American English. "Get in now."

"How do I know you're for real?"

"What choice do you have? Besides, if you ever want to collect on your World Series debt, you'll get in now."

Nick grabbed Georgina, threw her in and jumped in the van. Two bullets grazed the back door as it took off. They came from the dazed guard who had just arrived at his commander's side to see Nick jump into the getaway vehicle.

The van took off down the alley to the next street, still hidden by the semi-truck. The dazed guard staggered around the truck and to the mouth of the alley to find nothing. He ran back to find his two dead colleagues and a moaning boss, just regaining consciousness. The guard cursed his escaped quarry and feared the inevitable retribution from Hussain, for failure.

A lone pedestrian witnessed the escape. He just turned and shuffled away, having learned long ago that when you see such things it is better to ignore it and not ask questions. No one wants or needs a prying visit from the police. They always search your small apartment and find restricted goods in the kitchen pantry. It is better not to have to answer where they came from. It was simply better not to get involved.

A few blocks from the scene, the van to a halt. Hatim opened the doors. He hustled them into a different style van of a different color. This van squealed its tires as it accelerated in a different direction. The first unmarked van continued on its way to divert any attention.

For the first time, Nick closely inspected his rescuer. Nick thought him to be about forty years old. The man looked like a British aristocrat from Grosvenor Square. His features were classically chiseled, with high cheekbones, a sharp nose, bright eyes and stylishly cropped light blond hair. He was of medium height and build and was dressed in a charcoal turtle neck sweater and black trousers. The serious but calm look on the man's face showed his resolve and concern for their current situation.

Nick spoke up. "Thanks. I was beginning to wonder how many lives I had left."

"From the looks of you, I think you've used a few of them up. Manny asked me to watch over and help you if I could. You're a difficult man to keep track of. You're also ticking off a lot of Libyans."

"Yeah, and thanks to you, I'll be able to tick off a few more."

"You won't have time to. I've got to get you out of the country, like pronto."

"I'm not done here yet. Take me to Krasivwye Cemetery."

Hatim looked at Nick in disbelief.

"No way Jose. There's no time. The LIS will think the CIA busted you out of that field prison. Now you're creating an international incident just by breathing. This whole city is going to be crawling with secret police looking for the both of you. These LIS guys we just waxed can already taste your blood. We don't have a moment to lose. And I have strict orders to evac you two, like yesterday."

Georgina then spoke. "Maybe he's right Nick. We've pushed our luck too far. We'll be fortunate to get out with our lives."

Nick insisted.

"No! I came here to get something. I'm not leaving here without it. Now take me to the cemetery."

"It's suicide! Do you know how difficult it will be if we delay? I cannot guarantee that we'll be able to get you out if we wait another minute."

"I'm not asking you to guarantee that. I promise it will only take a few minutes."

Hatim scowled, looked hard into Nick's eyes, then slid open the window to the cab.

"Krasivwye Cemetery and step on it. But don't get stopped."

Nick grinned at Georgina, who rolled her eyes in disbelief.

"You'll need these." Hatim pulled out two sets of typical clothes worn by city dwelling Libyans. Hatim turned away so Georgina could change into her outfit. It consisted of thick black, winter pants, a white pullover sweater and a blue corduroy jacket. Nick changed into dark blue trousers, a white turtle neck sweater, a heavy brown leather jacket and a workman's cap.

As Nick changed, he explained something to Hatim. "Those weren't

LIS guys. They were Libyan Army Special Troops."

"Army? Hmm. That's strange. Army Intelligence ambushing LIS to free American spies."

There was a slight pause, then he continued. "There's something you should know. Manny told me there was something very wrong with this whole operation. He cautioned me to be careful. You should also."

Nick thoughtfully nodded. "Right."

Then, he finished dressing.

The van came to a halt. The driver slid open the connecting window.

"Three blocks."

Nick gave an instruction to the driver.

"Pull up to the back of the cemetery."

Hatim cautioned all of the people in the van. "They'll surely have LIS still at the front of the cemetery, just in case a lead surfaces there."

As they drove around the front gate, Nick cracked the back door open. He saw two men standing against their black car, smoking a cigarette.

"You're right. Do you have any weapons?"

The man gave each of them a Czech-made pistol.

"Here. We'll watch the back."

Nick popped the gun's magazine, made sure it was full, firmly palmed it into place and chambered a round. He placed it in his front waistband. He had the dead guard's gun tucked in the small of his back. Georgina did the same. Nick and Georgina got out of the van and slipped unseen, into the back of the cemetery. Nick pulled the worker's cap further down over his face.

"Look for Farid's grave, F A R I D. Next to it is a little statue of

Napoleon."

"Napoleon? A Russo-Libyan cemetery with a statue of the little, French general?"

As they walked, each looked up and down the rows, trying not to be too obvious.

Georgina found it. "Here it is."

They kneeled at the headstone.

"Watch the goons. Tell me if they come our way."

Georgina read the inscription to him.

"F A R I D, 1840-1887, and in Arabic, the phrase 'Soul and voice of the Libyan people'."

Nick started to dig at the base of the stone. He found nothing. He felt the grave marker for any compartments or latches. He still found nothing.

"Am I wrong about the courier's words? Did I misinterpret them?"

He cringed at the thought that he would have to dig up the grave or go away with nothing.

He was becoming frustrated when he saw that "Soul and voice of the Libyan people" was chiseled into a discolored rectangular block set into and almost flush with the marker face. It was just below the surface, under some wind blown debris.

About that time, Georgina saw the two goons react to something they heard on their car radio. One of them reached inside the car's window and apparently acknowledged the message received. No doubt, they had just been told of the escape and instructed to be alert. It was only then that the men noticed Nick and Georgina in the distance.

One of the men started toward them. Nick pried the block out with his fingernails.

He remembered what the courier had said.

"He wrote with his soul."

In the recess he found one folded page containing twenty names of Libyan government officials and other Europeans.

Georgina whispered to Nick.

"Hurry up. He's almost here!"

Nick reached into his belt and clicked the safety to "off" on his Czech weapon.

The LIS man was about thirty feet away when he spoke.

"Papers. Show me your papers."

The LIS man was tall, solidly built, square jawed, with dark eyes and dark hair. He wore a smoke colored suit that gave away his secret police persona.

Nick recalled the phrase from the road block, but did not know whether he was asking for identification papers, or the list of names. He reached for the pistol. Georgina's hand stopped him.

She barked at the man in flawless Arabic.

"Leave us alone to pay our respects in peace! Isn't anything sacred any more?"

Nick's back was turned to the man, to hide his face.

Nick's eyes looked to the side, watching the man with the extreme edge of his peripheral vision. The LIS man showed a slight surprise at Georgina's command and stopped in his tracks. He looked at Nick, still hunched over the grave stones. He shrugged his shoulders, waived them off and slowly walked back to his car.

She sighed with relief.

"Sometimes, I think it's the peasant women who really run this country."

Nick replaced the block and they quickly walked to the back gate and got back into the van.

Hatim met them. "Glad to see you guys. For a minute there, I thought there was going to be some fireworks."

"There would have been if it hadn't been for my partner's quick thinking."

"Now, it's off to the airport with you two. And this time I won't take no for an answer. If I have to shoot you myself, I'm going to get you on that plane!"

Georgina protested. "The airport? They'll have the tightest security there!"

"Don't worry. You'll never even get near the terminal. I have someone who owes me a favor in the luggage section. You see, there was a slight matter of one of his drug shipments that I caught wind of. I didn't turn him in then. But, I could any day. I have photos. Heh, heh."

Georgina muttered to them. "I'm not riding in any luggage compartment. The wind would simply ruin my fancy hairdo and designer clothes."

Everyone laughed.

Chapter Seventeen

At the airport the van drove through a seldom used entrance at the far end of the runway. As the van approached, a man unlatched and opened the gate to let them pass. The gate man was one of several people that were conspiring to spirit Nick and Georgina out of the country to safety.

The gate opened onto the tarmac which led to the international terminal. The van headed towards a corral of baggage carts and lift platforms. A police car suddenly sped at them from behind. Its blue lights were flashing. Its familiar European style, high-low siren was blaring. Once again, Nick wondered whether he had voluntarily jumped into the arms of traitors, eager to deliver him to the secret police.

The warped howl of the receding, high-low, two-toned siren relieved Nick's anxiety, if only for the moment.

The ride across the flat, cement field of unused aircraft parking made Nick realize how vulnerable they were. Nick felt as if every eye at the airport was watching them.

He wondered to himself.

"Can I trust anyone but Georgina?"

He got the impression that he was a Christian slave being led down a path lined with silently smiling rows of Roman soldiers. Those Roman sentries knew that the slave would soon be thrown into a den of starved and voracious lions.

Nick looked over to Georgina. She was watching him, waiting for some clue from him. He reached over and took her hand. He gave it a squeeze and began buttoning his coat. He checked his shoelaces. He was just trying to steel himself for whatever was going to happen next.

The van finally rolled to a stop. The several seconds that passed during the drive across the tarmac, seemed like an hour. There were two knocks on the door, then one, then two more. Hatim opened the door.

A pudgy, unshaven Armenian with dark, curly hair and a bushy mustache, beamed a smile at them.

He spoke in heavily accented English. "I'm Costia. Get into cart please."

Costia motioned them to get in a luggage cart. Nick peered out of the van's back door and looked at his surroundings.

"Wait. We could be seen by the terminal windows."

Costia understood some English. "No problem."

He opened the burlap flap covering one side of the cart. The Armenian propped it open with a metal hinged pole attached to the cart. He did this, so it would appear that the luggage handlers were tossing bags in without having to hold the flap open. The flap created a tunnel from the back of the van to the cart. Costia smiled again, noting that Nick and Georgina's movement was now hidden. To Nick, the terminal seemed to be an elevated guardhouse surveying a prison yard.

"O.K., Georgie. Let's go."

They climbed in the cart, already half filled with bags and containers. They uncomfortably settled in.

Hatim helped them into the cart. He spoke to Nick.

"There's a flight leaving sometime over the next three hours for Cairo. The embargo didn't stop every flight. Just sit tight until they load the luggage. Once you're in the cargo hold, go to the rear. You'll find a hatch leading up into the galley. Once inside, go to the lavatory. Behind the towel dispenser are your stamped boarding passes and new papers. You'll be a married couple. There's also a Cairo address to go to for further instructions."

Nick marveled at the completeness of the man's quickly crafted plan.

"What is your name?" Hatim hesitated, smiled, then answered.

"Call me Mack."

"Well Mack, I owe you a lot more than a World Series bet. Thank you for everything." "Not a problem. Good luck to you two. And by the way, tell Manny he still owes me for the 1978 World Series."

The men firmly shook hands, then smiled at each other with the silent understanding of the bond forged between those who risk everything, every day, operating in a secret world, on the edge in life and death. Silent service is only appreciated by those that know and do it. Mack winked at Georgina and closed the van's back door.

The van pulled away.

Costia spoke. "Wait quiet."

He lowered the flap.

Georgina looked at Nick and whispered to him. "I guess I didn't like my hairdo anyway."

Ninety minutes is a very long time to wait, crouched in a luggage cart, expecting to be discovered. Trust is a cautiously tentative thing for a secret agent. At any second the flaps could be thrown open and there could be a dozen armed men with rifles, ready to shoot you or put you through excruciating pain.

A cold rain began to fall. Nick thought he heard faint footsteps approaching. He strained to hear them over the pelting shower that was rattling on the metal top and canvas sides of the cart. He slid the safety of his pistol to the "off" position and motioned for Georgina to bury herself further in the luggage.

There were two thumps, one, then two more thumps on the side of the cart. Nick had his gun pointed at the flap. Then, the flap was lifted. There was the smiling Costia. He opened his coat, showing two rows of wristwatches.

"Good price for you. Which you like?"

Nick looked in disbelief at Georgina and she at him.

Georgina answered him. "Laa,shukran sadik." "No thanks, friend."

Costia's smile disappeared. He lowered the burlap.

He flatly spoke to both of them. "Go now."

Nick remarked to Georgina.

"There's hope for this country yet. We're on the run from the LIS and our rescuer still has time to be a capitalist entrepreneur."

They both laughed. The tension of the moment was relieved by Costia's unlikely sales pitch.

Costia attached a small, dated tractor to the cart and pulled it for some distance until Nick could hear the whining engines of a parked airliner waiting to depart. Nick peeked through a crack between the flap. He could see that the cart was lifted several feet into the air by a burly man turning a hand crank.

The cart was on a platform attached to an accordion, criss-crossed braced lift. Up the baggage cart went until it was at the level of the plane's open cargo hold. With practiced mediocrity, Costia started tossing bags into the open compartment of the plane.

Nick peered out again and looked at the plane's passenger door. He saw a man, undoubtedly a plain clothes policeman, standing at the top of the walk up ladder. He was outside at the entrance of the aircraft, checking the papers, names and faces of every passenger who was boarding.

"C'mon, girl."

They crawled into the plane just as Costia closed the cargo door.

As he did, Costia flashed a toothy grin. "Good fly. Thank you fly Costia Airlines."

Georgina smiled at him, then shook her head in disbelief as the door latch turned.

The policeman at the top of the ladder looked at his list. Almost all the names had been checked off. The flight attendant wanted to close the door. The policeman authoritatively held up his hand. The door stayed open. There were two more names on the passenger manifest than there were people on the plane. He went into the aircraft and checked the lavatories, closets, the cockpit and quickly verified the list again. He could only think that they never got on the plane. He pulled out a radio.

"The plane is clear."

He took one, last look at the seated passengers, then headed out of the plane's door.

Inside the cargo hold, Nick and Georgina clumsily made their way to the rear. They crawled over the baggage, thrown helter skelter, into the compartment.

"Ow!" "Hurry up now, Georgina. We don't have much time."

"I don't have much room to move."

"Use your body to wade through the bags. Roll that big one over you, instead of pushing it. You'll move faster."

Nick found the hatch just as the plane began to move. The taxiing was rough. The runway seemed to be maintained as well as most of the city streets, which felt like covered wagon wheel ruts.

The latch was difficult to budge from Nick's awkward position as he reached over some luggage and turned his arm to get at the latch.

"One way or another, we have to get out of this cargo area and into the pressurized cabin before the plane reaches altitude. If we don't, the atmospheric pressure will cause our blood vessels to burst throughout our bodies. We'll either drown in our own blood or die from asphyxiation, due to lack of oxygen."

"Quit talking and get that damn hatch open!"

Nick continued to struggle with the latch as they left the ground.

"Argr. It's stuck!"

"We're airborne. Hurry up, Nick!"

He knew he only had a couple of minutes at best, until they would reach their physical limits.

Georgina heard the whir and clank of the raised landing gear as it locked in place.

"That's the landing gear. The pain is already starting in my ears. Hurry!"

Nick pulled out one of the pistols and started to beat the latch with the butt of the weapon.

He thought to himself.

"Had someone accidentally forgot to unlock the latch from inside? Had someone purposely not unlocked the latch?"

It finally gave.

"We have to get inside fast. We don't want to alert anyone to our presence by causing a significant decrease in cabin pressure."

Nick raised the hatch an inch or so and looked up into the galley. He whispered down to her.

"It's empty and the curtain is drawn."

Nick climbed up. Georgina followed him. As Nick helped her to her feet, a flight attendant entered the galley. She opened, then quickly closed the curtain behind her. The woman looked at them, nodded with quiet complicity. She went back to the passengers. Again, she closed the drape behind her.

Nick and Georgina brushed the dust from their clothes. They walked down the aisle to the lavatory. It was occupied. Eventually, a woman emerged. She suggestively looked at Nick admiring him. She straightened her skirt and walked to her seat, swinging her hips all the way. She glanced back to smile at him again. Nick smiled back. With a determined look on her face, Georgina pushed him into the lavatory.

"In, Romeo."

Once inside, they pried the towel dispenser apart. They found a plastic bag containing their new identities.

Georgina remarked to Nick.

"Hmm. Mr. and Mrs. Gestaldt. And wedding rings too."

Georgina slipped the slightly oversized ring onto her finger. She extended her hand out in front of her to admire the gold band.

She looked at Nick.

"Looks natural for us, don't you think?"

Nick smiled back, grabbed some paper towels and tossed them at her.

"I'd never be married to a woman as grimy as you."

Georgina turned and looked at her reflection. "Yuck."

Her face was a mess of bruises, perspiration and dirt.

"Well, at least we're a pair."

Nick looked at himself and realized he did not look much better.

There were two knocks on the door, then one, then two more. Nick fingered his gun then unlocked the door. It was the flight attendant whom they saw in the galley. She had brought them a paper sack with combs, toothbrushes, some make-up, a razor and some other toilet articles.

"Thought you might need these."

"Thanks."

She nodded, closed the door and left.

Georgina playfully elbowed Nick away from the sink and began scrubbing her face in the cramped washroom.

After they cleaned themselves, Nick and Georgina hurried to find their seats. The boarding passes showed them to be in aisle thirty-two, seats A and B. Just a few rows in from the galley, they took their seats for the first time. They were nineteen minutes into the flight.

As Nick sat, he examined their papers. The passports listed Mr. Gestaldt as a German industrialist, his wife as a school teacher. The passports bore several stamps and were moderately worn from use.

An old woman, in a flowered dress, sitting across from them looked at Nick with a confused expression.

"Takeoffs always make her ill."

Georgina rubbed her stomach, put her hand to her mouth and puffed her cheeks, as if she burped. The woman knowingly nodded and returned to her magazine.

Nick and Georgina looked at each other, then settled into their seats.

The flight attendant came to them.

"Coffee?"

Their reply in unison. "Please!"

The woman who smiled at Nick when she came out of the lavatory sat just two rows away from them. She again looked back, down the aisle and smiled at Nick. Georgina pushed his shoulder. The flirting woman then returned to her magazine. She flipped one page to see an eight by ten inch glossy photograph of Nick in an Army uniform. Verifying that he was the man in the photograph, she folded the photograph and placed it in her purse.

She picked up the in-flight telephone, located on the back of the seat in front of her. She inserted her credit card and dialed a number. She spoke in Arabic.

"Daddy, I think I finally found the right man. He's just a dream. I'll tell you all about him. Uh huh, uh huh. OK, see you when I get there. Love you, bye."

Her conversation had been with the man the Libyan General instructed to follow Hussain. The General was further hedging his bets. After Hussain's failure to get the list and Nick's escape, the General placed someone on every international flight, just in case Nick and Georgina somehow got on one without being detected.

A BASEMENT, TRIPOLI

Again, Hussain was called before his commanding General. This time, he was told it was for a situational update.

Even though the General already knew of Dentworth's escape, he nonetheless wanted to ask the question.

"So, Colonel. How are things going? Have you found him yet?"

Hussain delayed his answer, then decided there was no point in hiding the truth.

"General, he has temporarily been lost."

"What? Define lost. He has escaped? This is most unfortunate."

"General, this is merely a brief setback. I will find him again soon. Once I do, he will not escape again, I promise you."

Hussain said it in an apologetic tone of voice.

The General grimly looked out his window. "Comrade Colonel, let us hope for your sake that you do catch him. If you fail again, this could be the very last promise you ever make."

Chapter Eighteen

CHEVY CHASE, MARYLAND

Manny Martinez lived in Chevy Chase, Maryland, an exclusive suburb of Washington, D.C. It was also a relatively short drive to Langley, Virginia, where the Headquarters of the CIA was located. His beautiful wife Lorena had, over the years of military separation, managed to raise three marvelous children. The oldest, Reynaldo was at West Point, preparing to be an Army officer. Maria, a gifted musician, planned to pursue a career as a concert pianist. Leticia was a fifteen-year-old budding beauty planning a career as an international model.

"Snip, snip." Manny was out in his back yard, trimming some errant branches from his shade tree. It had overhung into the neighbor's property, dropping the last few leaves into his pool. The neighbor was a Washington lawyer who had a reputation for cleanliness.

He commented to Manny the previous day. "I am very unhappy to have to unclog my pool skimmer yet again, Mr. Martinez."

It had prompted Manny to venture out in the cold winter weather to trim his tree.

Leticia or Letty, was on the phone, as usual, with one of her teenage girlfriends, talking about the latest rumored breakup of a worshiped high school hunk. The split up was causing shock waves of gossip throughout her fourth period home room class.

Letty was a typical teenage American girl, always on the telephone. There was one difference, however. The phone she was talking on was not an average one. About the size of a small video cassette recorder, this was a top of the line secure STU III phone. It had the capability of securely communicating by voice or facsimile with any other similar phone anywhere in the world. In addition to its secure mode, it could be used "in the clear" like a normal phone.

Letty spoke with her friend Stacy.

"Stace, so like what did Bobby say, like when like, you know, Cheryl gave him, you know, the jacket back, you know?"

"Suzy told me, you know, that like, he told her ..."

"Click, click"

It was the sound of another incoming call on line two of four.

Stacy's juicy details were too good to interrupt.

"What's that?"

Letty explained.

"Forget it. So, like what did he tell her?"

"Click, click."

"Maybe it's Bobby. I saw the way he looked at you at the lockers the other day. You know?"

"Click, click."

"Damn. I wish, like, wouldn't it be totally rad if he did call me? It would be so bitchen. You know? But it's not him. I just know it. You better tell me what he told her, though."

"Click, click."

"Guy! Doesn't this dude ever give up?"

"Just a sec, Stace."

Letty pushed the "hook flash" button on the thirty button panel.
She impatiently answered.

"Hello?"

A voice spoke on the other end of the slightly static affected phone
line.

"Hello. Is your father there?"

Moody and self-centered, fifteen year olds can become inexplicably
brain dead at the most inopportune times. Letty was impatient and
anxious to get back to Stacy so she could hear every last detail of what
Bobby told Cheryl.

"No. He's not here."

She knew her father was in the backyard. But, it was far too much
trouble to go and get him, when Stacy was holding on line one.

"It's very important I talk to him. I'm calling long distance. Do
you know where he is?"

"No, I don't. Try the office. He's always at the office. Bye."

She hit the hook flash again, hanging up on the transatlantic caller.
She went back to Stacy.

"So who was it?"

"I don't know. Someone for my Dad."

"Oh well. Like, he told Cheryl ..."

Letty turned around in the easy chair, putting her back to the back
yard window. Behind her through the glass, arcadia door leading out to
the back yard, Manny could be seen stretching to snip a straggly stem
which jutted from the trunk of the tree.

Hatim was at the other end of the telephone, in a city on the other
side of the world. He crinkled his forehead and ran his fingers through
his hair.

205

He hung up the phone and thought to himself. "I wonder why Manny told me to call him at home? Something must have come up."

He called Manny's office. As it was Sunday, a CIA switchboard operator answered the phone.

"Central Intelligence Agency. May I help you?"

"Yes. Please check and see if there's anyone in the International Research Department, please."

"Who's calling please?"

"Tell them Mack is on the line."

"One moment, please."

The operator buzzed that office.

Samuel Gibbons was in the office, as he usually was on weekends. Sam was a bona fide workaholic. It was not a matter of spending an unusual amount of time in the office, raising the eyebrows of the security teams. They knew that each Sunday morning, they would find Sam Gibbons at his desk. He would be quietly working, with none of the usual noise, confusion and distractions of the busy work week. Here he could collect his thoughts, compose memos and coolly analyze things.

He picked up the buzzing phone.

"Yes?"

"Sir, there's a gentleman on the line wanting to speak to someone in your office. He said his name is Mack."

"Put him through, please."

"Sir, regulations state that … ."

"Just bloody well put him through, Madge."

"Yes Sir!"

"Mack, how are you? A bit unusual calling on this line isn't it?"

"I tried to get Manny at home but he wasn't there. But I'm glad I found you. Listen. I airmailed that package. I sent it to your third cousin. You know, the one you last saw in '79?"

"Yes, I remember him."

Indeed he did. Manny, Sam and Mack had prearranged the coded words for such a cryptic conversation over the open phone lines, should it become necessary. His third cousin was actually his third in command of the anticommunist cell Sam ran in Cairo in the 1950's. At the time, the newly formed CIA was providing arms and logistics to Middle Eastern ethnic groups trying to resist the Soviet control being exerted upon their homelands.

The third cousin, Simon Weatherby, was a British born businessman who joined the OSS and continued to assist the CIA from time to time. Once intelligence work is in your blood, no number of transfusions of age or years of other work can completely flush the system.

"The package will be well received. My first cousin will be delighted. Thank you for your help."

The first cousin was St. James.

"My pleasure. Give my best to the family."

"Will do."

After hanging up, Sam immediately called St. James and set up a meeting in one hour. St. James met Sam in the DCI's office.

"What's the latest, Sam?"

"Well, thanks to the able work of our support man in Tripoli, Dentworth and Matlock were delivered safely to Cairo."

"Really. What about the list, Sam?"

"Apparently, they have it. Our man didn't say he saw it. He just delivered them."

"What are they going to do in Cairo?"

"They're going to meet up with one of our contract agents. He'll help them get here, Sir."

"Who is he?"

"He's Simon Weatherby. I worked with him in …"

St. James interrupted.

"The plastics magnate?"

"Yes, he's done well."

"Great job, Sam. When can we expect them to get here?"

"Well, depending on when they contact Simon, I'd say by tomorrow if there are no snags."

"Well done. Please inform me upon their arrival. I would personally like to meet them."

In a cautious voice, Sam answered.

"Very well, Sir. But they're not completely out of the woods yet."

"Oh? Have faith Sam. They'll make it one way or the other. Thank you for coming, Sam."

Sam thought St. James was unusually upbeat as he dismissed Sam from his office.

After Sam had left, St. James visibly smiled.

"How fortunate."

Just one hour before Sam's call, St. James had talked with Hussain, from whom he got the bad news that Dentworth had escaped.

"Yes, very fortunate indeed." He said it aloud to himself.

CAIRO, EGYPT

The flight was uneventful, except for a painful jab in the ribs Georgina administered when Nick obligatorily smiled again at the flirtatious female passenger. As they stepped off the plane and into the terminal,

Nick and Georgina appeared to be the typical tourist couple. Nick kept his guard up, looking at the various people around the terminal. There was a man in a trench coat and hat leaning against a pillar, looking bored.

"Too arch typical."

Another man was standing at a bank of public phones, looking towards Nick. The phone suddenly rang. He picked it up and started arguing with someone, in quickly spoken Arabic,

"Your grandmother was not on the plane. No, there's no way she could have slipped passed me. With Allah's grace! She's eighty-five and uses a walker. I would have seen her!"

"No. He's calling too much attention to himself. He must be O.K."

Nick turned his attention to the exit.

Then he saw the young cleaning woman. She was an ordinary looking woman in an airport maintenance uniform. She had a walkman radio on her belt. Although Nick couldn't hear the type of music, he could hear enough to know she had the volume up very loud in the earphones.

She was half dancing, half vacuuming with a loud vacuum cleaner. It had a one hundred-foot cord. The carpet itself was very short. The only thing that caught his curiosity was that she was cleaning an area of carpet that was spotless. She kept going over and over the same area.

"Something about her, hmm."

He made a particular mental note of her.

The Egyptian Customs official eyed their German passports.

"Mr. and Mrs. Gestaldt. What's your purpose for visiting Egypt?"

"Again bitte? In German or English?"

"Why are you coming to Egypt?"

"Ah, ya. To see the Pyramids and history of your great country."

"How long will you be here?"

"Two, three weeks maybe. There's so much to see. What would you suggest we see first? The Pyramids, the Valley of the Kings, the Nile, or perhaps something else."

He was cut off.

"I am not a tourist guide. Go to the information booth."

He frowned and pointed to the information booth across the room.

"Yes, yes. Danke, danke."

Nick was successful in his ploy. The Customs officer stamped their documents and sent them on their way. He disliked foreign tourists pestering him.

Nick and Georgina performed another counter surveillance route before meeting their contact. They took a taxi to a restaurant that Nick knew would afford him a great view of the street.

"The tinted glass windows serve as a one way mirror looking out."

They took a seat by the window and ordered something to eat. It was about five o'clock, p.m.

"Look down the street. See the hot kabob cart? It just relocated from one side of the block to the other. Anyone could be part of a team sent to find and capture us. I suspect everyone. I can trust no one, but you Georgina."

A few minutes later, she pointed out a man she saw go into a bookstore directly across the street.

"That guy's dressed in a long coat and green plaid scarf."

He appeared to randomly pick a book out of the display. He opened the book and appeared to review it. All the while he faced out the window towards the restaurant. Nick could see the scarf through the shadowed glass.

"I'm starting to get an uneasy feeling in the pit of my stomach."

"What's wrong?"

"I'm not sure. I keep thinking of Manny's warning to Mack, that something was very wrong."

"Why? What are you sensing?"

"I don't know. Something just doesn't feel right. Let's take the back way out." They left through the kitchen door, apologizing to the protesting cook.

"Sorry, sorry. We're parked out back and we thought this was the rear exit."

The portly cook scoffed, and threw up his hands in disgust, flinging little pieces of dough from his fingers.

Once in the alley, they ran to the street. Nick and Georgina found a nearby taxi. They jumped in and took off. Looking back as the taxi pulled away from the curb, Nick saw the man in the green plaid scarf.

"Look."

The man coolly strolled around the corner of the building and glanced at his wristwatch. Nick's nagging doubts began to crystallize into a solid suspicion.

He pulled out the address of the contact that was supposed to help him, twenty-two Al Habibi.

Nick explained.

"This is an enclave of Cairo's privileged class. It's like New York's Central Park West."

He took Georgina on a roller coaster ride of changing modes of transportation. A bus, then another taxi, a short walk, then another taxi until he was convinced no one was tailing them. He had the taxi driver continue to drive passed twenty-two Al Habibi. Nick scoured the street for signs of surveillance.

It was now dark, and the alcoves and sides of the buildings were pitch black and mysterious. Out of the corner of his eye he saw a light in an alley near the building at twenty-two Al Habibi. He saw a pencil point of orange light move up, briefly grow brighter then dimmer. It then moved downward and disappeared. It was a cigarette being raised, inhaled, lowered, then hidden by a cupped hand.

"Smoking is bad for a guy's health. Thank goodness it's habit forming."

"What do you mean?"

"We're not alone yet."

He pointed to the alley, gesturing as if he were smoking a cigarette.

As they drove around the block continuing their mobile reconnaissance, Nick saw a car parked on a side street along a block wall for no apparent reason. Nick nodded in that direction for Georgina to notice. There were no walkways, doors or entrances near it, making the car seem out of place. Nick could just barely make out the shadow of two figures in the vehicle. They were just sitting there in the dark. Nick decided.

"I don't think we'll ask for 'help' from twenty-two Al Habibi after all."

He instructed the taxi driver to drive on. After another hour of counter surveillance tactics, Nick walked Georgina down a street.

"I'm sure that someone was waiting for us. Deep down I feel that Mack did us right. But hell, the more I think about it, the more I feel that someone has been watching our every move, always one step ahead of us. I don't know who to trust anymore. I think it's time to do the un-expected. A cardinal rule is that you never use the same contact twice. But I just don't trust the company plan. Let's go visit my uncle."

"Your uncle? I didn't know you had a relative in Cairo."

"Neither did I until a few days ago."

NAZHITNABE TRAIN YARD, TRIPOLI

Railroads have served as the lifeblood and veins of Libya, conduct-ing both commerce and defense through the most remote frontiers. Any place of significance has a rail line. Something was occurring at the Nazhitnabe Train Yard. Throughout the dark of night, members of the bomb conspiracy had been secretly arriving.

The old depot had been abandoned years ago.

The great hall of the building was cold and drafty. No one wanted to be there at this time of year. That is precisely why the conspirators chose this place to meet. No one else would think to find them there. As the last members arrived, one of the elderly participants mumbled.

"I'm too damn old and too damn cold for these cloak and dagger meetings."

Another spoke.

"Patience, patience."

When all had gathered, the meeting began.

The leader started the conversation.

"Gentlemen, our situation is growing more precarious by the hour. The list has not yet been recovered. We can't meet like this again. If the list is compromised, any one of us may be followed. We must all think about going into hiding now. However, it is not too late to find the list before we are exposed. We need to make emergency plans, backup plans now, even with a traitor in our midst. Perhaps a diversion or decoy to discredit the document's authenticity?"

A fat man with a greasy forehead, breathed laboriously with lung cancer, and puffed.

"We need to draw the attention away from the conference."

Another added his suggestion.

"Something like a coup attempt now, just before the conference. The list might be denounced as a plant, an overreaction."

The Commanding General, who had Hussain follow Nick, then spoke.

"Gentlemen, gentlemen, let's keep our heads. I don't think things are as desperate as you indicate. I have information that will lead me to the list. Unfortunately, the courier that originally had the list was killed. But the current holder is about to land in my spider's web."

With those words, one of the conspirators, "Daphne," felt a sudden, silent pang of sadness.

CIA HEADQUARTERS

The next morning, St. James had an emergency meeting of his own in his office. He had summoned Manny Martinez, Sam Gibbons and Kimberly Phelps. St. James opened the meeting.

"Gentlemen, Sam said Dentworth didn't show up at his designated contact last night. Does anyone know why?"

Phelps snarled a comment. He examined his fingernails.

"The opposition must have snatched him. He was lucky to have gotten as far as he did."

Manny glared at him.

Sam spoke up to break the tension. "He definitely knew where to go if Hatim's meaning was understood. Hatim's a good field man. If he said he delivered the package, I'm sure he did a good job. We didn't hear of any unusual happenings or incidents at the airport."

Manny asked a question. "Sam, did you say you talked to Hatim?"

"Yes. He caught me at the office yesterday. He said he called you at home, but that you weren't there."

"Hmm. That's weird."

Sam continued. "I naturally informed the Director at once."

Manny shifted in his chair, but said nothing.

St. James addressed them both. "Because of the sensitivity of this matter, I took the liberty of sending a safety team to the contact area to help ensure that things were not unduly interrupted."

Manny angrily queried him. "What? You sent a separate team in on your own, Sir?"

"Mr. Martinez, I am the DCI and I saw fit to send some help."

Manny detected some irritation in St. James voice. "Yes, Sir. It's just that without the case agent's knowledge, an action like that could screw things up."

He wondered why St. James had taken an unusual personal interest in getting his hands on Dentworth and the list. Uncharacteristically, Manny started to question the intentions of his superior. He began to wonder if the DCI had a different agenda.

"When you are DCI you can make the decisions, Mr. Martinez. Until then, I do."

Sam blinked twice at the intimation that someone else other than himself would succeed to the DCI throne.

St. James turned to Manny. "Mr. Martinez, you know Dentworth better than any of us. Why do you think he didn't show?"

"I think your team spooked him, Sir. It would sure as hell spook me. I think he'll find his own way out now. I don't think he'll trust the company plan."

St. James pressed him. "How will he do it?"

"He'll take a trusted route."

Manny was feeling a little cautious about his answers.

"Who will he use?"

Phelps chimed in more to be part of the conversation than to offer any assistance.

"Perhaps, he'll use the same people that got him inside. He knows that route will work."

Sam joined in. "Getting out is different than getting in. But it's possible."

"What do you think, Mr. Martinez?" "It's possible, Sir. But it's against the rules. You never use the same contact twice if you can avoid it. It can become a dangerous association for both persons."

"We are in a dangerous business, Mr. Martinez. My men are on the ground and can move the fastest. Who helped him get in, Sam?"

Sam opened a file, flipped a page and underneath a color photo, he read the name "Hassan, Ali Hassan, eighteen Nasser Boulevard."

Manny thought St. James' assertion of authority and exertion of case control seemed a little more like desperation than help.

CAIRO, EGYPT

As St. James' meeting broke up, it was late afternoon in Cairo. Ali had been happy to see Nick again. It was as if he was his son who had been away at university and who had returned on holiday. Ali welcomed Georgina.

"I can tell that Nicholas and you are 'together' by the way you look at each other."

216

Inside, Ali now doubted that Nick actually was married. But he let it pass for now.

Jasmina seemed more nervous. The evening before when Nick and Georgina showed up, she did not hesitate to feed them and prepare sleeping arrangements. But she remained on edge.

In the morning, Nick apologized to Ali. "I lied about being married."

Ali nodded his acceptance. "It's a shame, what this business does to us, eh?"

"Do you know of a quiet way to leave Egypt for Greece or the U.S.A.?" "I have a brother who is the Captain of a French freighter, the 'Isle de Paris', a transport that regularly carried oil equipment from Egypt to Greece. I can telephone my brother and arrange passage on the next ship to leave. Maybe twelve hours. After the boat, this gives you plenty of time to catch a flight to England or the USA. Yes?"

To relieve an otherwise tense situation, Nick and Georgina took a protesting but grateful Jasmina to the neighborhood clothes shop to buy her a new outfit. She hadn't bought anything new for years. It would be a small token of thanks for the maternal care and warmth offered to them.

A few minutes after they had left, there was a knock at Ali's door. He opened it. "Yes?"

A man and a woman stood before him. She flashed some sort of official looking police credentials.

"One of your female neighbors was assaulted in your courtyard earlier this morning. We'd like to ask you a few questions about what you may have seen or heard. We need to come in."

They started to enter before he had a chance to answer. Ali cautiously opened the door wider.

Rounding the corner on the way home, Nick and Georgina were laughing at Jasmina who was wearing her new, bright yellow and white robe style dress and sweater. She suggestively modeled her prize. Nick's smile faded as he focused his gaze up the street. Coming out of Ali and Jasmina's apartment courtyard, Nick saw the airport cleaning woman dressed in street clothes. She was accompanied by a man who removed his gloves and tossed them into a nearby trash bin. They got into a car parked at the curb and sped off.

Nick shoved Georgina and Jasmina against the wall hoping that the cleaning lady did not see them.

Both of the ladies protested.

Georgina blasted a question at Nick. "What are you doing?"

Georgina and Jasmina's smiles vanished as they saw the look on Nick's face.

"Ali!" Jasmina cried as she started to trot ahead.

Nick grabbed her arm and slowed her down. "You must walk normally. They may still be watching."

The three of them entered the courtyard. Everything was quiet. A child was bouncing a ball against a first floor wall. They went upstairs and carefully approached the apartment. The door was slightly ajar. They pulled their handguns.

Nick mimed a count from one to three. Nick and Georgina rushed inside, leaving Jasmina outside on the landing. They quietly swept through the apartment, ending up in the kitchen.

There on the floor lay Ali, on his back, in a growing puddle of blood. Nick scanned his body. Georgina gasped. She saw that the index finger on each hand had been severed at the second knuckle. This minimized the lack of feeling from shock and maximized the sensitized pain one could feel under interrogation. He had been shot twice in the chest and was bleeding profusely.

Jasmina entered her kitchen and shrieked at the sight of her husband. She fell to her knees and cradling Ali's head. Her new yellow dress began to soak up the pooled blood like a dry sponge, transforming it into a ghastly rag of horror.

Jasmina tearfully whimpered. "There's so much blood!"

Ali was still barely alive. He cracked his eyes open to see Jasmina. She smiled at him, silent tears streaming down her face.

He looked beyond her at Nick and sputtered, coughing up yet more blood. "I'm sorry. I told them of the boat."

"You did fine, Ali. You just rest. You have toys to make for my children, remember?" Nick told him this in a false voice of confidence. Nick knew Ali was finished.

Ali again sputtered. "You two marry, my son?"

"Yes, and you'll be there."

Looking back at Jasmina, Ali spoke his last words.

"I love … ."

He closed his eyes and died. His last breath escaping as a gurgle.

Jasmina squeaked out a tearful cry.

"I love you too, Ali."

She bent her face down and kissed his forehead.

She talked to his lifeless body.

"Oh, Ali, I just knew this would happen."

Nick cupped the side of Jasmina's face.

"I am sorry. We'll take care of him."

Jasmina looked at Nick. With tear filled eyes, she sadly shook her head. "No! You will leave us now. Go. There's been enough killing."

Georgina softly spoke. "But the police?"

Jasmina choked out a response. "These days, there are more and more street criminals."

Nick was dumbstruck. Even now, she was offering her help to save him and Georgina. After all she and Ali had been through. They had paid the ultimate price. She was still willing to respect the fight for freedom that Ali so deeply believed in.

Nick, leaned down and looked at Jasmina's face. "Thank you, Jasmina. I will never forget you or Ali."

Jasmina just stared at him, then sadly returned to her Ali.

With nothing left to do, Nick and Georgina left. As they quickly walked, Georgina tried to stop him.

"We, we just can't leave them there like that!"

"We can't do anything for Ali now." Nick used an emotionless tone of voice. Nick gritted his teeth, spun around and smashed an empty flower pot on a gate pedestal with his fist.

"Damn them all to hell! I'll find the bastards who did this. I swear it Ali! Now, we go through my people, my way!"

Chapter Nineteen

At a public phone near Ali's residence, Nick dialed a number. "Hey Ace, this is Dentworth. How are you doing?"

"Nick Dentworth. Geez, I haven't heard from you since, since El Sal. Man! We went through some deep squat there, didn't we?"

"We sure did. And I'm up to my eyeballs in it again."

"What's up Nick? Is there something I can do?"

"As a matter of fact, yes, there is. Are you still flying?" "Oh yeah, everything from plastic doggie doo-doo to Chinooks."

"Great. How about meeting me at that old Mediterranean restaurant? You remember? The one with the blue and gold pillars out in front. Me, you and Bud went there a couple of times when we were in transit to the States. You were supposed to meet us there, but were tied up. What was her name again?"

"Cindy, the embassy cipher clerk. She sure deciphered my code. You mean the one that serves all those beers from around the world? I didn't think they were allowed. I'll finally get to collect on that beer you owe me?"

"You bet. They'll serve just about anything you want for the almighty dollar. But I'll owe you a six pack for this one."

"Uh oh. There must be a woman involved, huh?"

"Yeah. But she'd kick your butt."

"Oooeee! I can't wait to steal this one away from you. One hour then."

Ace McCullough was a brand new, cocky Air Force pilot when he was assigned to support the Southern Joint Command, Special Operations Group. He met, then Captain, Dentworth on a mission in El Salvador.

Nick's Special Forces team was airdropped in the jungle, about fifty miles outside of San Salvador, the capital city. The team set up booby traps, explosives and anti-personnel mines along a trail that soon would be clogged with leftist rebels. The rebels were intent on seizing an upper class neighborhood of San Salvador in their quest to take the battle to the cities. They hoped to destabilize the right wing government. It was a classic insurgency tactic.

The ambush by the Green Beret advisers and El Salvadoran Special Forces decimated the one hundred man guerrilla unit. They did fight valiantly. The few rebels that survived escaped back into the jungle. They were actually allowed to live. The El Salvador government wanted them to take a message to their colleagues.

"The Army will win, with overwhelming force." It was part of the Army's psychological war against the rebels.

The Special Forces soldiers arrived at the pick up, landing zone. They awaited the two, U.S. built, U.S. flown helicopters that were to recover them from their mission. As Nick was about to climb into the helicopter, the pilot, Second Lieutenant Jeffrey "Ace" McCullough saw something move in the distance. A surviving, rebel sniper leveled an AK-47 from the tree line, directly at Nick's back. Ace yelled and motioned at Nick.

"Hit the deck!"

It was just in time for a couple of bullets to miss Nick. They plunked into the metal at the door gunner's feet. As the helicopter violently rose up and out of the jungle, Nick turned to the young pilot.

"Hey, thanks. You saved my life back there. What's your name?"

"McCullough. Ace McCullough, Sir."

"Well Ace, I owe you a cold beer."

"No problem, Sir. About now, that beer sounds good."

On returning to the base camp, Nick was immediately sent to Tegucigalpa, Honduras. Ace did not get a chance to drink his beer. Over the years, they had talked to each other several times. Ace was eventually transferred to fly fixed wing transport planes. He was now a Captain and was officially assigned to the U. S. Air Force, Southwest Asia Transport Command. He actually worked for a Defense Intelligence Agency special operations unit. He flew strange equipment and strange men to strange places within the middle eastern theater of operations.

Nick and Georgina arrived early at the restaurant, taking one of Nick's habitual, circuitous routes. He chose a table in the back of the room from which he could watch the entrance and be able to grab Georgina and lose themselves in a crowd of merrymakers if necessary. Nick kept an eye out for Ace. Nick stood and gave a small wave as Ace entered the room.

Nick gave him a hug. "Ace, it's great to see you. And congrats on your promotion."

"Thanks. It's great to see you too."

Ace was a short, handsome, devilishly confident, hot shot pilot. His dimpled baby face made him seem younger than his actual age. Consequently, he was able to develop quite a reputation as a lady's man. His amorous liaisons, legendary among other flyers, ranged from experienced vixens to precocious young women.

"Ace, this is my partner Georgina."

Ace obliged, by taking and kissing her hand. "Nice to meet you, Ma'am. What are you doing with a bum like this? I'd be so much better for you."

"You're probably right. I'm unsuccessfully trying to keep him out of trouble."

"See? That's the difference between him and me.

I don't know. Something says, 'trouble', all over your forehead."

They all laughed and ordered.

"A large glass of dark German beer." A waiter instantly produced one, seemingly out of thin air.

"Aaahh!"

Ace swallowed a large gulp with utter contentment. "This country has many wonderful things. And imported German beer is one of them."

He drank all of it down, then put the glass on the table. He earnestly looked at Nick. "So what's the trouble? Need to hop a flight to Singapore, Iceland, Peru, Paris?" He gave a flirtatious look to a dark-eyed waitress, who twirled her hair and smiled in reply.

"We need to get to Washington."

"Washington?" Ace sounded puzzled.

"Yeah. But no one, I mean no one can know how we got there or even that we got there."

"Why not just jump on a TWA bird?".

"I think someone would be watching. Things have gone to hell in a hand basket. I can't trust the people I work for. This is a big one, Ace."

Ace growled.

"Must be the damned Agency. Can't trust those guys with their own sister."

"Can you get us there, completely in the black?"

"Both of you? No problem" Ace smiled as if he had just won the lottery.

"I'd need a chopper flight across the pond too. Can you arrange it for me?"

"Consider it done. When do you want to leave?"

"How about now?" "Grab your bag honey. The bus leaves in ninety minutes."

As they walked out together, arm in arm, Georgina turned to Ace.

"Why do they call you Ace?"

Nick slapped his forehead, dreading the familiar story that Ace was hoping she would ask about.

Ace's face broadening into a wide grin. "Well, It's interesting that you should ask about that. You see? I was in flight school. We were having target practice. A bull's eye was painted on the side of a big old barn. There I was, zeroing in on the objective when I lost the hydraulics on my trainer. I wound up crashing the bugger in the middle of the bull's eye. I walked away with only a broken ankle, but by God, I hit the target! The guys knighted me 'Ace' in honor of my tactical accuracy under pressure."

"That's a comforting thought."

Ace grinned again "Onward to Camelot!"

AL AHRAM (U.S. AIR BASE), CAIRO

As the empty C-130 transport prepared to taxi from the hanger to the runway, a young Air Force Airman flagged Ace to a stop, causing him to slow the engines. The Airman rolled a wheeled ladder platform to the cockpit window. He trotted up the stairs.

"Excuse me, Sir. I don't have a fuel authorization or a flight plan for your bird."

With an impatient look on his face, Ace answered him.

"What's the problem, son?" "Sir, according to the allocation roster, you're not cleared for fuel."

Ace countered with a big grin on his face. "Do you like the women, fun and frivolity here, Airman?"

The Airman smiled broadly. "Oh, yes, Sir. I like it here."

"This is a classified flight. Now, I don't know who screwed your paperwork up, son. But' if you don't drive that truck over here and fuel my aircraft in the next thirty seconds, you're going to be monitoring a one man weather station on a floating ice pack, somewhere in the South Atlantic. Your only sex will be with an occasional passing penguin."

The Airman's smile turned downwards, as he pondered the chilly prospect of the penguin.

"Unleaded or super supreme, Sir?"

Happy with his successful ruse, Ace cheerfully mocked him.

"Super supreme and check the oil."

A short time later, the plane left land on its way over the Mediterranean Sea. Ace spoke over the in-flight headset.

"Feet wet."

Some hours later, Ace's voice again came on the radio.

"Sir, we'll be landing at Andrews in a few minutes. A guy named Stilwell, in a civilian 'wop wop' will fly you to the Air Park."

"Stilwell? I know him. We did a job down south. He's a bald headed, ugly, two toothed, crazy S.O.B. and a damn good pilot. Then again, you gotta be crazy to be a pilot."

"That's the one, all right."

"Ace, did you steal this plane?" "Me? Steal? No, Sir! Me and my copilot, Joe, here, just temporarily relocated an already designated and allocated Air Force asset."

Joe turned and smiled knowingly at Nick, who was leaning into the cockpit.

"You did steal this plane. Damn! Does this make me an accessory to a felony?"

Ace explained. "All I know is that you were never on this flight. Someone called and said to deliver this baby A.S.A.P., to Andrews to receive cargo. I don't know who got their wires crossed, but hey. These things happen."

Nick chuckled. "You're a common thief."

Ace corrected him. "Sir? A thief? Maybe. But' common? No way."

Ace and Joe then turned to flying their aircraft. Nick and Georgina settled into the canvas net sling seats, for the landing.

"Feet dry." Ace's voice came over the headset, once again.

Soon, they landed at Andrews Air Force Base, located near the shores of the Chesapeake Bay.

The Andrews air traffic control tower questioned the lack of a filed flight plan. Ace told them a priority security code of numbers and letters, on a secure radio frequency. The message indicated that there was no time for a flight plan before takeoff. He said he would explain after landing.

Ace pointed to the waiting helicopter outside the security hangar, where important planes and cargoes were handled behind closed doors. Nick, Georgina and Ace got off the aircraft. They exited the hanger through a pedestrian door as the huge rolling hangar door descended.

Stilwell met them outside the security reception hanger. Nick turned to Ace. "What are you going to tell them?"

"If anyone can confuse and confound these turkeys into submission, it's me."

Nick grinned. "You're up to a case of beer now, Captain."

"And I'm going to collect on it some day."

Stilwell's helicopter was revving up as Nick and Georgina said goodbye to Ace.

Nick greeted Stilwell, slapping him on the back. Nick talked loudly into Stilwell's ear to be heard over the thumping of the chopper engine warming up. "Thanks for the hop. This is my partner." He pointed to Georgina.

"Ma'am." Stilwell was an action man of few words. He motioned for them to get into the helicopter. Once airborne, Stilwell maneuvered around the restricted Washington Military District airspace, circumventing the Capitol and the White House. A few minutes later, they landed in Langley, Virginia at the Executive Research Air Park helipad. They thanked Stilwell, jumped out and walked toward the hangar. They crouched to avoid the chopper's blades as it took off.

It was now just two days before the conference was to begin. They approached the open hangar. Two young, beefy security guards contracted by the Department of Defense (DOD), came running out from their dark windowed office, adjacent to the hangar.

The bigger of the two athletic looking men called out.

"Excuse me! Stop where you are."

Nick noticed that they both slowed to a cautious walk. They also had their right hands on their sidearms, ready to draw and fire if needed.

"This is a restricted area. You're trespassing on private property."

Indeed they were. The Executive Research Air Park was a cover for a DOD counter terrorist strike team base. It was used to support the D.C. area, if the Federal Bureau of Investigation's Hostage Rescue Team needed assistance in handling a terrorist incident. It was primarily a Delta Force base. It was one of several used by that Joint Service Special Operations unit.

"I'm here to see John Stevens. He's the manager of this place."

One of the guards responded.

"Listen, pal. Nobody just lands here without authorization and asks to see people that may or may not work here. You two will have to come with us until we sort this out."

"Please. We don't have much time. It's very important that we see John. It's a matter of extreme urgency."

The bigger guard spoke.

"I don't care if you're the King of Siam, here to save the rain forests and ozone layer. You're not going anywhere until I figure out who the hell you are and why you dropped out of the sky expecting the red carpet treatment. Now you two just slowly walk this way."

Nick turned to plead with the other man. In doing so, his half-open leather jacket exposed the butt of his pistol. It was silhouetted against his light-colored sweater.

"But, It's urgent. I'm... ."

One of the guards noticed the weapon and shouted.

"He's got a gun!"

The guards quickly drew their weapons and pointed them at Nick and Georgina.

The bigger guard ordered them.

"Freeze! Don't be stupid. Do exactly as I tell you or you're dead."

"This is unnecessary, fellas. It's all a mistake. If you just get John, you'll see."

"You're the one who made the mistake, pal. Now, both of you, slowly put your hands behind your head. Interlock your fingers. Now slowly drop to your knees. That's it. Now don't move, or I'll shoot you."

Nick calmly spoke to them.

"Each of us has two weapons, one in the front waistband, one in the back. Just stay cool, guys."

The smaller guard circled around Nick, grabbed his interlocked fingers and leaned Nick back onto his knee. Off balance and controlled by the guard, Nick was frisked. His guns, passport and the list of names were confiscated. The smaller guard did the same to Georgina, covered by the other guard. They then handcuffed Nick and Georgina, behind their back, and made them lay face down on the cold pavement.

The big guard looked at Nick's fake passport.

"Gestaldt. German huh? What are two Germans with four guns, who speak perfect English, doing walking around a private airport in the good 'of U.S.A.?"

The other guard used his walkie talkie to summon the Langley Police Department.

Nick talked to both of them.

"I wish you wouldn't do that."

"I'll bet you do, Mr. Gestaldt, or whatever your name is."

"If you just let me make a phone call, I can clear up this misunderstanding."

The big guard responded. "You'll get your chance for a phone call, pal."

An hour later, Nick and Georgina had been booked into the local county jail.

Nick assured Georgina. "Don't worry. It won't be long."

A Detention Officer pulled Nick.

"This way, buddy."

The jailer led Nick, still in handcuffs, into a holding cell. Here, inmates wait to be processed. The jailer removed the cuffs and gestured for Nick to go in the cell.

This cell was luxurious compared to his last one. The walls were painted brick, chipped and covered with graffiti. It was fifteen by twenty-five feet deep. A short, three foot wall hid a stainless steel, communal commode. Bolted to the longer side walls were two metal benches that ran the length of the room. The outside bars looked like something out of the old west. The whole corridor was noisy and it smelled bad.

Sitting in his street clothes in the holding cell, an enormous, fat, bearded, biker with an Aryan Brotherhood prison tattoo tapped Nick on the shoulder. The other seven or eight men in the cell started to snicker.

The biker snarled at Nick. "I don't like the way you look, pretty boy."

"I'm sorry to hear that."

There were oohs, aahs and more snickers from the others.

"I think I'm going to rip your face off, pretty boy, smart ass."

Nick was sitting on the bench. "I don't think so."

He knew there would be no way to talk the biker out of a confrontation. He was spoiling for a fight. Nick quickly punched the biker's groin twice, causing him to double over in pain. Nick then bounced the biker's forehead off the metal bench, knocking him unconscious.

The obese man was on his knees in front of him, his eyes rolled back into his head. A red welt was forming over his nose. Nick pushed the bearded, bear-like face. The biker sprawled back onto the cell floor.

There were no snickers, just a surprised and respectful silence. Nick adjusted his position on the bench, rested his chin on his hands and resumed contemplating the jam he was in.

A jailer came to the cell door. "Gestaldt! Someone here to see you. Let's go."

The deputy saw the biker on the floor.

"What's the matter with him?"

Someone in the back spoke up.

"Too fat to sleep on the bench, I guess."

Snickers from the group were heard again. The deputy suspiciously looked at the group, then at Nick. "Let's go, Gestaldt. I don't got all day."

In a nearby interview room, a stocky man with dark, thick hair and a clean-shaven face met him. He wore a grey suit and introduced himself with government credentials. He was assigned to the Foreign Counterintelligence Squad of the Washington Metro Field Office of the FBI.

"My name is Alphonso Grovers. I am a Special Agent with the FBI. I'd like to ask you a few questions, if you don't mind."

"Not at all."

"Before I do, I need to advise you of your rights." Grovers recited the Miranda rights warning. "You have the right to remain silent. Anything you say... ." When Grovers was done, he asked Nick a question.

"Will you answer my questions?"

"If I can."

"O.K., I was interested when I got a call, that there were two Germans with handguns poking around the Air Park, Mr. …Gestaldt."

Grovers had to thumb through his notes to find the name.

He continued. "Just what were you doing there?"

"I can't tell you."

"Who dropped you off in the helicopter?" "Can't tell you."

"The security guards told me you asked for a John Stevens. Who is he?" "He's the manager of the Air Park."

"Well, how do you know him?"

"Can't tell you that either." Nick conversed with Grovers with a friendly smile on his face. Even though Grovers was an FBI agent with a TOP SECRET security clearance, he had no need to know about the Air Park or his activities. Nick had a legitimate reason for refusing to tell him much. It would be the release of classified information to an unauthorized person. If he did, he would commit a felony.

"You're not being particularly helpful, Mr. Gestaldt."

"Sorry."

"Your passport has no visa entry into the United States. You speak English like an American. Are you actually a German national?"

"Can I make a phone call now?"

"To where, the German Embassy?"

"To someone who can give you some answers."

Intrigued by Nick's last response, the FBI agent nodded.

"All right. But, I'll watch the numbers you dial."

"Fine with me."

In the next room, Grovers observed Nick dialing Manny's office number. Something about that number was vaguely familiar to Grovers.

"Hey. It's me."

Manny answered the phone.

"Jesus Christ! You O.K.? Where are you?"

"We're in the county jail closest to you."

"What?"

"And there's an FBI agent asking me a bunch of questions."

"I'll be there in a few minutes."

Manny hung up.

Nick turned to Grovers.

"He'll be here shortly."

"Who will?"

"The man who will answer your questions."

"There won't be any undue excitement will there?"

"No. No worries, mate."

"You know, your wife was worried about you. She told me all about why you were here. It's not too late to arrange some sort of deal."

"Nice try. She would have told you less than me."

Grovers looked at the list taken from Nick's impounded personal property. "What's that list of names, your contacts here?"

"Sure could go for a cup of coffee."

Grovers opened the door and had a jailer bring a cup of coffee. Five minutes quietly passed.

Grovers looked intently at Nick and tried a harsher tone of voice. "You know of course, that foreign nationals can be prosecuted for illegally entering the U.S. and carrying concealed, unregistered firearms, trespassing, let alone providing false information to a federal agent. I didn't see any diplomatic immunity passport, if that is your passport."

Nick agreed with him. "You're right. A guy in that position would be in a lot of trouble."

"And you're not? Or are you? What do you mean?"

Nick decided that it was best to remain quiet until Manny got there.

"I think I'll just sit and enjoy this jail house brew for a while." Nick took another leisurely sip of coffee.

After a minute or two had passed in silence, Grovers was about to say something else, when there was a knock at the door.

"Sir, there's a gentleman here to see you."

"Very well." Grovers left the room upset at having made so little progress. The jailer stepped inside the room to observe Nick in the agent's absence. Nick raised his cup and saluted the deputy. He continued to sip his coffee, occasionally smiling at his guard.

Manny presented his CIA credentials to Grovers. After Grovers inspected them, he presented his to Manny. They stepped away from the closest earshot and quietly talked. After a minute of spirited whispers, onlookers had decided that Special Agent Grovers had lost the argument. Grovers re-entered the interview room.

"You and your companion are free to go. Release them and their property deputy."

The guard questioned him. "But, Sir ... ,"

"Just release them, deputy! And delete all references to them from the computer."

"Yes, Sir." The deputy complied, wanting to ask more but wisely deciding not to.

As he walked out of the interview room, Nick offered his hand to Grovers.

"No hard feelings, Grovers. For your own good, forget me, forget my companion, forget the list, forget the number I dialed, forget you even got up this morning."

Alone in the room, Grovers shook his head and muttered to himself.

"Damn spooks. It's getting harder and harder to tell the good guys from the bad guys."

Once all three of them were in Manny's car driving to CIA headquarters, Manny questioned Nick.

"What the hell happened to you two? You had me scared half to death."

"Well, we went to the safe house that Mack gave us."

Manny interjected.

"But it wasn't clean. It was hot."

"Yeah. How did you know?"

"Those were St. James' own men. He sent them as a 'security' team."

"Wait a minute. The DCI's own men? What's going on here Manny? St. James running an operation within an operation?"

"I'm not sure yet. But after your initial debrief, you both have a required audience with him. Do either of you need medical attention? You both look a little worse for wear."

Georgina spoke first. "No. Nothing that can't wait."

Only now, did she once again remember the dull pain in her ankle.

Manny had to ask the obvious question. "How about the prize. Is it safe?"

Nick patted his interior coat pocket.

"Right, here."

Georgina offered a comment. "All this, just for a piece of paper?"

Manny responded to her. "I wish that's all it was."

They soon pulled into the back entrance of the CIA compound. They were stopped at two armed guard gates, where Manny had to produce his photo ID access card. Each time, a guard carefully checked Manny's appearance with the photo, verified the expiration date, noted the car license plate and time of entry.

Once inside the compound, he drove down a ramp into an underground garage. Again, he produced his ID to a guard, who verified he was on the garage access list. Manny inserted the ID card into the gate box. The magnetic strip on the back of the card contained half of the gate lock code. He punched the other half of the code on the numerical keypad. A bomb resistant door of concrete and steel slowly opened. It was six feet thick and could withstand a small nuclear explosion. They drove in and parked.

At the security office, they each placed their palm on a machine that determined the true identity of the person, based upon previous palm print records maintained in the CIA computer.

They were signed in and given color coded badges.

The guard explained. "These badges authorize you only to be on the floors that correspond to that particular color."

The actual number of floors in the building is classified.

At the yellow floor guard desk, they signed in yet again. They went to a comfortable conference room, where a team of highly cleared and compartmentalized specialists awaited.

Even though they all had TOP SECRET clearances, not all of them had access to the same sensitive programs. This compartmentalization helped maintain the secrecy of certain projects.

Nick remembered another CIA school lecture about compartmentalization. "The same principle applies in the construction of a submarine. If a leak sprang in one compartment, the men would seal off that room limiting the damage to the boat, preventing access to the others. In the case of the CIA, it is to keep others from learning about a specific project or case."

There were strategic debriefers and document exploitation, or

DOCEX, experts in the conference room. Nick produced the list. The DOCEX people immediately boxed the list and whisked it away for a quick, but careful analysis.

One DOCEX expert explained why the document was rushed away.

"Such precautions are necessary. Depending upon the sophistication employed, the list could be on regular paper, or on one that was chemically treated to ignite or destroy itself upon the flash of a photocopier. The ink might irrevocably disappear if exposed to certain weather or room conditions.

DOCEX is a complicated and technical science, much more than the mere translation of foreign text. What a tragedy it would be to have this document vanish before their eyes, after all the effort and lives it took to get it there. Nick kept his eyes on the box containing the list as it left the room.

Chapter Twenty

At the room's large oak table, two CIA debriefers sat across from Nick and Georgina. The debriefers produced detailed, classified maps of Egypt and Libya for reference.

One questioner introduced himself, then looked at Nick.

"O.K., Major. Let's start at the beginning, shall we?"

The initial mission debrief lasted about two hours. It covered the mission highlights from start to finish. There would be a series of follow-up sessions to fill in the details. All information would be compiled into an after action report, used to judge the mission's success and to determine the utility of the equipment, personnel and techniques used. Manny sat next to Nick the whole time.

Having heard the debrief, Manny was bothered by the coincidences that seemed to indicate that someone or some group was always one step ahead of Nick. Manny was particularly interested in Hussain's remark that Nick would be surprised to know who he actually worked for. Manny was uneasy as all three went to the red floor, to see the DCI.

His secretary spoke to them. "The Director will see you now."

They entered the office. St. James rose from his chair and walked in front of his desk to greet his guests of honor.

"Ah, welcome. Welcome home Nick and Georgina. I'm delighted that you made it back safe and sound. I'm so proud of you two. A fantastic job, fantastic. In honor of your skill and courage, I am awarding you two the American Intelligence Medal for the success of this most important mission."

Nick initially responded. "Thank you, Sir. We're overwhelmed."

"Nonsense. You did a damn good job. It's the least this country can do to show its gratitude."

Manny had never seen the DCI so thankful or complimentary.

St. James continued. "And the DOCEX boys said you caused quite a stir with the list you recovered."

"I couldn't have done it without Miss Matlock, Sir."

"Quite a team indeed." St. James beamed a smile at Georgina.

Manny suddenly realized that in the short time since Nick gave the analysts the list, St. James had already been briefed on it.

Manny thought to himself. "That's rather odd."

"You both have done a great service to your country and the cause of freedom. The President will be very pleased."

St. James told them with a hand on their shoulders.

Georgina was visibly impressed by the remark.

Nick responded to the DCI, "Another day, another dime, before taxes."

St. James burst out in laughter. "Hah, hah, hah. Very good. Hah, hah. You two take a few weeks off, after you're done with Mr. Martinez. You've earned it."

In stereo, Nick and Georgina simultaneously spoke. "Thank you, Sir."

Manny led them from the office.

St. James muttered to himself. "Before taxes, hah, hah, before taxes."

The three went back to the garage entrance. Manny had only Georgina surrender her building badge. A limousine was waiting.

Manny turned to Georgina. "I'm sending you to a nearby safe house in the Virginia suburbs. Get some rest and we'll continue the debrief tomorrow."

Nick nodded to her, indicating everything would be all right. The limousine drove her away out of the garage.

Nick looked at Manny, expecting to be sent home for a rest, but Manny was not ready to let him leave.

"We're not done yet. I told Hatim. Now I'll tell you. Something is very wrong with this whole set up."

"Hatim is his name, huh? What do you mean?"

"I gotta hunch. Follow me."

They went to the DOCEX document custodian.

Manny asked the clerk. A question. "Can I see the log book?"

He found that item 3014A, was the last item to be catalogued.

"It was entered and checked out all within seven minutes, with no copies having been made. Item 3014A is the list you brought back."

The DOCEX boys had done extensive tests on the document. They satisfied themselves that it would not be destroyed upon handling or inspection.

Nick looked at the custodian. "They were supposed to release it to the TOP SECRET catalogue room for temporary storage. Right?"

"Oh, yeah."

Manny then questioned the clerk. "When and where did item 3014A go?"

"Top Dog, eyes only. You just missed the messenger by thirty seconds."

"Nick, Top Dog, eyes only means it's an item to be seen only by the DCI. It's been checked out."

Manny glanced at the courier's initials and ID number in the log book. He spun the clerk's computer console around and furiously pecked his way into a restricted personnel file. He pulled up the ID of the messenger. A digitized photo of the young man appeared.

The clerk complained. "Hey. You can't do that with that work station."

"Sure. You can. I just did."

Nick and Manny raced to the stairs.

Manny exclaimed to Nick as they hurried. "We can still catch him."

They had to run up four flights of stairs.

"What for?"

They started jumping two steps at a time.

"You'll see."

Manny coughed. They exploded out of the stairwell, in front of the elevator. As they caught their breath, the elevator doors opened.

A fresh faced, young courier clerk stepped off the elevator and made for the DCI's office.

Manny stopped him. "Hey, Douglas, isn't it?"

"Why, yes Sir."

"Yeah. I thought it was you. The DOCEX supervisor pointed you out to me in the hallway the other day. He had a lot of fine things to say about you."

"He, he did, Sir?"

"Oh, yeah. He said he wants to keep you for promotion. Yes, Sir."

"He did?"

"Yeah. Say, what you doing up here in eagles land? Not trying to get a job transfer, I hope."

"No, Sir. A delivery for the Top Dog, I mean the Director, Sir."

"Really? I'm heading in there right now. I'll drop it off for you."

Manny threw the hook and line into the water.

"I don't know, Sir. It's eyes only." The fish nibbled at the bait.

"That's all right. His desk is only ten steps from here. There's no use in bothering him twice."

"You think it would be O.K., Sir?"

"Sure. Go on." Manny took the envelope from Douglas.

"Well, O.K., I guess. Thanks, Sir."

Manny reeled in his fish. "And keep up the good work."

He watched Douglas close the elevator doors.

"Come on."

They flew back down the stairs, one level to Manny's office floor. They went into his office.

"Close the door." Manny put on some surgical gloves and tore open the envelope. He kept surgical gloves in his desk.

"This keeps me from getting my fingerprints on any forged documents I might handle."

He took the list out and went to his personal copy machine. He made one photocopy, which he handed to Nick. He folded the list and put it into his pocket.

"Just a second."

Manny opened the copy machine door and pushed the numbered copy counter back one notch. He then quickly repackaged the list in another eyes only envelope and sealed it.

"O.K.. Vamos!"

Off they ran up the stairs again, to the DCI's office. As they arrived, they heard the secretary's speaker phone erupt.

"Where's that messenger? I sent for him minutes ago."

It was an irritated St. James.

Manny gave the envelope to her and whispered in her ear.

"I was talking to the guy at the elevator. I'm dropping it off for him."

Manny winked at the secretary. She responded on her speaker phone.

"It's just been delivered now, Sir. I'll bring it to you presently."

Manny pulled the single red rose out of the vase on her desk, handed it to her, smiled and left.

"Nick, Let's go back and check the DOCEX analysis. It might tell us something."

Nick instinctively patted his pocket, to make sure the copy was still there.

The secretary brought the envelope into St. James' office. When she left, St. James got up and locked the door. Walking back to his desk, he removed the list, read it over and smiled to himself. He picked up his telephone and dialed a long distance number.

"I have it." He hung up. He took a lighter from his desk and lit the paper on fire. In his garbage can, he watched the list of conspirators burn into oblivion.

When Manny and Nick got to the DOCEX desk clerk, there was a different man on duty than the one they had seen just a few minutes ago. It wasn't yet shift change.

Manny made a request of him. "The analysis on item 3014A, please."

He presented his building clearance ID as his authorization. The clerk looked at the log book for the storage number and shook his head. "Sorry. There is no 3014A yet. Maybe it's still in the shop."

"What?" He turned the log book around and looked for himself. The last item entered was 3013Z, checked in hours ago and not yet fully processed. Manny showed Nick. They looked at each other.

"O.K., thanks. I guess I'm a little early. I'll check with you later."

"O.K. chief." He snapped his chewing gum.

Walking away, Nick cautioned Manny. "Forget your car. Let's take the tunnel to the Air Park. We need to see John for a trusted, clean ride."

"Good idea."

Down they went in the elevator, an unspecified number of floors. Then, there was a "Bing." The doors opened.

They boarded a monorail, pushed an intercom button and instructed the driver. "Air Park."

Obediently, the futuristic vehicle picked up speed, passing other tunnels leading to other unknown destinations in the National Capitol region. After a few minutes, the monorail gradually slowed to a complete stop. Without saying anything, they exited the train through the hydraulically activated doors.

They walked through an underground passageway and got into another plain looking elevator. Up it went with a quiet hum, stopping with a slight jerk. The doors opened onto an office area, buzzing with noisy activity. Some people were in military uniform. Others were in civilian clothes, but obviously military. Still, others were unmistakably fat civilians.

Nick walked over to a glassed-in office and tapped on the window. The occupant was on the phone, but motioned them to come in. Manny and Nick heard the end of his phone conversation.

"O.K., O.K. But just get it there by tomorrow. O.K. Harry? Fine, Bye."

He dropped the phone down onto the receiver. The man in the office looked at Nick's obviously foreign clothes.

"Hi, guys. How the hell you doing? Hope your day's been better than mine. Been traveling, have we, Nick?"

"John Stevens? Manny Martinez. You old goat. Still in the federal express business, huh?"

"Yeah. Overnight delivery of mega firepower, when it absatively positutly has to be on target, by sunrise. I'll tell you. There's no lack of terrorists. And there certainly is no rest for the weary."

Manny chimed in. "What you need is a three hundred-pound Geisha with spiked shoes to run up and down your back. That will sure as hell relax ya."

"Hell, If I wanted that, I'd just call the Sec Def over and tell him to bring his golf cleats."

"Manny, I do believe he's talking about our illustrious Secretary of Defense."

Nick got to the point. "Old buddy, we need some clean wheels and some toys."

"Sure. Do you want to drive a Soviet Embassy staff car or a Lamborghini? One gets better gas mileage. Guess which one?"

Manny jokingly clarified their needs. "A rental, low miles, non-smoking, with an air bag and very strong seat belts."

Stevens was a high energy, type-A personality.

"I got just the ride for you. C'mon. You're gonna love this one. I love this one."

They meandered through a maze of partitioned, five foot high, office cubicles. They moved into a large airplane hanger.

Nick, Manny and Stevens passed by a bank of television sets tuned to news stations in eight countries. They were constantly monitored around the clock to keep abreast of fast breaking crises.

Just as they left the office area and entered the hangar, one of the televisions, always switched to an American, twenty four-hour news station, announced an hourly bulletin.

"Investigator's indicate that this morning's sinking of a Egyptian transport ship, the 'Isle de Paris', was caused by a boiler room explosion. The incident occurred in international waters about one hundred fifty miles north of Egypt. The ship was on its way to Greece when it went down in the Mediterranean. There were two survivors picked up by an Italian fishing boat. The Italian boat heard the ship's distress calls, just before it sank. Three bodies have been recovered, while twelve are still missing and presumed lost. In other news today, Georgia Senator …"

In the hangar, there was an executive's luxury jet, a King Air twin turbo prop, a helicopter and several cars parked against a wall. The spotless hanger floor was painted with a shiny, white enamel.

Stevens snatched a set of keys from a selection hanging on the wall. He tossed them to Manny. "It's the black one."

Manny grinned, because the only black car was a brand new, top of the line Corvette. It was sleek, shiny, with blackened windows, a cellular phone and every imaginable option.

"We'll take it."

Stevens described it for them. "It does zero to jail in four point five seconds. But don't speed. Tickets are expensive these days, if they can catch you. There's a B-bag of weapons and stuff in the storage compartment for fun and games."

Manny could not resist his temptation.

"I'll have her back by midnight, Mr. Cleaver."

"Yeah, yeah, yeah. I've heard that one before. 'Just a quick test drive around the block. I'll be right back in a jiffy. I promise.'"

Stevens watched as Manny drove Nick out of the hangar. As they pulled out onto the tarmac, Nick told him to stop. Nick rolled the window down.

"Those are the two guards that got me arrested today."

Nick waived Stevens over to his window.

The guards, were about to end their shift for the day. From a distance, they eyed the car with envy. They then focused on the passenger.

The big guard spoke to the other.

"Uh, oh. Our ass is grass. That's the guy we caught today. And he's talking to the boss."

The Corvette then peeled out, squealing its tires. Stevens threw his hands up with worry at the way they sped off. Then, he walked over to the guards. They braced themselves for the worst.

"I understand you tangled with that guy this morning."

The smaller guard swallowed hard, expecting the worst.

"Yes, Sir."

"He's a very important man and an old friend of mine."

"Yes, Sir. But ..."

Stevens held up his hand to silence them.

"He told me you did a damn fine job of keeping riff-raff like him out of here. He said that you two should be commended."

The guards blinked their eyes, wondering if they heard Stevens correctly.

"You both just earned a $1,000 bonus. Keep up the good work." Stevens smiled, turned and walked away.

The guards closed their eyes, then opened them, breathing a

sigh of relief. They grinned and punched each other's shoulders, like high school football players in a locker room celebration after the big win.

"Yes!"

Chapter Twenty One

Nick found a D.C. area blues station on the Corvette's surround sound stereo system. It was playing a hard driving song with a heavy rhythm guitar. "All right, B.B. King. Do it to me!" Nick shouted. Half dancing in his seat, he was really glad to be home.

Manny smiled and shook his head. His fingers tapped out the same rhythm on the steering wheel. Manny drove the car out of the Air Park and onto the outer beltway surrounding D.C.

Manny turned the radio down and blurted out his thoughts to Nick. "Nick, I think St. James is behind all of this."

"What? What are you talking about?"

"I know it sounds crazy. It's the only thing that fits."

"Wait. You are crazy. If you can't trust St. James, who can you trust?"

"You know as well as I do that the only people we trust are each other, us, not them. He's one of them. Sure, he's a career man. But there have been too many strange things with his fingerprints all over them."

"How do you figure?"

"Well, for one, he sticks his own watchers in the middle of my operation. Why? He knows that's dangerous. Two, from what you told me, I don't think the LIS knew what they were looking for. Why would the Libyan Army rescue you from LIS? If LIS didn't know what they were looking for, that means someone had to tell the Army. And that means someone told Hussain."

Nick looked at his longtime friend. "Are you saying that the Director of Central Intelligence is a spy for Libyan Army Intelligence? You're nuts!"

"Just hear me out on this one. You yourself told me that it seemed like someone was always one step ahead of you. No offense, but you made it through insurmountable odds. How? Only a few people even knew of the existence of this operation. St. James was thoroughly briefed on almost everything.

Third, an important document like the list suddenly vanishes without a trace and lands in his hands. Only minutes after it arrives. The log book is doctored and a new clerk takes over in the middle of a shift. It would take the DCI, or at least the DDO to pull that off on such short notice."

Manny made his way down the Rock Creek Parkway to enter the Capital Mall area.

Nick patiently listened. "Hmm. O.K. Granted, it doesn't look too good. But why? What's in it for him to let so many diplomats blow up in the world's face?"

"That I don't know, Nick. But I do know that someone ought to be told about this."

"That could be a death warrant, if not professional suicide."

"I know. Now, I've worked with Bart Rollings, the Assistant to the National Security Advisor. What do you say we give him a call and see if he can get us in to see his boss? Bart owes me."

As Manny pulled off the Parkway, he called Bart Rollings on the secure cellular car phone.

"Hey, Bart. It's Manny Martinez. Listen. I have an unusual favor to ask. I really, really need to speak with the boss."

"No problem. How's tomorrow at dinner?"

"Well, this is urgent. How about one hour?"

"An hour! Geez. I don't even know where he is."

"Can you find him? I'd sure appreciate it. This is close hold and time sensitive, Bart. We truly need to see him, like yesterday."

"I'll find him, Manny. I've known you a long time. You wouldn't ask this if it wasn't necessary. One hour, his office?"

"Thanks, Bart. You're doing a fine job. There's a big raise in this for you. Go ahead and take the rest of the day off. It's O.K. I'll sign for it."

"Ha, ha. Oh, yeah. You got a lot of pull around here."

"Hey, by the time they decipher my hieroglyphic handwriting, you'll be long retired."

They both laughed.

"Thanks much, Bart. Goodbye."

WASHINGTON, D.C.

The National Security Advisor is retired four-star General, Stanley Stadwick. He had been a Marine Corps officer for forty years. He distinguished himself in Korea and Vietnam, then took on his toughest opponent, the Pentagon bureaucracy. He had earned the reputation as a common sense conservative. Over the years he had become everyone's ally and everyone's nemesis. Through it all, he retained everyone's respect. He was also known for being able to make command decisions and to act on them, while most others wet their pants, wrestling with indecision.

Only five feet eight inches tall, Stadwick nonetheless emanated "General." At age sixty-four he still ran five miles per day. His bearing and lean physique made his civilian suit seem more like a starched and creased uniform.

Manny extended his hand to the National Security Advisor for the President.

"Thank you for seeing us on such short notice, General."

"Quite all right. I don't like the stuffed shirts at that get-together, anyway. To what do I owe this visit? My Latin-American travel brief isn't for two days. Has something come up?"

"Yes, Sir. Something has come up. But it's not about your travel brief. It's about another sensitive matter that is also supposed to happen in two days."

"Go on."

"First, I'd like to introduce my colleague. General Stadwick? Army Major Nicholas Dentworth. Nick is on loan to us from Special Operations Command. He's one of the best Special Operation Techniques men we have."

The General made it a point to get up. He shook Nick's hand.

"Major, you look a little beat up. Been messing with some of my Marines?"

"Pleased to meet you, Sir. But no, Sir. I learned to steer clear of the Marines and stay on their good side, ever since they took over hell. I need them to reserve a place for me when I finally retire."

The General grinned and let out a quiet chuckle.

Manny went on with a serious tone of voice. "Sir, you know enough about me to know I'm loyal and that I don't go off half cocked. I have information that leads me to believe that DCI St. James may somehow be compromised. And that a great disaster will occur in two days time unless we can get a handle on this."

The General calmly directed him. "And what is the basis of your concern, Mr. Martinez?"

"Sir, the Agency found out through a well placed, high-level source, that a group of Libyan Army and Intelligence Service hardliners are planning to explode a large bomb at the upcoming G-7 Conference."

"Yes, I'm familiar with the importance and attendees of this conference."

"We sent Major Dentworth to Tripoli several days ago to retrieve a list of the conspirators from our source. That's when things started to go haywire."

The intercom buzzed. "General, the Chief of Staff is on his way for your meeting in fifteen minutes."

Stadwick instructed his secretary. "Call him and cancel. Continue, Mr. Martinez."

Manny detailed his initial operational plan, after which Nick recounted the important parts of the mission. Stadwick listened carefully and patiently, asking a quick question now and then.

Manny concluded. "Sir, Perhaps now you can see the delicacy of our coming to you on this matter."

"I do. And what do you propose to do about this problem?"

"I suggest we quickly draw the players out into the open, to test my sad suspicion. We'd need your full support if it actually went down. We'd also need sharpshooters and clean up teams, to sanitize the whole affair. Most important, we'd have to keep all knowledge of this completely out of CIA channels."

Nick offered a comment. "Sir, I can provide the secure rifle team, if you wish."

The General leaned across the desk and looked intently at the two men. "Do you know what you're asking me to do? You want me to mount a sting operation against the head of the entire American intelligence community."

Nick answered for both of them. "Yes Sir. There's not enough time to gather the evidence needed to prove our case. By the time we did that, it would be too late. And a lot of people would be dead. There would surely be terrible, international repercussions. If we're wrong, nothing would come of this and the conference would be a success. You could have our hearts for breakfast. If we're right, you will have saved the world from the worst terrorist incident in history. The conference would be a success. You win both ways, General."

"Do you know what you'd be personally risking?"

Manny answered. "Yes, Sir. At least our careers, at most, our lives."

Stadwick paused then made a decision. "Tell me the details of your plan."

CIA HEADQUARTERS

St. James looked at Manny from across his desk.

"Yes, Mr. Martinez? You had something you just had to see me about?"

"Yes, Mr. Director. I just received a communication from a source of mine in Tunis. He's going to meet me at the Lincoln Memorial tomorrow at two o'clock p.m., to give me a second copy of the list that Dentworth got."

St. James blinked.

Manny continued. "But this one has a note about the time and location of the bomb."

With an undefinable edge in his voice, St. James queried Manny. "Don't you think that proper notification, based on Dentworth's list, would be sufficient to thwart the bomb?"

"Perhaps, but I can't call my source back. He's already on his way. As I see it, I'd better meet him. If I don't see him, he'll think something is terribly wrong. I don't know what he'd do. He could do something unpredictable with the list. He could give it to the media, the British, who knows? I'd rather control what happens to that information. What do you think, Sir?"

"Yes. That information must be controlled. We wouldn't want the publicity or panic on our hands. O.K., meet him. Take Dentworth. But keep me informed."

"Good idea, Sir. Thank you." Manny left the office.

St. James looked at his American flag and thought for a moment. He picked up the phone and dialed a long series of numbers.

The voice on the other end sounded like he just awoke from sleep. "Hello?"

"Have you ever wanted to fly on the Concorde?"

Chapter Twenty Two

CHEVY CHASE, MARYLAND

Manny looked at Nick.

"I think it was wise to stay here last night. Was the guest bed comfortable?"

"Terrific Manny, thanks. I was really wiped out."

"What about Georgina?"

"I'd prefer to leave her out of this. She can hold her own, believe me. But it's just unnecessary danger for her. I've already pushed the limit way too far. Besides, she needs to stay off that ankle for a while. We'll have plenty of help. Speaking of help, I need to call John, to verify our mission brief time. And, I need to call Bud."

"The phone is over there."

Manny looked at his lovely wife Lorena, hustling their daughter Letty out the door to catch the school bus at the last possible moment. It was the standard morning routine.

As the door closed behind her, Letty called out to Manny.

"See you later, Daddy."

Manny talked to the closed door. "See you, honey."

Lorena went into the bathroom to put the final touches on her makeup.

Nick dialed Bud Harlington's number. "Bud? This is Nick Dentworth. How are you today, Sir?"

"Great. Things go O.K. on that job?"

"Well, that's what I'm calling about. Are you on the STU III?"

Bud turned the secure phone key to the "on" position and answered. "Yes. I'll push."

Bud pushed the "secure" mode button causing the two phones to technically link up on a privately coded frequency.

"Go ahead."

"Bud, a little problem popped up where I need to get my claws on some SF teams this morning."

Bud waited for a moment for the characteristic, but slight, audio delay between the speakers. The voices were heard with a slight waiver.

"O.K., How many do you need?"

"About thirty, a prep, sniper, evac and counter surveillance team."

"Jesus Christ! What country are you attacking?"

"Funny you should ask that. Today, I'm wondering myself. Look, I know it's asking a lot on a short fuse. But it's really important that I use our people only. Do you think you can swing it, Sir?"

Bud thought for a moment then answered him. "Yeah, I can swing it."

"Terrific. And Colonel, I don't mean to sound cocky. But no one at all can catch wind of this."

"On whose authority is this based?"

"The National Security Advisor, himself. The paperwork is about to arrive at your door by special messenger."

"Good enough for me. Where and when?"

"Executive Air Park, Langley, zero nine-thirty hours."

"They'll be there if you provide the donuts."

Nick laughed. "Roger that. Thank you, Sir."

"No problem. Let me know how the girls do. Ciao."

Nick warmly thanked Bud again and bid him goodbye as they hung up. Nick then telephoned John Stevens and coordinated things with him.

Nick informed Manny when he was done. "All set. The brief is at 10:00 a.m. We'll have a prep, counter surveillance, sniper and evacuation team there."

"Good."

Lorena came back into the room and kissed Manny on the lips.

"Got to go dear. Whatever you boys are doing today, be careful. Our insurance policies aren't paid up yet."

"Or the house, or the cars, or Letty's braces."

Nick had to throw in his comment. "Or my World Series bet!"

Lorena hugged Nick, kissed Manny again and flew out the door to her Volvo warming up in the driveway.

Nick and Manny had some English muffins, jam and tea. About 9:00 a.m. they headed out to the Air Park.

This time Nick had no trouble gaining admittance to the facility. Inside, Nick went over to a computer and looked into a retinal scanner. The ocular device matched ten thousand points in Nick's eye, with his retinal records held at CIA.

The sophisticated computer also required the additional match of the voice that belonged to the eye print.

"Computer, on. Major Nicholas Dentworth, U.S. Army, voice print, Top Secret, Crypto clearance, verify."

The computer was a DPS-2 or Digital Photo Scenario-Model Two.

This was cutting edge technology that could provide digitally enhanced, clear photographs, video or virtual reality graphics of just about anywhere in the world. This giant computer had trillions of images stored in its memory. Combining the features, you could walk, run, drive or fly anywhere you wanted to, from your office or living room.

Given the parameters, the computer could show a customized route between any number of locations. It was linked to many other national intelligence, police and government computers.

The computer responded to Nick's voice print and command.

A sultry, female voice answered him.

"Access authorized. Good day, Major Dentworth. Awaiting your command."

Because of the voice, the computer program was called "Marylin." Nick looked at Manny.

"If only all women could say that."

"That comment is not recognized. Try again, Major."

Manny chuckled. Having been put in his place by the cyber woman, Nick got down to business.

"Marylin, route, Executive Air Park, Langley, Virginia to Lincoln Memorial, Washington, D.C.? Use most direct route. Include current weather, construction sites, area events, traffic conditions, for this afternoon, using auto transport. Virtual mode please, engage."

"Program ready, Major Dentworth."

"Thank you, Marylin."

"You're welcome, Major."

Nick turned to Manny. "Definitely faster than the prototype."

"Thank you, Major." Marylin was grateful.

Nick wanted to end their conversation, so he instructed the computer.

"Marylin, pause."

Nick picked up a pair of specially designed eyeglasses that when worn, displayed a virtual reality image. These glasses were named Virtual Reality Glasses or VRGs. They looked like stylish sun glasses. But, when viewing through them, you could move up, down, forward, back, turn around and see everything in a three hundred and sixty degree, three dimensional view . You could walk, run, start, stop or fly like Superman.

In the briefing room, Nick reviewed the room setting. He made sure each chair had a pair of the special glasses. He double checked the list of needed personnel and equipment.

John Stevens came into the room. "Everything squared away?"

"Yeah. Thanks for pulling this all together so quickly."

"No problem. We're here to serve. Ah. That's what I forgot, my coffee. Now, where did I put that mug?"

Stevens wandered back out toward his office.

By 9:55 a.m., all the necessary people had gathered.

Manny took Nick to the side. "I liked your 'save the world from the worst terrorist incident in history" remark. Nice touch. I think I saw that in a Peter Sellers movie."

"You liked that, huh? It sounded good at the time."

"Well, smooth talker, it's show time!"

Nick nodded and stepped up to the podium. Everyone was in their seats and murmuring amongst themselves.

"Quiet, please. Thank you. Good morning, ladies. Thanks for coming. I believe everyone here knows who I am. This briefing is TOP SECRET. We're not here and you're not hearing this. As a matter of fact, all of today's activities will never have happened. This operation is completely and plausibly denied. Understood? O.K., everyone. Put on your VRG's and we'll get started. Marylin, display destination, please.

This is the Lincoln Memorial. A meeting is going to take place here, around 1400 hours. Mr. Martinez here and I will be meeting with one of you. And that lucky person is going to give us this envelope containing a piece of paper."

Nick held up an envelope.

"We will be using trade craft, clandestine communication techniques for this meeting. We expect some uninvited guests to show up. They'll try and obtain this paper. We don't know who it will be. We do know that they will be extremely dangerous. You will be divided up into four teams: preparation, counter surveillance, snipers and evacuation. Marylin, run route from starting point."

The scenes seen by them all, showed Washington, D.C. area streets leading from the Air Park to the Memorial.

"This is the route Mr. Martinez and I will be taking to the Memorial. Once there, we'll make a 'drop and switch'. Hopefully it will be uneventful. We'll return here for the debrief. Prep team, you'll be leaving in a few minutes to scout out the area. Counter surveillance team, you'll have time to familiarize yourself with the route and its surroundings. There is a construction site as seen right here. Marylin, freeze image. Here's a construction site, last updated ten minutes ago. Traffic is a little congested there. So, we'll want to go one block south of there. Marylin, continue. There are several vantage points. Marylin, continue route.

Snipers, You'll be positioned at these locations around the Memorial."

Nick used a digital pointer to identify the sniper positions. Marylin depicted the spots with blinking red lights.

"Remember, there will be innocent bystanders all around. Only hit the known threats. We don't know who they'll be but you'll be able to see us with your scopes and hear us. We'll be wired with a listening device. We'll also be armed. Should the need arise and if we're lucky and have time, we'll be pointing our guns at the bad guys.

Evac team, you'll have to be quick. You'll take this route. As you can see, it's a quick getaway, around the back of the Memorial. If things go to hell, we won't have much time before the cops arrive on the scene. All those that need them will have a headset. The left ear will be the tactical frequency, the right ear will be our conversation. Both are secure channels. We'll be handing out your team packets and splitting you up into your sub groups. Are there any questions?"

A man from the evac team raised his hand and spoke.

"What would you like done with any prisoners or injured?"

Manny interjected his comment. "Don't let them die, or let them kill themselves. They may have a cyanide pin prick, or poisoned tooth. Yeah, it's old, simple, but effective. We'll want to talk to them. Take them to the Alexandria safe house seen here at the end of the route tape."

Nick again asked those gathered. "Any other questions? Good. Then we'll pass out the packets. Listen up for your team designation. And gentlemen? This is an extremely important mission. Aren't they all? Be aware, alert and safe. Good luck to everyone. That will be all. Marylin? Stop program."

They all took off the VRGs. The tactical team Commander stepped up and called out the name and team designations. The men separated into their groups. They went over their tasks, checked and double checked their weapons and equipment. Before long, the preparation scout team was ready to go.

Manny turned to Nick. "You know, here we are swimming Salmon against the stream again. And the waterfall is just ahead."

"Yeah. I just wonder whether we're swimming toward quiet waters or a curtain of fish hooks."

Manny, Nick and the soldier who would give them the envelope went over their planned actions. Then they sat and waited. Then, they waited some more. This was always the worst time before a mission. You are prepared, ready and anxious to go. As soon as you start, you forget all of your doubts and fears. You just do it right.

Nick and Bud had brought together the country's most skilled specialists. They were his kind, people he literally trusted with his life. They were experienced Special Forces urban intelligence operatives. They were totally dedicated to accomplishing the impossible, pushing themselves further and doing their jobs with exacting precision. Manny and Nick wired themselves with the microphones and prepared to leave.

SAFE HOUSE, MACLEAN, VIRGINIA

Georgina wondered why it was taking so long to get the follow-up debriefs going. She spent all morning waiting for someone to come and get her. She had already wasted half of the day. Her mind was full of things to say, situations to retell. She wanted to get on with it and get it over with.

Her hosts at the safe house had taken very good care of her and were as gracious as they were discreet. Only the guards posted in and around the house reminded her that this was no ordinary bed and breakfast.

About twelve-thirty p.m., one of the guards knocked, poked his head into the drawing room. "Ma'am, We got the word. A car has been sent for you."

"Thank you."

A few minutes later, the same man knocked and entered. "Time to go, Ma'am."

Georgina was escorted through the lavishly furnished Tudor style house and out onto the gravel driveway. A black limousine, with dark windows pulled to a stop. An American luxury sedan with two guards was behind it. A guard from the limousine opened the door for Georgina to get in. In the back seat, she sat next to a man who smiled and nodded at her. The car door was closed.

There was a dark glass partition dividing the driver's compartment from the roomy back seat.

Georgina commented to her muscular riding companion. "Taxpayer money paying for this, huh?"

The man silently smiled and nodded. They drove on.

The glass partition slowly lowered with an electric whirring sound. The man in the front passenger seat turned to meet Georgina.

"What a pleasant surprise to see you again, Miss Matlock."

Georgina shouted in disbelief. "Hussain!"

Frightened and shocked, she lunged for the door handle, throwing her shoulder against the window. Leaping out of a speeding car was preferable to being with Hussain. The door wouldn't budge.

"It's useless, Miss Matlock. The door can only be opened from the outside."

Hussain now trained a pistol on her. Her riding companion also had a gun pointed at her. He was not smiling now.

In crisply articulated English, Hussain confidently explained her position. "This time, there will be no escape, no miraculous rescuers. Miss Matlock, please sit back and enjoy the ride."

His satisfied chuckle abruptly stopped in silence, as the glass partition rose to the fully closed position.

Chapter Twenty Three

WASHINGTON, D.C.

As they drove toward the Lincoln Memorial, Manny listened to the tactical frequency on the portable radio headset. The counter surveillance team reported no signs of surveillance of Nick and Manny in the Corvette. Nick parked on a side street just off the Capitol mall, a few blocks from the Memorial. They put coins in the parking meter.

Nick and Manny walked passed the Washington Monument. The stark, white obelisk beautifully contrasted with the clear, blue sky. They continued across a grassy area, next to the Reflecting Pool. The grass was a healthy, dark green color. They stopped out of ear shot of the nearest person.

In a conversational tone and normal voice level, Manny talked to the sharpshooter team.

"Everyone in place and ready? Testing to see if you can hear my question."

The microphone strapped to his body worked perfectly.

On the headset, Manny heard each of the four marksmen respond.

"Ready, one."

"Ready, two."

"Ready, three"

"Ready, four. Heard you loud and clear."

Nick asked the teams a question to test his equipment.

"Can you hear me as well?"

Manny was listening on the headset and nodded "yes" to Nick. Nick then gave the green light.

"Go."

This meant the operation is now in progress as planned. They continued to walk along the Reflecting Pool. Nick and Manny looked hard at each person or couple that passed them, in the opposite direction. They searched for anything giving them away or indicating "threat."

Manny remarked to Nick.

"Everyone and everything seems normal, so far."

They got to the foot of the steps that led to the larger-than-life statue of the seated President. Nick glanced at his watch. It was exactly 1:55 p.m.. There were several tourists and sightseers sprinkled on the long ascension of steps.

"Well, Manny here we go."

Slowly, Nick and Manny climbed the stairs, one by one.

By the time they had reached the top, they had heard five languages being spoken: Japanese, German, French, Arabic and yes, even English. The magnetism of American history draws people from around the world. Nick's thoughts drifted for only the briefest of moments.

"If only more Americans would rediscover the wisdom of Abraham Lincoln's teachings, like these foreigners have, this country would be in a lot better shape."

Gathered around the base of the impressive statue was a uniformed cub scout troop from neighboring Maryland. Their necks were arched back in awe of the silently powerful figure before them. Around them was a mixture of people of different colors and nationalities. All of them were there for the same reason. All gazed at the sorrowful eyes, enigmatic smile and curious expression of the man known the world over as one of the fathers of freedom.

With a tourist map and guide book in hand as props, Manny raised the camera hung around his neck and snapped a photo. A half dozen people jockeyed and swapped positions to get a snapshot of themselves with the famous President. Nick was casually glancing around to see if anything was out of the ordinary.

After about two minutes of admiring the statue, Nick looked at his watch. It was four after two.

A man with a cultivated British accent stopped next to Manny.

"A marvelous statue isn't it?"

"It sure is."

"Nothing like this in Northampton, except of course for the likeness of Churchill's Steel Minister, Lord Applebury."

"He was an amazing man."

"Lord Applebury?"

"No. President Lincoln."

"Quite, quite. Um, excuse me, but would you please take my photo? I would very much appreciate it."

"Sure."

He took the Englishman's camera and focused it. "How's this?"

The Englishman smiled.

"Looks great."

Manny clicked the shutter.

"Splendid! The folks back home will love it."

The man shifted the weight of his camera case. It had maps and tour tickets bulging from it.

The Englishman was actually the Green Beret soldier sent to meet and pass them the envelope. He had arrived there, after making his own way through the city. The Englishman reached to retrieve his camera from Manny. He fumbled the bag, almost dropping the camera. In the process, he "accidentally" dumped the contents of his camera case and knocked the tour map and book from Manny's hand. It all spilled together in a cluttered pile, onto the cold, marble floor.

"I'm terribly sorry. How clumsy of me." The Englishman apologized.

"No harm done. It's all right."

As the Englishman picked up Manny's tour guide, he deceptively inserted the envelope containing the list, with a slight of hand. He gave them both to Manny. The Englishman collected the last of his things.

"I'm dreadfully sorry. It's a wonder I didn't drop my camera. Many thanks again for the photo."

He then walked over to the wall where Lincoln's inaugural address was inscribed.

Nick and Manny turned to make their descent down the steps. There, at the top of the stairs, they suddenly found themselves face to face with Colonel Hussain dressed in a long tan raincoat. He was closely clutching, an obviously stressed, Georgina. On Hussain's right and a couple of steps down, was the muscular guard that sat next to Georgina in the limousine.

On Hussain's left, to the other side of Georgina, was the "cleaning woman" from the Cairo airport. She was one of Ali's assassins.

Hussain whispered while smiling. "How good to see you again, Major Dentworth."

He then spoke in a louder, more threatening voice. "Don't be foolish, or I'll blow her heart out."

As he said this, he pushed the barrel of his hidden gun, into Georgina's ribs, causing her to wince in pain.

Standing at the entrance of the Memorial, Manny and Nick realized that only two of the four marksmen could see them. They could not shoot yet because their view was partially blocked by the gigantic white marble columns. Standing behind Nick and Manny, were the tourists, the cub scouts and other sightseers. Any shot would be too risky.

"Let the girl go, Hussain. Her long, blonde hair doesn't have to be hurt."

Nick said these words to try and communicate to the snipers, that the girl with blonde hair, Georgina, was an innocent and not to be shot.

Hussain raised an eyebrow at Nick, trying to decide if his English was less than perfect, or whether Nick's words had some other significance. He opted for the prior.

"I saw the switch. She doesn't have to die, if you give me the list."

"Let her go and I'll give you the list. It's right here."

He said this as he started to reach inside his jacket pocket.

"Ah! Ah! Move one millimeter and she dies, having a terrible fall down these steps. You think I'm a fool? You don't have the list. He does. Mr. Martinez isn't it? Give me the list now, or I pull the trigger. Gentlemen, you know I will."

Nick nodded to Manny, who carefully pulled the envelope from his coat. He extended it to Hussain.

"No. Open it."

Manny did so and handed the paper to the Libyan Colonel.

Keeping the gun at Georgina's ribs, he quickly glanced at the list. He saw names, a time and a place noted.

Hussain ordered the American agents. "Now slowly, ever so slowly, walk down and around in front of me, with your hands at your side. We're going to take a little sightseeing tour together."

Nick and Manny did as they were told. At that moment, Hussain had the drop on them. They looked at the other two Libyans with their hidden guns pointing out through their coat pockets. They wanted to direct them away from the innocent visitors.

They slowly walked down the steps. A small group of chattering tourists happened to walk with them on either side, thus shielding them from the snipers. The sharpshooters followed them with the cross hairs of their rifle scopes.

Nick thought to himself.

"Don't shoot! Not yet!"

He trusted the marksmen's judgment.

No bullets came.

At the bottom of the steps, they crossed the street together with the tourists. Then the chatting sightseers split off in different directions. Hussain was limping, still hurting from Nick's kick to the knee the other day.

An English accent from behind was heard. "Excuse me, but did you drop?"

The accompanying Libyan gunman pulled out his weapon, spun and fired. The bullet struck the American soldier in the left eye, far from the protection of his bullet proof vest, hidden under his shirt. His quick thinking effort was an attempt to distract Hussain and his two assassins. He bought crucial time to give the snipers a better shot. The Green Beret sealed his own death warrant.

At the same time, Georgina pushed away from Hussain, diving for the pavement. The cleaning lady turned to fire at Nick.

Nick was faster. He shot her two times, once in the chest and once in the throat as she stumbled. Two sniper shots finished her off.

Manny was not as fast, but was moving. The Libyan gunman, that shot the soldier, hit Manny twice. He got hit once in the arm and once in the side, just above the belt line.

As soon as the Libyan man had squeezed off his second round, he was blasted three times by distant sniper fire. He was hit twice in the head and once in the chest.

In the split second of confusion, Hussain had turned to fire at Nick. He was instantaneously killed by Nick. Two quick shots went through his forehead. His eyes were wide open in astonishment. The surprised look on his face lasted only a moment. His limp body crumpled over the short retaining wall and into the Reflecting Pool. The large waves dramatically rippled the famous, glassy surface that gave rise to its name. Unfortunately, there would be no one left to interrogate. All of the combatants used silencers on their weapons to dampen the sound of any gun shots.

Nick then leaped to Georgina's side. She was unhurt except for a few bruises.

A groan from behind him said Manny had not fared so well. Nick ran over to him.

"Are you hit bad?"

"Bad." Manny was lying on his back. Nick applied pressure to his side wound as Georgina did the same to his arm.

Everything had happened so fast. Although the sniper's bullets were unheard, the silenced "splats" of the close-quarters gun battle were only now catching the attention of a passing female pedestrian. She shrieked at the fallen bodies and the pools of blood that were quickly spreading wider and wider.

Nick impatiently gritted out a curse.

"Where are they, dammit?"

No sooner had he said it than on the scene came two ambulances, with sirens blaring. They screeched to a halt.

The doors burst opened. Six men in Emergency Medical Technician uniforms, jumped out and quickly collected the bodies. Two men carefully put Manny on a stretcher, then into one of the ambulances. One retrieved Hussain's floating body, or what was left of it. A couple of guys threw him into the other ambulance, with the other corpses. Yet another man collected all the shell casings that had been expended at the scene. Nick and Georgina jumped in with Manny.

The ambulances raced off, sirens wailing, leaving only a few pools of blood.

The fight had lasted only a few seconds. The recovery took fifty. About a minute later, a crowd had gathered and was gossiping amongst each other. The first D.C. Police car stopped to see what all the fuss was about.

As the ambulances flew through the streets, Nick comforted Manny. His wounded friend, received the very best emergency treatment by the Green Beret trauma doctor.

As Manny lost consciousness, he heard Nick talking to him.

"Hang in there, Manny. You can't get out of your bets that easy. Besides, Lorena would kick our butts." As blackness descended upon him, Manny kept hearing the echo of "Lorena, Lorena, Lorena."

CIA HEADQUARTERS

St. James sat at his DCI desk, thinking to himself.

"One way or the other, the deed must be done by now."

The conflict inside him intensified as he wrestled with the justification in his mind. It was as if he was trying to convince himself, that what he had done was right.

"In my heart of hearts I know, I know damn well, that the Arab-Israeli peace initiative is just a clever ploy to lure the West into letting its guard down."

St. James had a complicated and convoluted perspective on political realities in the Middle East.

"Peace between the Arabs and Jews is the largest deception operation in history. This G-7 Conference is the perfect vehicle to further play out their act. They will surely and quietly draw power from the West's appeasement. Then they'll spring the trap, catching us unaware and impotent to the Arab's control over oil sales and regional power.

But in order for us to keep their power in check, we need to maintain the tension between Arabs and Israelis. So, that bomb must go off. The peace process must be crushed!"

For St. James, the extremists behind the bomb plot, have been his life long, arch enemies. He needed them to remain as enemies, for his world to stay together.

He needs to deal with the known enemy, the monolithic Arab block. He needs one he could battle spy for spy, wit for wit, life for life.

He suddenly spoke aloud.

"By God, I'll show them that what I have been preaching all these years is true! One way or another, I will be vindicated!"

It was for this reason that he paid particular attention to the Daphne information.

St. James' office door opened. Four muscular men in suits entered and walked over to him at his desk. Two of the men wore black shouldered bags containing machine guns and drugs to render him unconsciousness if necessary.

One of the men spoke to him.

"Sir, you are to quietly come with us by order of the President of the United States. If you resist, we will take you by force."

St. James' face turned pale. He instantly realized that the meeting at the Lincoln Memorial must have gone terribly wrong. He calmly rose to his feet. He noticed that his legs were a little wobbly. He straightened his suit coat and turned to the men with a confident bearing. "Very well, gentlemen."

The men escorted him on all four sides. As they moved out of his office, they passed his secretary.

"Sir, what's happening?"

Another guard who had been watching the secretary fell in behind the others.

St. James looked back over his shoulder and spoke to her.

"Don't worry. I'm not yet done here."

TRIPOLI, LIBYA

Hussain's Commanding General, the one who had him followed and one other member of the conspiratorial group had just returned from an official function. The phone was ringing at the General's luxury home, as they came through the door.

The General was irritated by the incessant ringing.

"You see, my friend, this is why we fly falcons, to get away from the phone."

Disgusted, he yanked the phone off the hook to silence the loud ringing and squawked at the caller. "Yes!"

It was the tall, dark man, assigned by the commanding General to follow Hussain.

He filled the General in. "I followed him since before the Americans escaped from Tripoli. They went to Cairo. On one occasion, Hussain made a long distance call, probably international, with a security code. He dialed more than eighteen numbers.

This was Hussain's call to his contact informing him of the escape and that they had disappeared into the Tripoli streets. I saw Hussain travel to Cairo. Then, he got on the Concorde to Washington, D.C. I just had time to have "an associate" in Washington follow the Colonel in his travels throughout the D.C. area. I caught the first available flight.

It was only as Hussain arrived at the Lincoln Memorial that I visually reacquired him. I saw the whole thing happen before my eyes. Hussain descended the steps. He was embroiled in a gun battle. He and his guards were killed. Realizing that I could not follow the speeding ambulances that carried him away, I decided to notify you, General."

"Thank you."

The General then slowly and deliberately hung up the phone. He reflected on what he had just been told.

He turned to his co-conspirator. "Well, my friend, it looks as though we're going to be taking an unexpectedly long vacation this year. Grab your things. We must leave instantly."

The other man worried. "Why? Go where? What has happened?"

"There's not a moment to lose. I'll explain it on the way."

Chapter Twenty Four

WASHINGTON, D.C.

Two hours after the gun battle, Nick found himself once again in front of the National Security Advisor.

"Please sit down, Nick. May I call you Nick?"

"Yes. Of course, Sir."

"First of all, how is Manny?"

"I don't know, Sir. When I left him, he was in critical condition. The bullet seems to have damaged some internal organs."

A caring question came from Stadwick. "All arrangements adequate?"

"Yes, Sir. He was admitted to the VIP wing at Walter Reed Hospital as a patient with an ulcerating spleen. A special team of doctors are tending to him."

"Good. Now how are you?"

"Fine, thank you."

"Well, fortunately, or unfortunately your plan worked. Too bad that all were killed, especially Hussain. I would like to have had a chat with him. But, that leaves us with two issues. One, how to best forestall the bombing. Two, what to do about St.James. Is there any other way at all that the Libyan could have found you?"

"None, Sir. I was totally clean. And the only one we told was St. James."

"I reviewed the names on that list. I know all but a couple of them. DIA is pulling up their biographies as we speak. A few of the names surprised me. I'm going to ask the President to contact the Egyptian President directly about this matter. He can choose to do with it what he will. I'll be briefing the President in one hour. You'll be there to answer any questions that arise."

Nick rather nervously looked at the General. "Me? Sir? But I …"

"Cork it, Nick. There's no one else who knows what the hell's going on. I'll take responsibility for today's actions. But you'll need to fill in the blanks."

"Yes, General."

"Don't look so glum, Nick. He puts his pants on each day the same way you and I do. And he even flips the seat up. When this is over, you're going to take a much needed vacation with Georgina, was it?"

The General almost had a photographic memory. He feigned to falter on mnemonic details.

"Yes, Sir. Georgina Matlock."

"And where is she?"

"She's with Manny."

THE WHITE HOUSE

"Mr. President, I'd like to introduce Major Nicholas Dentworth, Army Special Forces."

The amiable President Terrance Carlton extended his hand.

"Major.".

Nick shook hands with him. "It's an honor to meet you, Mr. President."

He had a firm grip. Nick noticed that the President had many wrinkles, more than he remembered seeing on television. The heavy burden of world responsibility had taken its toll. Yet, the gentle businessman had risen to the demands of the highest office in the land, without losing his enthusiasm and public appeal. His wavy, white hair and tired eyes made him look much older than Stadwick, even though they were just a few months apart.

Stadwick started.

"Mr. President, we've come to inform you of a grave and urgent matter. Major Dentworth has just successfully completed a complex mission that indicates CIA Director St. James has been compromised, or is otherwise cooperating with Libyan Military Intelligence."

President Carlton looked shocked and fixed his stare on the National Security Advisor. He didn't say anything. He let Stadwick talk.

"It gets worse. The mission Major Dentworth just completed was the recovery of a document from Tripoli. It lists the names of a secret group of hard line, high level LIS and Army Intelligence officials. They plan to detonate a powerful bomb at tomorrow's G-7 Economic Conference. Yes, Sir, the same conference you'll be leaving for in a few hours. They would blame extremist Zionist groups, opposed to any compromise with the Arabs. They'd use the incident as an excuse as to why they can't trust the Jews. They'd reassert their control claiming security reasons."

President Carlton looked stunned, then slightly irritated. He demanded an answer from Stadwick. "Why wasn't I told about this sooner, Stan?"

"That's a damn good question, Sir. Apparently for unknown reasons, St. James took it upon himself to micro manage Major Dentworth's operation. And shortly after it arrived at CIA, the original list disappeared under mysterious circumstances. One more thing, Sir. On my authority, four hours ago, I ran a disinformation operation against St. James, here in D.C."

The President excitedly barked at his National Security advisor. "Christ, Stan! You did this without even telling me? This is not good." "Mr. President, I wanted to give St. James the benefit of the doubt. I needed to be sure, before I alarmed you."

"So what happened today? Did he defect to the Libyan Embassy, or what?"

"Worse."

The President rolled his eyes. "Worse. Great. Lay it on me, Stan."

"Major Dentworth's case officer, Manny Martinez, told only St. James that he had been contacted by another source who would provide an additional copy of the list. The meeting was at two p.m. today, at the Lincoln Memorial."

The President asked a question for clarification purposes.

"Did you say the list disappeared?"

"Yes, Sir. But the case officer was suspicious enough to copy it first."

"O.K.. Go on."

The President was holding his head in his hands, rubbing his temples.

"The meeting took place between us and us. That is, we had Major Dentworth meet with one of our own agents who acted as a foreign informant with the copy of the list. They were met by a Libyan Army Intelligence Colonel and two shooters. The final tally was all three Libyans and one U.S. Army Captain dead. The case officer Manny

Martinez is at Walter Reed in critical condition with gunshot wounds. Everything was done outside Agency channels for obvious reasons."

Nick was happy to keep his mouth shut and to let the General take the heat.

The exasperated Carlton shouted. "God, damn! My chief intelligence officer is a spy for the Libyans! We have the shootout at the O.K. Corral on the steps of the Lincoln Memorial! Damn! Am I going to see this on the news tonight, Stan?"

"No, Sir. I took the liberty of sanitizing the whole affair. I don't want to bore you with the details."

Carlton's flashing eyes implored Stadwick. "Bore me, Stan. From the beginning. Bore me."

Nick spoke up. "Mr. President, perhaps I should preface the General's comments with a quick review of my mission."

"Proceed, Major."

President Carlton impatiently waved him to begin.

Nick retold the events of the last several days, skipping over the things the President said he did not want to know. Stadwick then laid out his operation, paying particular attention to the cover up of the shooting incident.

By the time Stadwick had finished, Carlton had become perceptibly more calm. Now that he had the complete picture, Carlton closed his eyes and recited a remembered passage.

"Good God. 'Alas, he is betrayed. And I, undone.'"

This line was from Shakespeare's "Othello," where the decision to act upon betrayal could no longer be delayed.

The General offered a thought. "Mr. President, I suggest, you call the Egyptian President. His name is not on the list. He is one of the intended victims." The President looked directly at Nick.

"What do you think, Major?"

Nick answered his Commander in Chief. "Mr. President, I believe that if this bombing is not stopped, the Middle East peace process will be stopped cold in its tracks, perhaps forever. I agree with the General."

The President thought for a moment. He looked at Stadwick, then at Nick. He reached over and picked up the red phone.

"Get me Cairo."

TRIPOLI, LIBYA

It was now the day of the conference in Cairo. Within hours of President Carlton's phone call, all but two of the Libyan officials had been exposed. The two escapees, the commanding General, that had Hussain followed and his falcon flying friend, were lucky. They caught wind of the impending detentions. They quickly fled, ostensibly "taking an extended holiday." They left no forwarding address.

Although their lives of privilege were ruined in Libya, they were able to escape. Many, if not all of the others would probably be shot by Quadaffi, not for the heinous bomb plot, but for bungling the plot and embarrassing him. The price of such a grand failure was death or imprisonment for life. That would be the case, if Quadaffi liked or was related to someone.

The General and his friend disappeared into thin air by adopting a completely different identity. His false person was meticulously maintained over the years by the General for just this sort of emergency. It would give him enough breathing room, to allow him to start a new life, somewhere else in the world.

But there was still one nagging question for them all.

"Who was the traitor among the conspirators?"

The Libyan General swore to himself. "If the traitor lived, I will make him pay and pay dearly."

The more he thought about it the angrier he became. Being a firm believer in vengeance, the General began to plan his revenge against those that ruined his distinguished life in his native country.

Thanks to some quick thinking by Samuel Gibbons, one other conspirator escaped. Daphne was "kidnaped" and spirited out of the Libyan capital, to live a new life as someone else in America. The other conspirators would naturally think that one of the three escapees betrayed them.

The whereabouts of the bomb and those preparing it was soon discovered. The plan called for the positioning of four tractor trailers full of several kilotons of directional, high explosives. One trailer was to park at each corner of the main conference hall. They were to be there for "security." They would simultaneously explode by using a very sophisticated electronic detonator, developed by the CIA, stolen by the Russian KGB and given by them, to the LIS. If exploded, the blast would have leveled half the block, reducing the conference hall, its dignitaries and a regional peace to a mass of rubble and death.

Chapter Twenty Five

Nick and Bud Harlington entered Manny's hospital room and took Lorena aside.

"How's the old man?"

In a whispered voice, so as not to wake Manny, Lorena answered. "The doctor said he's out of danger for now. But they're not sure how long they'll have to keep him here for observation. Maybe six weeks."

"It'll be a cold day in hell, when I stay in a hospital for six weeks."

Lorena rushed to his side. It was the first time he had regained consciousness, since his arrival at the hospital.

"Mi Manuel!" She bent over and kissed his face, trying to keep her composure. Manny whispered something to her in Spanish and ran his fingers along the path of one of her tears, then put his finger to his lips.

He whispered little louder to her. "No more tears."

Manny looked up at Nick. "I'm not that much older than you, pal. And we're both saplings compared to that antique dinosaur standing next to you."

Bud scowled and grinned at the same time.

Nick taunted him.

"Oh yeah? Looks like you're getting slow in your old age to me.

You'll do anything to get out of doing the chores around the house."

Manny tried to laugh, but painfully coughed instead. Nick looked at his close friend and cringed at all the tubes and devices attached to him to sustain and monitor his vital signs.

After a few moments of silence, Nick tossed a Washington, D.C. newspaper to Manny.

"You made the papers, Mister media hound."

Bud joked with Nick, loud enough for Manny to hear. "He's always loved the limelight."

Nick agreed. "Just has to be the center of attention, or he'll throw a temper tantrum."

Lorena held the paper up for Manny to see.

The front page headline read, "EGYPT UNCOVERS CONFERENCE BOMB PLOT."

The subtitle of the article was, "Several Libyan fundamentalists arrested as peace destroying bomb plotters." The article detailed how the conference had gotten off to a good start.

Manny offered a comment on Egypt getting the credit.

"Doesn't surprise me. Sometimes I wonder who I really work for."

Bud urged him. "Read on, read on."

The second biggest column showed, "CIA CHIEF RESIGNS, CITES HEALTH AND POLICY DIFFERENCES WITH WHITE HOUSE."

Nick laughed. "That's the understatement of the year. Gibbons has been appointed as interim DCI, until the Senate confirmation hearings can get underway to make it official."

Manny smiled.

Bud sarcastically added his two cents worth. "Hell, in this town, we're lucky they didn't promote the S.O.B. They could never expose what really happened. It would be too politically damaging."

Nick looked to Lorena. "I give him three days until he starts pinching the nurses; one week before he's running the place."

She gave Manny a stern look. "Oh, no he's not! I've already seen to it that his nurses will be big, ugly, hairy, men, with their knuckles dragging on the ground."

Nick cheerfully laughed. "Nothing like a little motivation to get well, eh, Manny?"

Manny solemnly answered him. "I think it's going to be worse at home."

Nick laughed again. He was truly happy to see Manny alive and in good spirits.

"Ha! Well, we'll leave you two lovebirds alone. Georgina and I are taking a little time off. The Florida Keys sound nice this time of year. Get well, my friend. Oh, I almost forgot. Here's that collection of Howlin' Wolf's Greatest Blues Hits. Lorena, take care of him. He still owes me money."

Nick flipped a compact disc onto the foot of Manny's hospital bed, waved goodbye and headed out the door. Bud smiled, then went with him. He stopped, turned and around to Manny.

"Martinez, I want a complete report on this screw up, on my desk in the morning. No wimpy excuses, this time."

Manny painfully pulled himself up to a sitting position, smiling all the while. It took all the strength he had, but he saluted the Colonel.

"Count on it, Sir! Bye, Bud, Nick. Thanks. And you and Georgina have fun in Florida."

CIA HEADQUARTERS

Sam Gibbons did not have the luxury of knowing St. James' personal motivations. To the interim DCI, it looked like St. James was simply the biggest spy that the CIA ever had. For Sam, it really was frightening to think what would have happened if St. James was not discovered and had been left to seek the White House. With all the death and misery caused by this entire affair, Sam truly was relieved that St. James had finally been caught.

A SAFE HOUSE JUST OUTSIDE WASHINGTON, D.C.

About an hour after St. James was led from his office, he found himself in one of his own, or formerly his own safe houses. This time however, the house was not intended to keep him safe from harm. This was a place where St. James could be put on ice, kept out of trouble. General Stadwick and Sam Gibbons would have St. James interrogated to make a damage assessment of just how many secrets St. James had given away, how many operations had been blown, how many lives had been lost or put at risk.

The handcuffs removed, St. James sat at a table set only with a pad of paper and a pencil, for any statements or confessions. The place was buzzing with activity in preparation for the expected "extended stay" of St. James. Two armed guards watched him at all times.

The security team chief, Harry Burns was an unhappy but nevertheless extremely professional man. He strode into the main room where St. James was being held. He had to make just one more check. He looked around to see the rather bleak furnishings. The walls were brown, with no pictures or decorative hangings. There were two wooden chairs that the guards were sitting in. They did not need to be comfortable, just alert. The adjoining bathroom door was shut. Harry made sure there were bars inside of the windows. Harry looked around one more time. His eyes fixed on the only remarkable feature of the room, a huge fireplace and Rococo style mantlepiece around it.

Harry walked over to St. James and in his perpetual surliness talked to him.

"Well, well, well. If it isn't Director St. James! Guess you stepped in it, huh?"

St. James said nothing, choosing instead to give him a contemptuous look.

Harry goaded him further. "Cat got your tongue? No worry. You'll be spilling your guts about whatever you did soon enough. You see, whether you repent or we drug your ass to loosen your tongue, embarrass you with fake photos of you and some goat or whether we give you a gastrointestinal inflammatory substance to make you feel like your innards are turning inside out, you'll talk."

Harry motioned one of the guards to give up his chair. He pulled it across the table from St. James, sat down and looked him in the eyes.

"Oh yes, I'm sure that eventually they'll provide convincing proof that you embezzled or abused your position or something like that, eventually. But the fact that you're here and that I'm in charge of your ass means that, at the moment, you're outside of our constitutionally guaranteed criminal justice system. So don't blow your one and only chance, Mr. Director."

St. James tersely replied. "Oh, I won't, believe me, I won't miss my one and only chance." He was already scheming on ways to escape this arrogant security man's grasp.

As Harry left the room to check on the other security arrangements, he felt slightly uncomfortable about St. James' remark.

293

The next person to enter the room was one of the CIA's best tech men, a communications engineer. He was pushing a furniture dolly stacked with cases of sophisticated voice recording, video, human sensory and bio-monitoring equipment. The interrogators would know everything about St. James' body instantaneously as they questioned him in a few hours. They would be able to know when his voice wobbled imperceptibly to the ear, when he sweated a millisecond after he heard or even thought something. They would monitor his heart beat, his adrenaline, his eye movement, his muscle twitches, everything about his body as it occurred. Computers would then align this information with the interrogator's and St. James' recorded words to give an incredibly accurate analysis of the truth of his comments to the interviewers. Simple polygraphs were long ago discarded as the ultimate truth tellers.

The tech man was Gary Tomlinson, a twenty one year veteran of the CIA who has spent ten years before that as a communications expert in the Air Force. St. James knew Tomlinson in London when he worked for St. James, installing the Agency's secret radio equipment in the vaulted London Embassy communications room. Tomlinson had just started working for the CIA and was quite impressed with St. James' position and the attention he gave Gary in his performance evaluations.

Tomlinson was now ready to retire and live on a boat in the sunny Gulf of Mexico. The only problem was that with the alimony and child support to pay, it would be hard to play on the beaches on what was left of his $1,500 a month pension. Now fifty years old, he would have to continue to work until his children reached eighteen and his ex-wife remarried. Only then, would he have enough money to comfortably live out his days.

When Tomlinson looked at St. James, there was a surprised look of recognition from him. Tomlinson quickly looked away, realizing St. James was not there on a social basis.

Gary addressed the guards. "This will only take a few minutes."

They nodded.

St. James quietly tried to get Tomlinson's attention by whispering. "Tomlinson, isn't it? Tomlinson!"

Gary heard but ignored him. St. James was pleased with himself that he had remembered the man's name after all these years. No response.

Tomlinson just continued to set equipment up and test circuitry for impedance and signal conductivity.

St. James picked up the pencil, tore a piece of paper from the pad and wrote on it against the hardwood of the table so as not to leave an impression on the next sheet of paper for someone else to read. He scribbled furiously as Tomlinson finished up and began putting the large equipment cases on the dolly.

Although some of the cases were as big as guitar amplifiers, Tomlinson handled them with ease.

St. James crumpled up the paper as if he was displeased with what he had written and threw it on the floor in Tomlinson's direction. St. James then began to scribble again as if he was starting over. One of the guards glanced up at him and then back at Tomlinson who was hooking bungee cords around his cases, securing them in place on the dolly.

Just before he left, Tomlinson glanced over towards St. James. St. James was motioning with his eyes toward the crumpled ball of paper by his feet. The paper was hidden from the guards' view by the dolly. Tomlinson gave St. James a questioning look.

"What?"

St. James continued to gesture with his eyes. Tomlinson followed St. James' eyes down to the paper. Out of curiosity more than anything else, he knelt down to adjust a clasp on one of the cases and scooped up the paper, feeling strange as he did so. St. James breathed a sigh of hope.

Outside, in his van preparing to leave, Gary took the paper out of his pocket, smoothed out the note and read it.

"Tomlinson, I squirreled away one hundred and thirty five-million dollars of untraceable Agency money. Thirty-five-million of it is immediately yours, anyway you like it, anywhere you want it, if you get me out of here today."

Gary thought to himself. "Thirty-five-million dollars! I could prepay my family obligations and buy the boat for cash."

Tomlinson thought about a Gulf Coast lifestyle and his dream boat with his dream girl.

"Thirty-five-million dollars would buy a lot of dreams."

He snapped out if it and shook his head. He again, thought to himself. "This guy would do or say anything to get out of whatever jam he's in."

Tomlinson looked at the paper again and folded it up. "Nah."

He drove off.

A little over an hour later, Gary pulled up to the security entrance point and showed his identification to the gate guard. He checked the name and the access list on his clipboard. Tomlinson spoke. "Got to replace some equipment I put in a little while ago. When I tested it, a bad solder joint caused a power surge that fried the whole main unit, printed circuit card. I'm gonna have to send the old one all the way to Texas to get it fixed. Texas! Can you believe it?"

The guard looked beyond Tomlinson into the back of the van where he saw one large equipment case.

"O.K." He waved Tomlinson on through.

Once again, Tomlinson entered the room where St. James was being held, awaiting his interrogators.

"Sorry, guys. I gotta fix a bad circuit. It won't be long."

At the sight of him, St. James' spirits inwardly jumped. Outwardly, he just closely watched Tomlinson as he unpacked another smaller piece of equipment to replace the one he had set up a short time before. Tomlinson produced a line tester with its alligator clips and circuit probe. Similar to an ohm meter he uses to test the simple circuitry under the hood of his car. Then, he attached another device, plugging it into the standard wall socket. It had a cord attached from it into the equipment he had first installed.

While fiddling around with the machine, he produced a crumpled piece of paper from his pocket. Tomlinson subtly caught one of the guard's attention, then quickly threw it with disgust, at St. James, harmlessly hitting him on the side of the head. The guard seemed to remember St.James' having flung the paper toward Tomlinson before and smiled as if pleased to see Tomlinson taunting a caged beast in a zoo.

St. James showed a contemptuous face and squeezed the paper in his fist, causing the guard to smile bigger than before. What the guard did not notice was St.James quietly opening the paper to see what was written on it. His heart began to pound harder as he opened it. He closed his eyes before reading it. Would he see only his handwriting? He opened his eyes and read it. His facial expression did not change.

He called to the guard nearest him.

"I feel sick. I have to use the toilet."

The guard acknowledged and pointed at the bathroom door.

"Remember. I'm right here."

St. James went inside and closed the door. The door had no lock. He had taken the pencil with him.

Tomlinson checked the connections, then flipped the new set on. A current went through the set. The power went into the "line tester" plugged into the wall. From there, the current went through the house wiring, out from the house electrical cable that was suspended from the roof. It was strung to the nearest transformer some two hundred fifty feet from the house, hidden behind some trees. The device in the wall plug was actually a progressive voltage amplifier. It took a small charge and kept exponentially magnifying it, like a snowball going downhill, until it overpowered the transformer's surge protectors. The tremendous charge caused it to blow itself to pieces.

The loud booming sound of the transformers exploding sounded like a grenade to those both outside and in the house. The transformer's connections to the power line kept snapping, popping and spewing sparks in all directions. To an unfamiliar ear, it sounded like there was a small attack underway. A tree was set ablaze by the spewing, crackling sparks.

The guard outside the bathroom door, started to open it to check on St. James.

He protested to the guard.

"Do you mind? I have diarrhea."

The guard closed the door, not caring to verify St. James' statement.

The guard reassured the other one.

"It's O.K. I'll watch him. You go see what's happening."

The loud popping, sputtering and sparking continued outside. Another loud boom was heard.

St. James queried the guard outside of the bathroom.

"What's all the noise?"

He flushed the toilet.

The lone guard replied to St. James through the closed door.

"No concern of yours. Now, hurry up."

The guard's sentence was unfinished as he was knocked unconscious by Tomlinson and his hard rubber mallet.

Opening the door, Tomlinson exclaimed to St. James.

"Hurry. We don't have much time."

St. James mischievously smiled as he emerged from his faked sickness in the bathroom. Tomlinson took him to the large equipment case containing a smaller machine and undid the back panel of the case, opening a compartment. It was just large enough for St. James to barely fit in.

"Get in!" He quickly did as he was told. Tomlinson latched up the case, then went to the guard.

Tomlinson dragged him into the bathroom and closed the door again. He quickly gathered his tools and wheeled the dolly and case out to his van. A few men were trotting cautiously toward the blown transformer to see what was happening. They had guns in their hands. Tomlinson laboriously lifted and pushed the heavy case into his van and laid it on its side. He threw the cart into the back and jumped into the driver's seat to go.

The second guard that had left to investigate the explosion returned to find an empty room.

"What the? Phil? Where are you?"

He drew his gun and went to the bathroom. He pushed open the door. Something blocked it. He stood back and kicked it open to find Phil crumpled on the floor, out cold. The second guard cursed and yanked out his radio to report.

Tomlinson arrived at the gate just as word of the escape made it to the gate guard. A man burst out of the gate house and ran toward the main house.

The gate guard halted Tomlinson.

"Get out of the van."

Tomlinson started to sweat as he complied.

"What's wrong?"

The gate guard opened the back of the van, shouldering a machine-gun. He looked under the van and behind the equipment case.

The guard looked at the large case and ordered Tomlinson.

"Open it!"

Gary climbed in and removed the case cover. The guard looked inside. Gary was sweating.

"Just equipment, see? This is the broken one I told you about."

The suspicious guard looked at the machine in the case, then at Tomlinson.

Although cramped and uncomfortable, St. James did not even breathe. He could only listen.

"Hey man, let me out of here. I don't want no part of whatever is happening here. I'm just a slide ruler commando."

The guard paused then replied to Tomlinson

"Go on."

Tomlinson obliged and drove through the gate and away, forcing himself not to push the gas pedal to the floor.

Safely into a D.C. suburb, Tomlinson pulled into a grocery store parking lot. He went into the back of the panel van and lifted the case up on its end. He unclasped the back half of the case. St. James came tumbling out with a grunt.

Tomlinson excitedly exclaimed. "I did it!"

St. James caught his breath. "You sure did. Brilliant, just brilliant!"

Tomlinson quickly took his opportunity and pointed through the windshield at the store front.

"You see that phone over there? We're going there. You're going to call and set up a Cayman Island bank account for me and my thirty-five-million dollars."

St. James smiled broadly, sticking his hands into his pockets.

"Sure enough. Fair is fair. You sure pulled my fat out of the fire. And now it's time to give you something in return."

"Yeah, baby. Give it to me!"

"Yeah, baby." St. James mimicked him.

With lightning speed, St. James pulled the pencil he had taken out of his pocket and jabbed it deep into Tomlinson's right eye.

Reeling back against the interior wall of the van, Tomlinson's hand reflexively shot up to his punctured eye. He screamed with terror.

St. James gritted his teeth with ferocity and placed his hands around Tomlinson's throat to choke him. He kept squeezing harder and harder, with all his might to kill Tomlinson and stop that hideous animal like screaming.

Finally, the screaming stopped.

St. James calmed himself for a moment, breathing hard. He untucked Tomlinson's shirt and used it to wipe the blood from his hands. Now free, St. James's focus turned to his new obsession, Nick Dentworth.

"A phone call, indeed."

He looked down at Tomlinson's corpse. "Got some phone

change, buddy?"

He searched Gary's pockets and pulled out some coins.

"It's time to call in a few favors before word gets around of my unfortunate situation."

The blood continued to drain out of the engineer's eye socket. St. James stepped outside the van and closed its doors. He sighed, wiped his brow and straightened his tie. He slowly walked to the phone at the store front. He flashed a toothy smile at a passing woman with a cart full of groceries for her family. He picked up the receiver and dialed.

WALTER REED HOSPITAL

Manny Martinez picked up the phone next to his hospital bed. Lorena had left him an hour before. "Hello?"

He had a slightly groggy voice. It was General Stadwick.

"Manny, St. James escaped. Is Nick with you? In case St. James comes after you, I'll send guards there, right away."

Manny sat up in his bed. "Hold on a sec. Nick's not here. What did you say? St. James escaped? How?"

"We don't know exactly how yet. But I know one thing. If I were him and loose, I'd be coming after you and Nick. His life is finished. What's he got to lose?"

Manny shook his head. "For Christ's sake! Can't those CIA bastards do anything right?"

"My guards will be showing up at your doorstep shortly. There will be four. I'm at the office. Call me if you hear anything."

"Right. Nick was staying at my house. He's got to pick up his gear. I'll call right now. Bye."

Manny unsteadily dialed home. His fingers shook from his weakened condition. Letty answered.

Manny abruptly spoke first. "Put your mother on."

"Daddy! We were so worried! We thought you were hurt bad."

"Dammit, girl. Listen to me! Put your mother on now!"

He had never talked to her like that before. She went and got her mother.

A worried sounding Lorena got on the line. "Manuel?"

"Is Nick there?"

She didn't quite understand him. He had spoken a little too fast, with too much of a slur from the pain medication he was given.

"What?" He emphatically repeated the question.

"Is Nick there?"

"No. Letty said he left a couple of hours ago."

Manny cursed. "Damn!"

"I know your voice. What is it?"

Manny carefully enunciated, "Did he say where they were going?"

"The Keys, I think." Lorena answered with concern in her voice.

"Think very carefully, honey. Did he say anything specifically about where they would be staying, a hotel, an island?"

Lorena closed her eyes to concentrate. The phone in her hand began to shake. "Let's see. He called a cab. Letty! Come here right now! Did Nick or Georgina say anything about exactly where they were going?"

Manny could hear his daughter tearfully speak, scared by her father's tone of voice. "I don't know. Nick said he had everything and that they were off to the Keys for some 'fun in the sun'."

"Did they mention a hotel or island?"

"No. Uh, uh. Oh, yeah. They said the boogaloo on the beach was going to be so nice."

Manny interrupted.

303

"Boogaloo? Bungalow! Ask her if it was 'bungalow'."

"Was it a bungalow, honey?"

"Yeah, that's it."

Manny spoke to himself. "Can't be that many places with bungalows on the beach. Oh God, I hope there's time!"

"Time for what?" Lorena implored.

"Nick and Georgina may be in terrible danger."

Lorena was exasperated and scared. "Manuel, isn't this ever going to end?"

St. James' men had watched Nick and Georgina take the cab to the airport. They took a plane to Miami.

THE KEYS, FLORIDA

Nick and Georgina slowly and lazily walked hand in hand, along the seashore. Their pants were rolled up to let the tide lap around their bare legs. The weather was perfect. The breeze was warm and gentle. They could be completely carefree, making love on the beach, or in their bungalow. They laughed, danced and made serious plans for the near future.

"Oh, Nick. This is just pure heaven. I've never been happier. Are you really going to put a ring on my finger? I mean one I can keep?"

"I made that mistake once. I'll never let you go again."

Nick stopped her, dropped to one knee and took her hand in his.

"Georgina Matlock, will you marry me?"

Georgina looked in his eyes.

Hers filled with tears of joy.

"Yes, yes, yes!"

The relaxed and nondescript man slowly laid down on the sand dune in the distance. He focused the telescopic image until it was crystal clear. Although he couldn't hear them, he could see them on the beach. The beautiful woman was laughing. The man saw Nick on one knee.

Nick glanced upwards at her face.

"You know something? I can't believe I'm looking into the lovely eyes of my fiancee. I feel warm all over seeing your smile. I wonder how we'll spend the rest of our lives, till death do us part."

The man lying on the sand took a deep breath, exhaled and remained motionless. The intersection of the lines was directly between Georgina's shoulder blades. He smoothly and steadily pulled the trigger.

"Splat."

The smile on Georgina's face was replaced with a look of surprise. Nick felt a warm splash on his own face. It was immediately cooled by evaporation. It wasn't ocean spray. It was her blood. The high impact bullet blew away half of her heart. A large red spot appeared before Nick's eyes as her knees buckled. She limply fell forward into his arms.

The assassin got up, brushed the sand off his clothes and calmly walked away. With his rifle in hand, his job was finished.

One of several helicopters sent by Manny to search for them appeared around the island trees. They had been searching every resort in the Keys for several hours. The passenger was looking through binoculars. He spotted something on the beach.

"Hey, down there. It looks like them. Pull it down."

The pilot pushed the stick forward and lowered the helicopter.

"Seventy-five feet."

The wind of its blades fanned sand in every direction.

The passenger got on the loudspeaker. "Are you Nick Dentworth?"

No response.

He repeated the question. "Are you Nick Dentworth?"

Still on one knee, in shock, Nick suddenly, unbelievably found himself cradling his murdered love.

"Sir, Are you Nick Dentworth? Oh, no! We're too late."

The aviators now realized what had just happened."

From the depths of his very soul, Nick yelled his cry up into the uncaring and indifferent wind of the chopper blades. "Nooooooo!"

Chapter Twenty Six

FORT BRAGG, NORTH CAROLINA

Nick was given a few weeks convalescent leave after Georgina's death. After several days of feeling painfully low and miserable, he did what anyone would do under the circumstances. He called his mother, Emma Pauline Dentworth. Her friends called her "Pauly."

"Hi, Mom. How are you doing? What? Not so good. I just lost someone very close to me. Yeah. I'm sorry too. Say, listen, I was thinking of coming out there to see you next week. I should get in about seven, on Monday. What?"

"Honey, I'd love to see you. It's so rare that I get a chance. But, well, some days ago I finally met a man. We've been seeing each other all week. He's a retired oil company executive. And he's asked me to go on a Mexican cruise next week."

"Oh."

"Honey, I know you're going through a tough time right now. Believe me I know. I was destroyed for months after your father passed away. God rest his soul. And I want to be there for you. But is there any way you could make it the week after next?"

"Sure Mom, the week after next."

"I'm sorry, dear. But, don't you worry. We'll be seeing each other before you know it."

"O.K., Mom. See you soon."

"Thanks, honey. Oh, where are you?"

"At Bragg." Fort Bragg seemed to be a surrogate mother for SF soldiers in need.

"Bye, hon."

"Bye Mom. Out of here."

Then he thought to himself. "Out of here? Jeez, I can't even keep the military lingo out of a conversation with my own mother! Oh well. I guess I should be happy. It's been almost twenty years since she took an interest in another guy after Dad. I can't see myself ever seeing anyone else other than.... Oh, Georgina. I'm so sorry. I miss you. If only I could have done something, maybe ..."

He cleared the top of the table with an angry swipe of his arm, sending a plate of cold breakfast he did not eat, glasses and silverware crashing against the wall.

For days he moped around his Bachelor Officers' Quarters room. He alternated between fits of anger at himself over Georgina's death and the loneliness of being without her.

He punished himself again and again by saying talking out loud to himself.

"We were so close to having it all."

On Tuesday of the next week, he received an overnight letter from his Mom in Mexico. He tore it open and saw a photo postcard.

He read the note.

"Hola! We're having a wonderful time down here. Yesterday we saw a lovely church in a quaint coastal town and pigged out on fresh lobster, right off the boat! Friday, it's off to the Aztec temples of Cancun. What a gentleman! Then we fly home. Love you, Mom."

He flipped the card over, expecting to see some touristy photo of his mother and her beau sitting on a donkey or dancing with maracas in their hands. Instead, Nick saw his mother in a sombrero with her "beau," the "gentleman." The photo had their faces crammed, cheek to cheek, into the frame of an instant photo booth.

Nick was horrified.

"St. James!" His face stared back at him. St. James had a sardonic grin on his face, a taunting look in his eyes. They challenged Nick. "Come and get me if you dare!"

"You Bastard!" He glared with fury at the photo. A sick feeling came over him.

"Son of a bitch! I'll kill you if you even think of hurting her. I couldn't bear the thought of losing another, not to you! What to do?"

He picked up the phone and dialed.

A recording machine answered. "You have reached Walter Reed Army Medical Hospital. All of our lines are busy. If you know the extension of your party, press the number followed by the pound sign now." Nick punched in Manny's room number. The line rang five times without an answer, then transferred

"Intensive Care Unit, nurse station fourteen."

Nick made an effort to remain calm. "Room three eighty four, please."

"I'm sorry, Sir. There is no patient in that room."

"What? Where's the man with the, spleen condition that used to be there?"

Nick hoped Manny had not taken a turn for the worse. Manny was supposed to be laid up for at least four more weeks.

"Let's see. A gentleman checked out of there this morning."

"Checked out? He could barely move!"

The busy nurse snapped at him. "That's what the chart says, Sir."

"O.K., O.K. Thanks." He hung up, then called Manny's house, hoping not to surprise Lorena with the news that Manny was no longer in the hospital.

"Hello?" Manny's voice answered.

"What the hell are you doing home?"

"Nick, I have to tell you something."

Nick interrupted Manny. "St. James has my mother in Mexico!"

"Say again?"

"He tricked her. They're on a pleasure cruise off the coast of southern Mexico."

"How do you know that?"

"The bastard sent me a photo postcard to rub it in. He obviously wants me. I'm going."

"Not alone, you're not. I'm going too!"

"You can barely stand up! What are you doing out of the hospital?"

"You know me. I'm not one for playing defense. As long as that pendejo is out there, I couldn't rest anyway. I've always been on the offense. Listen, I'll let Sam know. I have some friends down there that can help."

"O.K. Tell Sam, but no troops or federales. He'd kill her in a heartbeat. It's me he wants and it's me he's gonna get. By the way, what were you going to tell me?"

"They went through his things at the office. They found your complete personnel file. He learned everything about your schooling, your family, your career, everything."

MEXICO CITY, MEXICO

Stepping off the ramp of the jumbo jet, Manny half-stumbled trying to adjust to the high altitude in his weakened condition. Nick caught him and helped him along the rest of the way into the terminal.

"Woa, woa. Take it easy, old buddy."

Once inside, Manny regained his composure and prepared to meet an old friend. "Reynaldo! My old friend! Como esta usted?" Manny smiled broadly and warmly embraced the other man.

"Manuel! Mi amigo! How is my beautiful Lorena?"

Reynaldo Gama Bustamante was a Mexican Secret Service Agent and second cousin to Lorena.

"She is very well. And she is looking forward to seeing you and your wife this year. They can spend all of our money, while they're shopping. We'll sit and drink Napoleon brandy until we're blind."

The men laughed and gave each other a hearty bear hug.

Manny turned to introduce Nick. "Reynaldo Bustamante, this is my close friend, Nicholas Dentworth. He's in the business with me."

They shook hands. "Pleased to meet you. Please call me Nick."

"And you must call me Reynaldo. Manny named his oldest son after me. It is a great honor for me. He will be a great Army general one day. I am proud that I was his godfather at his baptism, you know."

"He will make all of us proud, just like his stubborn father."

Nick knew that being a child's godfather was one of the highest honors in Latino culture.

Reynaldo laughed.

Manny chafed. "Stubborn? Me? Surely, you jest."

Nick looked again at Reynaldo. Even after this brief meeting, he genuinely liked and trusted this man. "You know? I like you already, Reynaldo."

Manny warned Nick. "Don't let him fool you. Reynaldo's kind, brown eyes and affable nature hide his skills and connections he has established over his many years of service to his country. And he cheats at cards."

Reynaldo formally and politely asked them a question.

"Will you both do me the honor of staying at my Rancho de Gama?"

"I wish we could. It's one of the most beautiful spots in the hemisphere. But this time we need your official help, for Nick."

"Come, come. Let's go where wee can talk." Reynaldo led them to a nearby airport executive lounge. In the room were a bartender, a busboy and two customers loudly talking about their awful flight. Reynaldo simply nodded to the bar keep.

The bartender took his cue. He ordered the busboy, "Hustle the customers up from their table and out of the room. I'm closing and locking the door."

The bartender gathered the protesting customers. "Come along, Senores. There's been a gas leak. You must leave now."

Alone now, with only a local talk show host on television to cover their conversation, the men chose a table in the center of the room. "Here, over here. Sit down, please."

"You have quite an effect on the bartender and busboy. You're obviously someone to be reckoned with, someone who wields quiet power."

Manny grimaced a little as he sat down in his chair.

"Aiy!"

"Manuel?"

"Slight hernia."

Nick decided to divert further inquiry. "Reynaldo, we need your help. It's a sort of personal matter. But it's also business."

"It's not exactly an official matter. But it's very important to me and Nick."

"If it is important to you, it's important to me. You know, Manuel, that I will do whatever I can to help."

Nick thankfully nodded.

Manny pulled out a copy of the cruise ship itinerary that he had brought with him. "We need to get to this ship while still at sea. On it is a very bad man who would hurt an innocent woman traveling with him. He is one of ours. She is Nick's mother."

"Dios mio! Su madre? Your mother?", Reynaldo gasped.

Manny continued. "This guy is sick and a dangerous. He's already killed. If we could do it quietly, it would be better."

Reynaldo reflected for a moment. "I have two questions. Where is the ship now and does it have a helipad?"

Manny and Nick smiled at each other.

"You're already living up to your reputation. The ship will approach Cancun tomorrow. Yes, it does have a helipad."

"May I see the cruise ship brochure for a few moments, please? I think I know of a way. Tonight we fly to Cancun by jet. Tomorrow we go to the ship."

He paused for a moment longer and set the brochure down on the table. A broad smile came across his face.

"Manuel, tell me, how are the children? What are they doing?"

With things obviously in control, Manny sat back, rubbed his chest and started filling Reynaldo in on the Martinez children. Nick relaxed too, for the first time in what seemed like weeks. It was nice just listening to the family talk between the two men so close, but separated by geography.

Reynaldo went to the door, opened it and called out for the bartender. The man appeared from nowhere. A few words passed between he and Reynaldo. The bartender trotted away. Reynaldo walked to the bar and poured tequila for everyone. About ten minutes later a sumptuous gourmet meal was brought to them. The three men spent a pleasant hour eating and becoming better acquainted. They finished dinner.

"O.K., gather your things and follow me. We go to a hangar. There, we board a Lear jet and fly south. Pronto!"

A few hours later, they arrived in Cancun. Reynaldo checked them into the best suites at the finest hotel in the resort town. Manny and Nick were impressed by the lavish furnishings and service.

"Not bad, eh, Manny?" They settled in for the evening. Nick was tired and retired to his bedroom. But even the old world furniture and freshly starched and ironed sheets did not help Nick's peace of mind. He slept fitfully. The sound of the nearby pounding surf conjured up dreams of that last moment with Georgina. He layed awake for an hour then dozed off. In a dream, he saw St. James aiming a rifle first at Georgina and then at his mother in a wild, psychedelic sort of shooting gallery. In the dream, Nick saw himself trying to catch the bullets with his own body. He threw himself from left to right. Each time he was shot instead of his loved one.

He screamed at St. James. "Not this time."

Fortunately the wake up call came from the desk rousing him from his dreams just as a bullet went screaming past him toward Georgina. Thankfully, he did not have to watch her die, again. Nick rose slowly gathering his senses.

As he showered and shaved he reflected to himself. "By the end of the day I will be with either one of the women I adore; my live mother or my dead sweetheart."

He answered a knock at the door wearing a plush, white, complimentary bathrobe. A bellboy handed him a tray. "Sir, muffins, hot coffee, juice and your pressed ship's officers uniform."

It bore the emblem of the cruise line, Pacifico Royale. The uniform had epaulets and logo patches and resembled a white, U.S. Navy officer's uniform, complete with gold braid and wheel cap.

"I hope all is satisfactory, Sir."

"It's great. Thank you. One moment. I'll get a little something for you."

"Oh, no, no, Sir. Senor Gama has taken care of everything. Have a good day, Senor."

"Thank, you." Nick dressed and was pouring his second cup of coffee when Manny knocked and entered his room.

"Jeez, Manny, you look like the Captain of the Love Boat."

Manny was also dressed in a uniform. "Ahoy, Ensign. Is there any coffee left?"

"Si, mi Capitan. How are you feeling?"

"I'm fine."

Nick could see by the wince of pain on Manny's face as he sat at the breakfast table that he was not fine.

"I'm not going to discuss the matter further, Nick."

"If you say you're fine, that's it. But how effective can you be in the clinch?"

"I'll do my best, O.K.?"

"O.K., O.K. It's just so soon."

"Just don't worry about me. I'll get along just fine."

"Ring, ring." Their conversation was interrupted by the telephone.

"It's Reynaldo. What? Sure. O.K." Nick hung up the phone.

"Fifteen minutes in the lobby. Let's get a move on, swabby."

Nick mocked Manny's appearance with an inter-service rival competition term. They referred to each other as dogs, swabbies, jarheads and fly boys, respectively for the Army, Navy, Marine Corps and Air Force.

Reynaldo, met Nick and Manny and shook hands in the lobby.

"Were the accommodations to your liking?"

Nick answered for both of them.

"They were, le mejor, excellente, the best, excellent."

"Let us go then. Our ride has already arrived. This way."

Reynaldo led Nick and Manny out to the back lawn.

"Wop, wop, wop." There was a Pacifico Royale helicopter. They all got on board. The chopper lifted off and headed out over the sea.

Since the ocean liner would be in Mexican waters, Reynaldo went along to invoke his authority, should it be needed. Reynaldo produced a suitcase from the back of one of the seats. He opened it for them. Inside was a host of weaponry. There were knives, a variety of pistols, dart guns and garrotes.

Reynaldo looked over the assortment. "If there is one thing my country has too much of, it's guns. Just like yours. We need good work, not more pistoles".

Nick and Manny knowingly nodded. "Yeah."

"Take whatever you need."

Manny and Nick each picked a small nine shot semiautomatic pistol and a throwing knife. Nick motioned to the square packages stacked in the helicopters.

Reynaldo answered the unspoken question. "Food and mail for the ship. This is a routine flight for the cruise line."

Nick smiled and pointed to Reynaldo. "Nice job, Reynaldo!"

A few minutes later, the pilot got their attention. He pointed down and out through his Lexan canopy toward the ship. It was anchored a couple miles offshore.

As the helicopter landed on the aft helipad, two crew members ran out to meet the supply chopper. They opened the door from the outside and immediately began removing the square boxes of supplies.

Nick, Manny and Reynaldo hopped out and headed for the bridge, where they would find the Captain. Manny lagged behind a step or two. On entering the bridge, where the ship's wheel and nerve center were. Captain Laggerson turned to meet them. He was dressed in a white uniform, but in warm weather shorts. True to the sailing tradition, he was smoking a pipe. He looked like a tropical version of a British Navy Captain. "Can I help you, gentlemen?"

He paused a moment, looking them up and down. He thought it strange to see three unfamiliar faces in his ship's officers' uniforms.

"Who are you? What are you doing in those uniforms and why are you on my ship?"

Chapter Twenty Seven

ON THE CRUISE SHIP

Reynaldo stepped forward immediately, showing his credentials to the Captain.

"Pardon our intrusion on your ship, Sir. But a delicate situation has arisen concerning two of your passengers. May we talk to you in private about this?"

The captain was particularly wary of these strangers in his company's uniform. One look at them and he could tell they had done little if any sailing.

"Anything you have to say can be said in the presence of my Executive Officer, here."

He turned to the other crew member on the bridge, Karl Furstenstadt, an expert boat pilot himself. The Captain had recently lured Karl away from the Rhine River Luxury Cruise Line in Germany. He had come to admire Karl for his seamanship as well as his unerring good sense.

"Very well, Sir. One of your passengers is a very dangerous and violence prone man. He unfortunately lured an innocent woman into accompanying him on this cruise. We ask your permission and assistance in finding and arresting him before any harm comes to the woman, or anyone else on board."

Reynaldo saw no reaction from the Captain or Karl.

Reynaldo continued. "Such a tragedy would undoubtedly spoil the wonderful vacation you provide for your other passengers. Not to mention the unfortunate publicity that would result."

Reynaldo's last remarks hit home. The Captain and Karl exchanged worried glances. "Yes, you're right. Any such incident would be most unfortunate. What is it that you need, specifically?"

He was now eager to assist and get these intruders off his ship as fast as possible.

Nick broke in. "Sir, it would be a great help if your Executive Officer would show us your passenger manifest and take us to the man's room. I can promise you any action we may take would be very subdued and uneventful."

The Captain pursed his lips then agreed. "Very well. Karl, will you please assist these gentlemen with anything they need?"

Karl saluted and reached for the manifest.

The Captain spoke to the intruders. "I say again, what are you doing in those uniforms?"

Manny spoke up. "Captain, hoping for your permission, we thought it best if we would blend in with the rest of your crew as we traveled your ship. It would limit the disruption of your operations. We don't want to upset your passengers or crew."

"Ah, yes." The Captain suspiciously nodding his head.

"Right. Karl, you go with them. I'll take the bridge."

"Aye, aye, Captain." Karl replied with his German accent.

He turned to the others. "Gentlemen, will you please come with me?"

They left the bridge for the Executive Officer's ward room. The Captain puffed his pipe and surveyed the instrument panels.

He wondered to himself. "What's going to happen on my ship?"

At the Executive Officer's table in his cabin, Karl addressed the men, "What is his name, this passenger you seek?"

"He's probably not using his real name. But the woman he's with is Pauly Dentworth."

Karl scanned the list with his forefinger.

Nick thought it strange that the ship did not have a computerized list.

"Ah, here she is. Cabin one sixty-two, the deluxe corridor. His name is Peter Van Pelt. Come mit, I mean with me. I will take you."

As they traveled to the other side of the ship, the four uniformed men occasionally saluted, tipped their hats and opened doors for the passengers.

After they saw a pair of beautiful women in string bikinis stride by them, Manny made a joking comment. "You guys go ahead. I'll catch up with you. I'm going their way."

Nick responded. "Old man, in your shape, you'll be lucky to even catch them."

Reynaldo added to the conversation. "What a terribly frustrating job this must be. I missed my calling."

Nick and Reynaldo grinned and craned their necks backwards to watch the women walk a few more shapely steps.

Outside Room one sixty two, Karl prepared to knock with the knuckles of his fist. Nick stopped Karl by grabbing his hand. He led him to the side of the door. Nick gently tried the door handle. It was locked. Nick, Reynaldo and Manny pulled their guns out and prepared to rush in.

Karl looked worried and whispered to Nick.

"I thought you said you would be subtle?"

"I lied." Nick kicked in the door. He, Reynaldo and Manny ran in, guns at the ready. Nick went through the cabin and into the private bathroom. Neither St. James nor Pauly was in the cabin. But all their things were still lying about.

Nick stated the obvious. "Not here."

He turned to Karl, who was now eyeing the damage to the door jamb.

"Where might they be, right now?"

"Anywhere on the ship." Karl excitedly worried out loud.

"What will the Captain say when I tell him what happened?"

Nick pressed him.

"Are there any special activities planned for this time of the day?"

"Yes. The shore excursion. Some passengers go shopping or sight-seeing. They'll be listed in another section of the ship's log. Here, I brought it with me."

Karl began flipping through other pages on the clipboard he he carried.

"Yes, here they are. They went ashore about an hour ago on one of the courtesy launches."

Manny looked at Karl.

"Do you have another launch?"

"Yes. But we must hurry. It's also about to leave."

"Karl, can't you contact the pilot and tell him to wait for us?"

Manny was not looking forward to running through the ship in his current state of health.

"No, the launches are not equipped for radio. We have never had a need."

Nick turned to Karl. "Until now. Luxury Cruise Ship, huh?"

Karl said, "Follow me, gentlemen" as he sprinted from the room.

Nick, Reynaldo and Manny raced out of the room behind him, tucking their guns into their front pockets. They ran through the maze of corridors and decks, dodging passengers and equipment as they followed Karl. They got to the launch just as it was pulling away from the ship.

Karl barked the order. "Stop the launch."

He waved at the helmsman as he ran down the steps leading to the launch. The helmsman saw him out of the corner of his eye. He cut the engine and put it into reverse.

Breathing hard, Nick, Reynaldo and Manny made their way aboard the launch. Manny was visibly shaken and holding his side.

Nick put his hand on Manny's shoulder. "Are you all right?"

Reynaldo noticed Manny's discomfort. "Manuel, this is no hernia."

Manny was so out of breath that he could only shake his head. He waved their concerns away.

The two miles to shore seemed like two hundred miles to Nick. Even Manny's condition was forgotten as his thoughts focused on St. James' deception.

"He led her like a trusting lamb to the slaughter."

Once ashore, the three men started to cautiously look around. Nick physically described them to Reynaldo. "He's in his sixties, white, six feet, one hundred eighty, light brown, green. She's sixty-six, white, five foot one, brown with gray, green with thick, round glasses. I hope the ship's uniforms will offer some momentary distraction to St. James. He'll be watching for my face."

The sun was very hot. They were almost on the equator. Nick helped an exhausted Manny along through the tiny coastal village street.

Reynaldo looked at Manny. "It is more like a gun shot, que no, right?"

"I was shot twice several days ago." Manny's voice was pained.

"Days ago! This man who has Nick's mother did that to you?"

Manny nodded, not caring to go into all the details.

"We will find him, old friend." Reynaldo jaw tightened. His eyes narrowed.

"I cannot guarantee that I will not kill him."

They passed under the shaded veranda of a cafe and cantina. Manny had to sit down. "Sorry, I have to sit. I think I'll stay here in case they come back this way. I can see the waterfront pretty good, from here. I would only be a burden from here on."

Nick and Reynaldo nodded in agreement then set out to search through the shops and bars that made up the main street of the village. After looking through several of the shops and cafes, they decided that St. James and Pauly must have gone to the ancient Aztec ruins.

They entered the Great Plaza of the ruins. There were several smaller, stepped pyramids around the complex. At the end of the impressive courtyard that led to its base, the largest pyramid was the focal point.

Nick scoured the area for any tourists walking out in the open. Although he could not see him, he could almost smell St. James. "He's here, somewhere, I feel him."

Reynaldo nodded and split off to the left to check through a group of buildings and the grounds around them. "I'll go this way."

Nick went through those to the right.

Nick progressed through each building, gun poised, ready to fire on his first sight of St. James.

Nick whirled around a corner into one room. He came face to face with an older couple that closely resembled St. James and his mother.

Nick did not raise his weapon, but kept it pointed at their feet, "at the ready."

The couple was surprised, then scared, when they realized Nick had a gun. They quickly scurried out of the old, stone structure and ran across the courtyard to avoid any contact with him.

Nick went through the remaining rooms of the ruin. No one else was there.

St. James and Pauly were atop the summit of the main temple overlooking the whole courtyard. St. James thought to himself.

"It will be particularly fitting that I will meet you here at the site of ancient, ritual, human sacrifice. I wonder what it must have been like for the Aztec high priest as he prepared himself to take an innocent life."

As he was looking out at the courtyard below, he noticed the older couple who were surprised by Nick. They were looking over their shoulder as they hurried away from him. St. James licked his lips with anticipation.

Pauly interrupted his concentration. "Oh, Peter. Look at this room. It has some sort of table or altar. Do you really think they used to sacrifice people here? Right here, on this very spot? And it's so cool in here compared to outside."

St. James barely heard her voice. He was looking at the building down below that the older couple had been running from.

He smiled to himself. "A few seconds more."

In five seconds, he saw Nick emerge from the building, carefully looking around. Even from that distance, St. James recognized him. "Finally, you have found me."

He saw Nick's face turn up towards the summit.

"Now I will have my revenge, Nick Dentworth!"

Nick had to shield his eyes from the sun as he looked up toward the summit. Although he could barely make out the face looking down at him, he knew it was St. James. St. James gave him a little salute with his right hand, verifying his identification.

Nick's eyes never left that distant, shadowed face atop the summit as he began a slow, deliberate walk across the courtyard towards the temple steps.

In his peripheral vision, Nick saw Reynaldo just entering the last of the buildings on the left. Nick knew St. James could kill his mother at any moment.

He thought to himself. "No time to get Reynaldo for back up."

Even if he yelled to him, Nick knew he would only confirm to St. James that it was he who was coming after him.

"Reynaldo would not get to the main temple soon enough to make any difference anyway."

St. James gave a smile and a little, friendly wave as Nick began the labored climb up the temple steps. He could have walked around the temple and take the long, winding path. It would be an easier climb. But Nick opted for the most direct approach to minimize the time it would take to get to St. James.

Pauly impatiently addressed St. James. "Peter, are you coming?"

"Yes, Pauly. I'm on the way." He broadly smiled as he saw the determination on Nick's face. He turned to join Pauly.

Nick's pace picked up as he saw St. James disappear into the temple. For Nick, each tick of the second hand seemed like a Chinese gong. He began to lunge up the steps, climbing with his hands and feet. Once again, he spoke in a rising, determined tone of voice." "Noooooo!"

Two eternities passed before Nick was halfway up the stairs. The blocks were uneven after centuries of use and erosion. Nick had to pick his way carefully. He could quickly lose his footing as his thoughts ran to his mother.

In his mind's eye, he saw her tucking him in bed when he was a child, singing to him his favorite lullaby. He remembered her crying while mopping the kitchen floor on the day John F. Kennedy was shot. He saw her building a birdhouse with him for Cub Scouts. There were so many memories that rushed through Nick's mind.

"Lunge, step, lunge, step."

Nick saw her smiling face the day he graduated from high school and her weeping face at his father's funeral. He felt her arms around him, welcoming him home from one of his more harrowing military tours.

Just as he reached the top step he dropped to a prone position, lying on his side. He used the last row of the steps as cover. He pointed his gun at the expected blast of gun fire from St. James. No one was there.

His body was dripping with sweat. His chest heaved with the exertion from his climbing run. Nick leaped over the last steps.

He quickly moved over to the wall framing the short door into the darkness of the altar room. He then snapped around to the outside of the square room, ready to shoot should St. James try to surprise him from the rear.

No one was there.

Nick heard his mother's voice echoing from inside the chamber. "Oh, look Peter. Here's an ancient hand print."

Nick heard no response from "Peter."

Nick drew himself close to the door's edge, preparing to jump into the room where he knew St. James was waiting for him. Nick would have no element of surprise. Short of calling out to his mother, Nick knew there was nothing he could do to improve his chances of getting St. James before he got his mother. But he also knew that if he did that, what little surprise he had, would be lost. He did not like the idea of losing that small advantage. He would not be able to see St. James' position.

Nick closed his eyes briefly then opened them, as if saying a brief prayer. Sweat dripped off of his brow in the high humidity. He jumped around the door frame and into the room.

"Mom, get down on the floor! Now!"

His eyes quickly adjusted to the darker interior.

St. James and Pauly were standing behind the stone altar positioned in the middle of the room.

Pauly wheeled around at the loud intrusion. She could not believe her eyes or ears. She could not believe she was seeing her son, pointing a gun at her, here, in Mexico.

Nick yelled his command again. Stunned, Pauly instinctively reached her hand back toward St. James for support. She had grown close to him over the past few days. In this strange place, under these circumstances, Peter was the only thing around her that seemed immediately familiar.

Yet, she wondered to herself. "What is it about that voice?"

St. James, expected Nick's entrance. He cleverly positioned himself behind Pauly. She moved slightly to the side, reacting to Nick's sudden appearance, St. James matched her movement, maintaining her as a perfect, human shield.

"Get out of the way, Mom!" Nick ordered his mother in vain.

Pauly finally realized it was Nick. She also saw he was dead serious. "Nick, honey! What are you doing here? What are you doing?" She was suddenly frightened. She did not understand what was going on.

Nick kept his gun trained on St. James' center mass, through her. "Mom, Van Pelt is not his name. He's a murderer."

Pauly still did not completely comprehend. She turned her head back and looked at St. James. "What?" She looked back at Nick. "What are you talking about?"

As she said this, St. James brought his hand up from his pocket area exposing a Walther PPK semiautomatic pistol.

He quickly grabbed Pauly around her left side with his left arm crossing up and across her chest. His hand went around her throat. His right hand put the gun barrel end against her right temple.

She gasped, then tugged at St. James' hand around her throat. St. James tightened his grip and pressed her closer across his body. The barrel made an indentation in the side of her head.

Through gritted teeth, St. James clenched her tight enough to hurt her.

"That's right, Pauly dear. I've murdered people. And, I'm about to kill you."

Pauly could not believe what was happening to her.

Nick was frustrated. He could do nothing during St. James' quick move. An attempted head shot at the moving St. James, so close behind his mother could end in disaster. All he could do was aim between St. James' eyes once he stopped moving. Even, if he shot and hit him, there was no telling if his finger would pull the Walther's trigger in a nervous response.

St. James spoke again. "Go ahead, Nick, honey, Nicky boy. Shoot!

Who knows what my trigger finger will do. Maybe you'll get lucky. Maybe you won't. It doesn't matter to me anymore. You already ruined my life. It's done. I'm a walking dead man."

"You got that right, bastard. You're a dead man."

Nick's mind raced. He debated his chances. His gun was pointed between St. James' eyes. He noted that his own breathing had almost returned to normal.

St. James sarcastically taunted him. "But before you do anything, I'm going to see the look on your face as I kill another woman you so dearly love."

St. James sighed and talked in an eerily cheerful voice.

"That will do it for me. I sound completely insane. Now, kindly put your gun down on the floor."

St. James pulled the hammer back on his weapon and screamed with pent up anger. "Do it!"

Nick knew that it only took a half pound per square inch of pressure from St. James' finger and a bullet would enter his mother's brain. The wait was agonizing.

"All right, all right. You win." Nick spoke in a quiet voice.

He slowly lowered his gun to the floor, never taking his eyes off of the former DCI's face.

St. James wryly smiled. Sweat beaded on his forehead. "That's it, Nicky boy."

Pauly had been silently shaking with fear.

Nick was returning to an upright position when Pauly took action to save her son.

Turning her head to the left, away from the gun, she jabbed her right elbow as hard as she could backward into St. James' ribs. He flinched in pain at the unexpected suddenness of the blow.

The gun went off.

At that moment, St. James' gun was then pointing up and to the left.

Nick instantly heard Master Zhu's voice again.

"Never unnecessarily throw all your weapons away. You never know when you may need them!"

Nick pulled the throwing knife from his waistband and hurled it at St. James. The sharp knife sank deep into the joint of his right shoulder.

The knife made a solid sound. "Thunk."

St. James reacted. "Ugh!" Injured, St. James painfully turned his weapon toward Nick and fired.

Nick somersaulted to the left, scooping up his gun as he rolled. St. James' fired again and again. His first bullet ricocheted off the floor and out the door where Nick had been standing.

The bullets landed just behind the rolling Nick. It was hard to hit a moving target with a knife in you.

Pauly was falling to her left as St. James' grip loosened.

She hit the ground.

Nick emerged from his roll on his right knee with his left foot firmly planted for steadiness. He fired twice at St. James hitting him in the chest. Nick was now presented with a full view of St. James, from the side of the altar.

St. James stared at Nick in disbelief after being shot. He looked down at his chest, then at Nick. He began shooting wildly, bullets dangerously ricocheting around the enclosed room.

Nick kept firing into St. James a third, fourth and fifth time as he rose to his feet and walked toward him.

St. James fell back against the wall with the force of the bullet impacts. The pistol circled around his index finger and fell out of his hand. He started to slide down the wall into a sitting position. As he did, he painted the wall with a broad red stripe of his blood.

Nick kicked the gun out of the way as he stood over St. James.

St. James was barely alive. Blood oozed from his mouth. His eyes began to glaze over. He raised his bloody, right hand and slowly pulled the trigger of an imaginary gun aimed at Nick.

He weakly spoke to Nick. "Bang, bang Nicky boy. You're dead."

Nick shot St. James twice in the head to finish him off.

He venomously spat at St. James. "Bang, bang yourself, you son of a bitch!"

Once the threat was gone, Nick jumped over St. James' body and got down on his knees. He, once again, found himself cradling a woman he loved, who had been shot by St. James. There was blood covering the right side of Pauly's head.

He looked down into his mother's face. Her eyes were closed.

"Mom! Oh God! Momma. Please live!" he pleaded. He was crying. His tears falling onto her cheek.

After a moment, she slowly opened her eyes. She swallowed and faintly spoke to him. "All right, dear. I'll live. But you have to promise me one thing."

Nick was happily surprised to see her looking up at him. He responded in a tearful voice. "Anything."

"Next time you have a problem with one of my boyfriends, just tell him to buzz off. Don't shoot him. O.K.?"

Just then, Reynaldo burst through the door with his gun drawn. He found St. James dead and Nick, on the floor with his mother. She was apparently all right. He let out a big sigh, smiled and lowered his gun.

Nick smiled, then he and Pauly laughed out loud. Tears of relief freely flowed from his eyes. He gently rocked her and held her close.

He repeated his response to her. "O.K., Mom. I won't shoot him. O.K., Mom."

Epilogue

WASHINGTON, D.C.

The audience of a few hundred people had gathered on the south lawn of the White House for a special occasion. On this brisk but sunny day Samuel Gibbons was being sworn in as the new Director of the Central Intelligence Agency.

He had successfully negotiated the politically charged inquisition of the Senate confirmation hearings. The position, so long beyond his grasp, was finally his.

The crowd was a mixture of foreign dignitaries, White House Cabinet, CIA heads, journalists, bureaucrats and their personal guests. Also there was Kimberly Phelps, Bud, Nick and Manny, who was making a speedy and complete recovery from his injuries.

The Chief Justice of the United States Supreme Court was swearing Sam in as President Carlton proudly looked on. Sam slowly repeated the oath of office as directed by the Judge.

The President was the first to shake Sam's hand. He had a smile made for T.V. He spoke directly to the cameras. "Congratulations, Mr. Director."

The crowd let out a small cheer and began to clap.

Sam's response was drowned out by the noise.

"Thank you, Mr. President. I'll do my best."

The videotape kept rolling. The cameras flashed with a barrage of photos.

Phelps was obligatorily clapping at half speed. His friend Tony, sitting next to him, was applauding with enthusiasm.

Bud, Nick and Manny were sitting together, with Nick in the middle. Everyone was giving Sam a standing ovation.

In the row just ahead of them they heard two bureaucrats talking to another, loud enough to be heard over the applause.

"I hate these affairs. Just another dog and pony show for some political appointee who probably raised fifty million for Carlton's campaign fund."

Nick, Bud and Manny thought the two men in front of them probably did not even know Sam and probably had never seen or heard of him before today. They were there just to "be seen" at this important political function.

The other responded to the remark. "Yeah, I know what you mean. In a few years he'll get booted out and probably become a lobbyist for the Japanese. The next President will put in his man. Does it really matter who? After all, how much damage can the head of the Central Intelligence Agency do in a few years anyway?"

Bud, Nick and Manny smiled at each other, silently savoring the irony of what had just been said.

After the ceremony, the three friends were walking back to their cars.

Nick turned to Manny. "Who's going to win the series this year?"

"The Yankees, of course."

"I'll bet you fifty bucks that they don't."

"You're on."

"Let's see. Then, you'll owe me a hundred dollars, a dug out seat and an autographed team ball."

"Aiyaa! Don't you ever forget anything?"

"Nope. Not important stuff, like this."

Bud had to jump into the conversation.

"Nick, I suggest if you ever want to get anything out of this hoodlum, you get it fast."

"You're right, Bud. O.K., Manny. Here's the deal. A hot dog and a cold one for all three of us, right now. And we'll call it even. Deal?"

"Done!"

They walked a few more steps. Manny patted his pockets.

"Hey, you know what guys? I think I left my wallet at home. Can you spot me twenty dollars? I'll pay you back first thing, tomorrow morning."

Nick half laughed, shaking his head. "Oh, ho, ho, no, no. I'm not falling for that old one. Uh, uh. Nope."

Manny then looked at Bud.

"No!"

"C'mon guys. That's not fair. I'm still a recuperating veteran. I've got braces and piano lessons for the kids to pay for."

All three spies started laughing, as they disappeared into the distance.

Printed in the United States
92502LV00003B/182/A